THE DEMON DIVIDED:
A DANCE WITH DEATH

ANGEL SERIES BOOK

BERNICE BURGOS

The Demon Divided

Copyright © 2022 by Bernice Burgos

All rights reserved.

Published by Red Penguin Books

Bellerose Village, New York

Library of Congress Control Number: 2022912023

ISBN

Print 979-8-20142-964-5

Digital 978-1-63777-282-9

No part of this book may be reproduced in any form or by any electronic or mechanical means, including information storage and retrieval systems, without written permission from the author, except for the use of brief quotations in a book review.

This book is a work of fiction. Names, characters, places, and incidents are the products of the author's imagination or are used fictitiously. Any resemblance to actual events, locals, or persons, living or dead, is coincidental.

To Author Gini Lee,
meeting you has been an inspiration.
You are a wonderful writer, human, and friend.
Cheers to the future!

PROLOGUE

The relentless waves crashed against the shoreline only to recede into calm ripples and noisy, frothy bubbles. Maggie's glossy eyes scanned the distance, admiring the beauty of the large mountainous stones that stood grounded in the ocean. In warmer weather, the water would have been rather inviting; instead, the brisk air lashed her cheeks to the color of blushing roses. She used the back of her wooly mittens to wipe the uncontrollable drip falling from her icy nose. Even in the frigid weather, she still found joy in playing a game of *"You can't catch me"* with the ocean.

Maggie giggled as she dodged the water to her own particular childish tune, trying not to wet the soles of her purple, rubber galoshes. At one point, the wind blew the crocheted hat from her head, sending it willy-nilly into the blackened sand dunes behind her. Gaggles of giggles escaped her mouth as she frantically chased after it. Each stride on the sinking sand felt as if she was trying to escape the inevitable dangers of quicksand. Her thin legs couldn't move faster than the wind. It was a race she was clearly losing.

Maggie, finally giving up all hope, stopped running and grimaced. She raised her mittens to her face in defeat.

"Aw, dang it!"

Her heart pounded and she breathed heavily while watching her hat become a lovely but soon-to-be memory within the dunes.

"I liked that hat."

Before she could register a subtle shift in physics, her tiny frame slowly rose and glided across the bumps of sand, her feet barely touching the ground. Delight lit her face as she shot her arms out, giggling and focusing on her target.

"Imma gonna get you now, hat."

She moved with such speed through the cool breeze that she hardly noticed the drip from her nose anymore, nor the brisk wind that had slapped her cheeks earlier. Her feet thumped firmly to the ground mere inches from where her hat rested. She tried to stomp it into submission, but the wind changed sides again. It whisked it away and almost out of her grasp.

"GOTCHA!" she happily and triumphantly yelled as she plucked it from the sand and shook it vigorously.

Maggie smiled and waved at the couple still walking along the shoreline before shouting, "Thank you, Ruby Jane." She placed the crocheted hat back on her head and dashed toward the water to continue her game.

Ruby Jane's rouge lips pressed together in a heartwarming smile as she returned the wave and replied in her most comforting southern accent, "Ya welcome, pumpkin."

Jack shook his head wondering when magic would stop solving all of life's problems.

"You know, you can't use magic for everything."

"Jack, quit ya worrying. It's fun. Kids love a little friendly push." she stated, trying to counter Jack's negativity.

Jack placed his arm around Ruby Jane's shoulder and nestled her close. He inhaled her familiar and enticing scent and dug his strong hands into her chinchilla for comfort.

He was ready to call their outing quits due to the frigid weather as it began to seep under his fur coat, but he couldn't bring himself to do so. Having Ruby Jane and his daughter Maggie by his side is exactly where he wanted to be. The salty air stung his nostrils, causing his nose to cringe as he deeply inhaled. It was the first time he had been able to take a breather while being on the run.

Usually, around this time of year, the Icelandic beaches were generally crawling with selfie-taking, human souls. Jack wondered if Ruby Jane had anything to do with secluding the area. She was the almighty powerful Ultra; her witchcraft came in handy for even the smallest task.

"I just don't want her to get too spoiled with the magic. I want her to be a normal kid and solve her little issues on her own," he continued.

"Well, it's too late for that! Maggie is far from normal. Besides, daddies are known to spoil their daughters, and you're no exception. It's only a little magic," teased Ruby Jane, waving jazz hands trying to lighten the mood.

She observed Maggie as she continued to play innocently by the shore as Jack's wandering eyes consistently remained vigilant, looking out for signs of danger. She gently placed her leather-encased hand on Jack's cheek, drawing his attention away from his constant surveillance, reassuring him that they were safe and secure. He gazed into her emerald eyes, losing himself in the little flecks of light that danced in the depths of her pupils. It felt almost hypnotic and desensitizing. Jack could feel the tension seeping from his tight muscles. His mind suddenly cleared as contentment spread throughout his body. Having his daughter and his lover by his side was a moment he wanted to live in forever, but knew it would be impossible in this reality.

They were on the lam from Maggie's mother, Angel, her band of Vs, and the Underworld. Jack had fucked up so badly that the bounty Master Anu placed on his head was high enough to buy a lucky fool two man-made islands in Dubai.

Knowing all of this information, and despite their past dumpster fire of a passionate relationship, Ruby Jane still agreed to help Jack disappear. He was a part of her history that she couldn't erase. She tried so many times to forget him, even seducing and subjugating numerous sexual partners. Her undying love burned so deeply that in anger she sent him back to Hell and ratted him out to the Vs. Yet, that betrayal was an awakening. No matter what she did, she couldn't fool herself any longer. She loved that idiot demon. It was a tug of war she fought internally for decades. So, when Jack showed up at her bookstore looking for refuge with Maggie in tow, she was compelled to help him.

Jack lowered his head and kissed Ruby Jane's rose-petaled lips. The softness of her lips against his melted his heart and warmed him inside like oozing lava. He embraced Ruby Jane, drawing her closer, fanning the flames of his repressed desire. The passion between them ended abruptly as Ruby Jane pulled away to examine her surroundings. The expression on her face read that danger was nearby; it was pressing up against them. The magic was persistent, pervasive, and unrelenting. There was an eerie force surrounding them that they couldn't shake.

Ruby Jane's next words came out in a low whisper, brushing along with the wind.

"We have to get going, something is near."

Jack furrowed his eyebrows and looked around, not seeing or hearing anything or anyone but feeling every sense of powerful magic. The beach was still except for the waves crashing and Maggie joyfully frolicking.

"Are they close?" Jack questioned on high alert.

"Yes, I can feel them."

"Shit! MAGGIE!!!" Jack warned.

Maggie's giggles halted as Jack's voice echoed in the short distance. She ran toward them and wrapped her delicate arms around Jack and Ruby Jane's waists, forming a tight circle. She gazed up at Jack with sad, puppy dog eyes.

"Is it time to go already, daddy?"

"I'm afraid so, baby girl. It's not safe here. Remember what I told you about needing to be safe, right?"

"Yes, But I was having so much fun. It's my first time at the beach," Maggie whined.

Ruby Jane tightened her grip around Maggie. "Don't worry darlin', the next time we see the beach, I promise you, it'll be nice and warm out. Enough for us to go rottin' and tottin' around in the ocean. How does that sound?"

"Daddy says never make promises you can't keep."

Ruby Jane smirked at Jack, then focused back on Maggie. "Trust me, pumpkin, I pinky promise," she reassured her while holding up her pinky finger.

Maggie wrapped her mitten over Ruby Jane's hand, indicating that her fingers weren't free to share.

Ruby Jane huddled everyone closer in the circle, tightening the gap between them. "Make sure ya hold on tight to ya daddy and me and don't let go. Let's close this up." She said to Maggie, drawing her in for a tight squeeze.

Jack tightened his arms around the only family he currently had, knowing that he was never going to let go. He gently kissed Ruby Jane on the forehead before they all bowed their heads in unison.

"Do-rentu, al-hira, Do-rentu, al-hira, whisk us away, farther away. Do-rentu, al-hira, Do-rentu, al-hira, whisk us away, farther away."

Ruby Jane chanted these words repeatedly, faster and lower. She continued her whispered spell until the sand lifted and swirled around them. Within seconds, they disappeared among the whooshing, twirling mini-sandstorm.

"What the fuck! There's nobody here. Why is there nobody here?!"

Angel paced along the shore furiously. She kicked at the water and punched her fist in the air in frustration.

Master Anu looked down at the sand, noticing small and large footprints. The *only* footprints on the beach.

"We must have just missed them," resigned Anu.

"How??? How is Jack moving so fucking fast?"

"He must have help," Anu surmised.

Angel thought for a split second, realizing Anu's statement was probably true. She walked back to the water and began kicking it some more, wetting her wings and soaking her boots. Master Anu took a few steps back, allowing Angel to wallow in her tantrum.

"FUCK! FUCK! FUCK!" she shouted up to the deep blue sky.

"When I find out who's helping Jack. I will KILL THEM WITH MY BARE HANDS!" Little did she know, she may never have the chance.

CHAPTER 1
MAGGIE OR MAGDALENA

It's quite impossible to put into words the exact way Maggie felt every time she woke up beside this particular lover. The closest would be the conscious feeling of being struck by cupid's arrow. It felt as if her heart had stopped and then kicked up to beating triple-time, all in the same instant. Maggie gradually opened her eyes to the few rays of sunlight peeking through the cracks of his heavy, blackout drapes. She rubbed her sleepy lids and quickly surveyed the room, trying to remember the events of the previous night, but everything seemed a blur. Pulling herself together, she tried to ignore the thumping of her heart and the correlated response of desire when she accidentally planted her palm on the naked, chiseled chest of the sleeping man lying beside her. The detailed, black-inked, dragon tattoo that covered his entire right breast and snaked up to his neckline heaved up and down soundlessly and peacefully. The slight hint of a shadow beard emerged from his sideburns and trailed down to his chin.

Maggie resisted the urge to gently run her fingers through his silky, dark hair. Instead, she dipped her head lower to get a whiff of his manly scent and wondered if that was the reason behind their obvious attraction. Flashes of glimmering strobe lights, whisky body shots, jumping to loud techno music, and tongue locking in a dark corner immediately exploded images in her mind, reminding her that she was so good at being so bad.

Maggie smiled sardonically then reached for her cell phone that had somehow wedged itself between them on the bed. It was 7:00 a.m. and she already had fifteen missed calls and eleven text messages. Two of the texts were from her best friend, Charlie, asking if she had made it home alright, but the rest were from her mother. That would usually have caused consternation, but right now, she had a more important task to worry about.

She needed to haul ass before her lover could make eye contact or, worse, conversation. Sneaking away before her lovers awoke became her thing, her game, her way of saying, *"You can't catch me."* She didn't know exactly when or how her version of this cat-and-mouse game started. What she did know was that with this lover her current record was seven to zero.

"Be home soon!" was the response she texted to her mother before flinging her long, sun-kissed legs over the bed and clandestinely tiptoeing toward the pile of clothes on the floor.

Maggie paused to send one more text message.

Maggie: Never made it home, it was my lucky night. Call you later.

She internally blushed while confessing her naughty behavior in so many words to her best friend.

Charlie: I want every little slutty detail!!!

She smirked at the message, thinking how Charlie didn't even have to ask. She was willing to confess all of her sins in exchange for a good laugh with her bestie.

Maggie continued to dress quickly and quietly but toppled backward after getting one of her legs stuck inside of her denim jeans. The wooden dresser against the wall mercifully broke her fall as her hip bone collided with its sharp edge, sending a stabbing, burning sensation down her side.

She paused, sucking in a breath and yelping in silence while biting down anxiously on her bottom lip.

"Fuuuuck!" she exhaled in a whisper.

She moved faster, struggling to don the rest of her clothing.

Shit, where are my damn boots? She thought as she scanned the bedroom for the rest of her items, hoping she would be able to silently tiptoe out of the apartment before her lover woke up.

For a bachelor pad, the apartment was surprisingly clean and organized, except for last night's passionate display of hastily discarded and entangled clothing scattered around the shiny hardwood floors. Finding her boots shouldn't have been this impossible.

Maggie snatched her footwear, found concealed underneath a pair of black boxer briefs, and swiftly made a beeline for the exit.

"Sneaking out already?" questioned a deep, soothing voice from behind her. He had spent a pleasant hour watching her sleep. As the sun began to rise, it appeared that it was getting too late for her to perform one of her many Houdini acts, so he dozed off. However, Maggie wasn't the greatest at creeping about; each heavy step she took creaked and vibrated the floorboards as if a two-hundred-pound man was tiptoeing around. He was inconspicuously watching her entire fiasco with one eye open.

"This is a first for you. The sun is up this time." A sexy smile played on his lips, mitigating any hint of resentment. He sat up on his elbow with one hand cradling his head, watching her lovingly as she discreetly tried to sneak away.

Maggie stopped short in her tracks and cringed. *Busted!* One thing she didn't want to do was engage in conversation. At the same time, she didn't want to seem rude. She slightly eye-rolled and cussed inside her head as she turned herself around and locked eyes with him. His high cheekbones, full smooth lips, and dark slanted eyes nearly turned her into putty. He reminded her of a K-pop singer, except he was taller and too physically toned to be prancing around on stage. He could have passed for a swimmer with his broad shoulders and toned muscles that tapered quite nicely to his gluteus maximus. Instead, he was just a DJ.

"Hey, you're up." she spoke while balancing on one foot, tugging her black ankle boot onto the other.

"Yes, I am, and so are you." He marveled at the absolute, stunning beauty of her. The more she fought their connection, their vibe, the happier he appeared. Working his way around the DJ circuit had gotten him a fair amount of adoration and worship, but being with Maggie was like an addiction. There was something about her that his human willpower could not fight. She was tantalizing.

Maggie stared at her lover awkwardly as he seemed to be mentally searching for answers she didn't have.

"I was just..."

"Leaving," he interrupted as he stood up to face her in all his naked glory. He was playing dirty to win this battle of will.

Maggie licked her upper lip sensually while staring at the fine specimen in front of her, *Damnnn, maybe just one more round,* pondered the voice that echoed in the left side of her head. She felt herself getting moist with excitement.

Not now, Maggie, we have to go! Mother, remember? shot the voice on the right. *Fuck!*

"I can't stay. I really have somewhere to be. How about I call you later, Tom?"

"Dom," he corrected her politely for what must have been the third time.

"Dom, that's what I said," replied Maggie reassuringly.

She pecked Dom on the lips and grabbed his aviators off the dresser. He tried to intercept her but missed her sticky fingers by inches.

"I'll make sure to return these next time I'm here," Maggie stated playfully as she walked out of the bedroom and into the sitting area, grabbing her fitted leather jacket off the loveseat and making her way toward the front door.

Dom followed her like a lost puppy, not wanting her to leave but also not reacting fast enough to make her stay.

"Aw, Magdalena, are you sure you have to go? Is there any way you can stay just for a little bit longer? I'll get us breakfast, and I promise to be so much badder than last night."

Dom held his hands to his heart, giving her his saddest love-struck expression. He sighed sarcastically.

Maggie gently pulled Dom's hands and brought them toward her lips. She kissed them softly and whispered, "No."

The air went dead as Maggie felt Dom's pride take a nosedive. She knew how much he cared about her. Although he never admitted it, his actions screamed louder than his words. Anytime Maggie felt lonely or in need of company, Dom made sure to clear his schedule. It was an invitation he generally welcomed with open arms, and he never disappointed her.

Maggie's prominent role as the lead singer of a popular, all-female, indie rock band was what lured Dom into this fascinating infatuation in the first place. He followed her band to every underground performance given throughout New York City. Locating her wasn't easy considering that the group performed at undisclosed locations on odd nights, packing the venue with young, drunken fans. It took commitment to become a groupie since the advertisement for each event was through word of mouth. It wasn't a show you could easily purchase tickets for on the internet.

Somehow, Maggie and her band became the hottest group in the underground circuit. Her long, dark, curly hair, and five-nine, slim yet curvy in all the right places, never went unnoticed. Her singing was hypnotic and her performance on stage was incredibly entertaining. She was hard to forget which was why Dom pursued her until she finally caved in. However, he didn't have her as he wanted. Maggie wasn't keen on letting anyone in. She held secrets she couldn't share. The less that people knew about her, the longer they would live.

Dom stared into Maggie's light brown eyes then gently pulled his hands away and placed them on her cheeks. He bent his six-foot-one-inch body closer to her, drew her forehead to his, and closed his eyes. Maggie's heart pounded slightly with anticipation of what was coming next. She thought about pushing him away and telling him to get over it. He could have any girl, just not her, just not now.

They had been sexually involved for months and Dom was head over heels for Maggie. He was genuinely sweet, witty, and a great party companion; but most importantly, he adored her. In respect for him, she decided to give him two extra minutes of her time.

"Magdalena, you have no idea what you do to me. One day—can you just give me one day of your undivided attention?"

Maggie pulled away, "What do you mean?"

"Let me take you out."

"You mean, on a date?"

"Yes, a date! Wherever you'd like to go. Dinner? A movie? Getaway weekend?"

Maggie slightly chuckled as all her anxiety ceased. *The man just wants to take you out. After everything you do to him, he still wants to hang out with you. He's so sweet,* thought the voice on the Right.

A date? OH, HELL, NO! We don't date. Tell him we're washing our hair, screamed the Left. Maggie felt conflicted.

Dom waited patiently for an answer, lowering his hands and rubbing Maggie's shoulders.

"Okay! Friday night. Let's meet at the steakhouse on 77th and Lexington. 6:30pm sound good? I don't have a gig this Friday, so you'll get your shot at a date!"

Dom grinned from ear to ear. He quickly darted to his room, nearly tripping over his own feet, and returned with his smartphone in hand. He spoke into the receiver, setting a calendar reminder.

"I will be there!" he squealed.

"Good." replied Maggie as she patted Dom on the cheek, turned on her heel, and walked out of the apartment. *What the fuck have you done? We don't DATE!* reminded the Left in a pissed-off voice.

"We will Friday night." she said out loud, grinning.

The New York City sun was blinding during the morning rush hour. A small fraction of humans occupied the streets with mere shorts and sweatshirts although it was a brisk morning. Maggie exited the apartment building and surveyed her surroundings. The streets appeared pretty much normal; the sounds of buses and cars roared down the streets, adding to the noise pollution.

The brightness of the sunlight sent a sharp pain through Maggie's eyes and then centered itself in the middle of her forehead. Her vision blurred slightly and faded in and out of clarity. She leaned against the brick building and quickly donned the aviators to protect her eyesight from experiencing another episode of temporary blindness. Suddenly feeling nauseated, she discreetly held her hand over her mouth and swiftly turned to empty her stomach of its contents. In a few moments, she was back to feeling normal.

Maggie made a sharp right on West 86th Street, nearly bumping into a baby stroller while turning the corner. The mother pushing the stroller gave her the dirtiest of New York City looks as if she were shooting daggers from the whites of her tired eyes.

"Oh, shit! I'm so sorry," Maggie sincerely apologized while holding out her hands to prevent further damage.

"You need to watch where you're going," berated the weary and irate mother.

"Sorry, I didn't see you."

"That's the problem with today's youth, you never see..." The woman's torrent of
words dried up like a teaspoon of water on a sunbaked desert floor.

The buses and cars could no longer be heard racing down the streets, and the joggers were left leaping in place. To the human eye, everything seemed as if someone hit the pause button on the remote control. In reality, everything was moving so slowly that a snail slipping by was moving at a faster pace.

Maggie knew the signs all too well. Her people were around, watching her every move, again.

"All right, Pierre! You can show yourself." The steel in her voice made her command unimpeachable.

Maggie's curls blew along with the gust of wind that burst around as two perfectly-winged, celestial figures stood before her.

Pierre's chocolate build blocked the sun from Maggie's view, leaving her standing in what she considered to be an "Angel Shade." She felt a hint of relief knowing the sun was no longer fatiguing her vision. Pierre surveyed the area, making sure that not one living thing was moving in real-time. He was the mastermind behind slowing time to a near standstill.

Gia's expression was burning a hole through Maggie's eyes; it was a look she was well accustomed to. She never understood Gia's irritation toward her. Ever since she was found and brought back to her mother, Gia treated her like a child who was a constant burden. That bothered Maggie to her core as she was a young adult of 21 years by human standards.

Seeing Gia and Pierre together reminded Maggie of the low-budget version of Batman and Robin or, as Maggie liked to refer to them, the Pale Woman and the Frenchman. They were attached at the hip and ordered to keep a close eye on Maggie, as per her mother's request. It was a duty that Gia was not fond of and often protested this assignment to her Queen Guardian. Unfortunately, it was a complaint that fell on deaf ears.

Maggie wasn't thrilled about her mother's constant monitoring. Even though she knew the Underworld was still searching for her, she resented the fact that her mother was wasting valuable resources. Gia and Pierre could be flying around Earth and saving humans. Instead, they were stuck babysitting her. And for what?! Was it really to ensure her safety or to keep tabs on her erratic behavior? Either way, she was bored with it all!

Most of the time, Maggie was either ducking and dodging Pierre and Gia or planning imaginative ways of amusing herself at their discomfort. The Underworld wasn't much of her concern anymore. She wanted the demons to find her; she was tired of running and invited the fight. However, that was a fight her mother and the rest of the Angels and allies wanted to strategically plan for. *It's been three years since they found me. How much more planning do they need?* It was a thought that the voice on the Left spun around in her mind, growing and spreading like a deadly spiderweb.

Gia crossed her arms defensively and retracted her wings. Her mesmerizing eyes narrowed as she noticed that they were once again dressed similarly. Both were sporting fashionably black, fitted leather jackets, tight denim jeans, and boots. Gia's platinum blond ponytail hung from the top of her head like a genie. It was pulled so tightly that it wouldn't allow the wrinkles on her forehead to move as she furrowed her eyebrows. Each step Gia took gave a menacing clink of steel on what would have been concrete if they were still interacting with the real world.

"Out all night again, Magdalena?" Gia's nose wrinkled in disgust. She appeared more frustrated than usual.

"Well, home isn't exactly where the fun is."

"And what is fun for you nowadays? Is it the bed of yet another lover or knocking over innocent babies?"

Gia's words pinched a nerve deep in Maggie's soul. The comment left her feeling personally attacked, judged, and irritated. By this time, she'd had enough of Gia's indirect and direct insults. She took two steps toward Gia ready to slap the cotton candy color off her perfectly-pressed lips. She despised Gia's choice of lipstick just as much as she despised her platinum blond hair. *How could anyone that pale think it's a good idea to have platinum blond hair?* Maggie's Left voice sneered inwardly that maybe one day she would take pity on her and tell her that it wasn't a good look.

"Do you have a problem with me, Gia?

"My problem is that you're an ungrateful little twat who needs a hard lesson." Gia drove her verbal poison dart straight into her opponent's heart.

"Yeah, and who's going to give me that lesson, YOU?!"

"THAT'S ENOUGH from you two!" interjected Pierre, stepping in between the two women, ready to defuse the situation.

The granite in his voice belied the fact that he was the kindest and gentlest of the group of angels. Pierre was now losing all patience. He rubbed his temples, indicating that they were on thin ice, as his tolerance for this shit had diminished. Maggie felt slightly embarrassed that she had stooped so low, especially in front of Pierre. She may not have been fond of Gia, but she highly respected Pierre.

"Apologies, Pierre," Maggie offered contritely.

Even the smallest things, such as their current argument over nonsense, could amuse Pierre. However, today he refused to let the bickering go on any longer. He rested his strong hands on Maggie's shoulder as Gia folded her arms across her chest, seeming to channel her internal peace. Pierre's mocha-tinted eyes transmitted a subtle calming sensation to Maggie's subconscious. She lowered her aviators to get a better look at the soothing glow radiating from his smooth, boyish face.

"We need to get you back to your mother. It is not safe out here."

Pierre glanced over at Gia who was staring at Maggie, indicating that the unspoken order was for her to obey or else.

"I'm going. I will be there in time for the breakfast meeting," Maggie promised, correctly interpreting his stern squeeze of her shoulders.

Pierre dropped his hands and took a stand next to Gia, patiently waiting for Maggie's next move.

"Magdalena, NO GAMES!" shouted Gia as she hurriedly made it her business to scold Maggie. "We have strict orders that you are to come home immediately."

Maggie shook her head from side to side and adjusted her sunglasses. She took two steps back before saying, "Pierre, do you mind hiding your wings." Pierre obeyed without question, and with one snap of her slender, delicate fingers, the business of the New York City morning resumed without skipping a beat.

Maggie had her back turned toward the woman who originally chewed her out. Seeing that Maggie was disinterested and was actually speaking to people who had popped out of nowhere, the woman huffed under her breath and continued to safely push her stroller across the street.

Pierre, stunned, was trying to comprehend how Maggie had been able to counteract his magic. It was the first in all the eons of his existence and very perplexing.

"How did you do that?" asked Gia, demanding answers.

"It's just a little magic," she stated, waving her best jazz hands and repeating the same words her caretaker, Ruby Jane often said. With an arrogant shrug of her slim shoulders, Maggie began making her way toward the crowded, dank subway.

Pierre and Gia stood flummoxed as if counteracting magic weren't bad enough, now Maggie was resorting to taking the human mode of transportation.

Gia called out to her, trying not to make too much conversation around the humans. "We have faster ways of getting home."

"Yeah, well, the demons won't be looking for me down here. I'm sure the subway is worse than Hell," Maggie stated sarcastically over her shoulder as she made her way down the gloomy, trash-smelling stairwell of the subway station.

Pierre watched Maggie until she was out of sight, expressing his concern. "Should we follow her?"

"No! She'll make her way home. And if she doesn't, her mother can deal. I'm done chasing her."

Pierre waved his hand slightly, slowing down time by seconds, giving them the window they needed to spread their wings and shoot up to the sky. The magic went unnoticed by the oblivious spawn of humans jockeying around to get nowhere in their mundane lives.

CHAPTER 2
ANGELS AND DEMONS

Maggie exited the apartment building and stopped short, squinting her eyes against the rays of the sun. She desperately put on her sunglasses, shielding herself from the sharp, fiery sensation that zapped her eyes. Her actions mirrored those of an addict recovering from whatever fashionable feel-good candies they used to fuel a raging party. She stumbled forward, then propped herself up against the brick wall. In a most unladylike way, she tried to retch and empty her stomach of its entire contents.

As the typical scene of Maggie's "walk of shame" played out, Lucifer waited patiently inside the cool opulence of his dark blue Maserati. His hypnotic yet dangerous eyes watched his niece's every move. He was parallel parked along with several vehicles that were sitting under a line of shaded trees. The scatter of humans moving about caused him to fume inside. Deep down, he wanted to torch every one of them and laugh as he watched their ashes blow in the wind, just because he could.

He took his eyes away from Maggie for one second to stare at an old man wobbling across the street with a cane.

"Look at that old fool. Lived his whole life as a slithering wanker, just to choke on a piece of steak and die. I'll be seeing you later this evening. Yes, I will," he mused.

The thought of the old man choking to death made him smirk as he sat back in the passenger seat stalking Maggie through his sea-green eyes. With an irritated glance in the direction of his chauffeur, he motioned his hand to his driver indicating that it was time to follow her on foot. His driver absentmindedly missed his cue. He was too busy admiring himself in the visor's mirror. He had been feeling his newly-formed nose and gushing over his charming smile, tanned skin, and slick dark hair. The nose is what he appreciated the most. His original one had melted off when the Prince of the Darkness was reprimanding another demon. The temperature in Hell was raised hotter than even the demons could stand. Several of their eyes, nose, and horns disintegrated in the fiery inferno. A new nose was never recreated for him. He'd been known as "No-Nose" Tommy ever since.

Lucifer soon realized that it was the demon's first time on Earth and his first time in human skin. He took a few seconds to stare at the demon and watch him as he pressed his index fingers against his gleaming, pearly-white teeth, noting that the sharp razor teeth he was used to were gone and replaced with human canines. In Hell, it wasn't uncommon for demons to take on the form of a human. However, it was only done in the simulated torture chambers as part of an illusion. They were never physically human but a manifestation of one. Seeing himself with skin explained why the demon couldn't tear his crystal-blue eyes away from the mirror. He was falling in love with himself.

The Prince of Darkness couldn't imagine what the demon was going through, nor did he care. He was on a mission, and his patience was rice-paper thin.

With a quick flicking motion of his index finger Lucifer quickly snapped the visor shut, startling the demon back into reality. His British accent thickened with each insult.

"You're not that handsome, Tommy. The mirror and I can't take much more of your ugliness."

No-Nose Tommy shot an expression of sadness at his master, taking the stern warning to bring his attention back to the task at hand.

"Apologies, Sire, the skin is just taking some getting used to."

"Yes, well, hurry it up now."

No-Nose Tommy stared at his master in confusion.

"Bloody hell, get out of the car." Lucifer asserted as he shoved Tommy out of the driver's seat.

The two men stood tall in their designer navy suits. Lucifer adjusted the collar of his jacket while steadily keeping an eye on Maggie walking across the street. He noticed that her demeanor was not as vigilant as it should be.

Two brunettes, taking a leisurely stroll toward Lucifer and No-Nose Tommy smiled and whispered to one another. One of them took a sip of her coffee, made eye contact with No-Nose Tommy and politely smiled. He paused to marvel at her beauty and awkwardly smiled back, seeming unsure if that was the right gesture to do.

"Good morning!" the woman stated casually as she walked by girlishly giggling with her friend.

No-Nose Tommy didn't respond. He stepped aside blushing like a timid school boy, and examined the ladies as if he was trying to solve a mystery. Lucifer stopped short, noticing that his demon was nowhere beside him. Annoyed, he mentally summoned Tommy using an invisible force that dragged him by the tie around his neck. His shoes scraped and scratched across the concrete pavement. The demon gagged as he was tripping over his own two feet trying to catch up with the powerful force pulling him toward his master. The two were now standing at eye level.

"Lose focus again and I will burn you into the void," Lucifer hissed between clenched teeth, balling his fist tightly.

Hearing the word 'void' made the demon straighten himself out quickly. The void was a place where lost souls went to suffer for eternity. It was a black hole of screams, despair, and emptiness. No damned soul or demon in the Underworld wanted to experience the void. It was worse than being tortured.

"I apologize, Sire. I have no idea what this place is doing to me," he quivered, trying to smooth things over.

"It's Earth. It will do a lot of things to you. Now stay focused, stupid! If there's one thing I hate most it's..." Lucifer's words fell short as he began to notice his surroundings slowing down.

No-Nose Tommy looked across the street, noticing that the buses and cars were moving slower than a sloth, much slower if it were even possible.

"What's happening, Sire?"

Lucifer felt the aura of magic cascading through the air. Even after being outcasted from Eden centuries ago, the sense of divine magic had never left him. The feeling sickened him.

"Angels!" Lucifer spotted two of them as they flew briskly above the skies. Their wings cast a brief shadow where he stood as they flapped above.

"This is a good thing. Isn't this what we want, Sire?"

"No, not now."

Lucifer watched intently as the two angels landed behind Maggie and engaged in conversation. He recognized one of the angels immediately. The sight of them turned his eyes into black coal and his skin a purplish red. Tommy, not sure what to do, morphed into his demon face alongside his master, ready to attack. Lucifer exhaled puffs of dark ashes from his nostrils.

He slowly turned to No-Nose Tommy and spoke in a low baritone, igniting with fury.

"We'll return soon enough."

With a wave of his hand, the two demons disappeared, leaving behind a mighty scent of sulfur.

The pungent ammonia smell of downtown Brooklyn hit Maggie's nostrils hard. It made her realize that she had reached her subway stop sooner than anticipated. She held her breath, suppressing the urge to cough out her lungs. The scent was stinging the back of her throat as she admitted to herself that this particular odor was not unique to Brooklyn—several parts of uptown Manhattan were notorious for this same perfume. Everything to her smelled like three homeless men had a grand old time marking their territory on the rundown streets. But even the foul stench couldn't change how she truly felt about the city. Out of all the varied and interesting places she had been for any length of time, nothing could compare to the glimmering lights and skyscrapers of New York City. It was always home. It was the city where she spent her fondest memories and the place that changed her family's life.

New York City is the devil's playground, it is the "city that never sleeps," and it's filled with people clawing their way to the top to be somebody or simply just to be. It's a place where the pretentious and desperate come to sell their souls to the devil, just to make it. It will bring out the survivor in anyone, just as it did to Maggie. She will never forget the day she discovered her powers. Her brother, Jesse, was preparing to take her to school when there was a sudden knock on the door. He urged her to hide in the basement and count. While in hiding, she could hear the front door get kicked down as if a battering ram had demolished it. Terrified, tears streamed down her six-year-old cheeks as the commotion above her head had her fearing for their lives. Something inside her kicked into full gear and prompted her to rush upstairs to protect her brother. It was her fight-or-flight instinct that awoke the supernatural being living inside her.

Maggie smiled at the memory and was grateful for the things she had learned and seen throughout the years. She survived a catastrophic event and had lived to tell the tale. What a world!

The Brooklyn streets were busy as usual with bumper-to-bumper cars and humans going about their individual errands—

their own pursuit of happiness. Maggie blended in with a crowd of ten preparing to cross a busy intersection. She adjusted her aviators and flicked the collar up on her leather jacket, sniffing from side to side discreetly. Powdered deodorant, cheap perfume, and cologne assailed her nostrils while confirming that no demons were hiding in plain sight disguised as a human. There was no masking the faint odor of sulfur that was emitted from the pores of a demon, no matter how hard they tried. Luckily for her, everyone in this gathering was mindless humans stuck in their ever-decaying, miserable bodies.

As the opposing light turned red and the pedestrian crossing signaled that it was safe to cross, Maggie took two steps forward before the sharp, shooting, yet familiar pain began. This was the wrong time for a massive migraine. The clobbering at her temples could not easily be ignored. She picked up her pace and walked half a block before turning into a darkened alley. She stood wedged between two tall brick buildings and firmly pressed her back against the wall as if trying to become one with the bricks. Maggie removed her sunglasses and lifted her head to the sky as in a silent prayer pleading to Eden for the pain to subside. The clouds were gathering and blocking the sun while simultaneously giving way to shade. She closed her eyes tightly, concentrating on anything other than the hammering happening inside her skull. Trickles of sweat rolled down her forehead, and her breath accelerated sharply.

Stay calm, Maggie, you know the drill. It will all be over in a few seconds, the voice to the Left convinced.

Shhhhh. The Left voice was soothing and almost calm. The Right had nothing to say, which was odd since both voices were always in constant battle.

"It hurts more than usual," Maggie painfully uttered out loud to the empty space.

I know, but it's all part of who we are. It's almost over. Just relax, reassured the Left voice.

After a minute, the pain vanished. The only remaining remnants of the attack were that her palms and forehead were still a little sweaty, and her breathing was still attempting to return to normalcy. Maggie slid the aviators into her jacket pocket and used her sleeve to rub the droplets of sweat from her forehead. She walked to the end of the alleyway toward a maroon brick wall and scanned her surroundings one last time before knocking three times.

The bricks crackled and swayed with powerful magic. Maggie could feel the intensity of its energy working on overload to protect what was hidden on the other side. The force was stronger than she remembered. She hesitated slightly before walking through it for fear of what it might do to her. Mild heat and static energy emanated from its aurora. The warmth didn't seem hot enough to burn. She pondered if it was safe to touch.

Something isn't right, said the Left voice.

"No shit," blurted Maggie. "Here goes nothing."

As Maggie inched her foot into the portal in an attempt to walk through, she was shocked and instantly jumped back in surprise.

"What the fuck?" She curiously watched as steam rose from the tip of her boots as if they had been roasting over a fire.

"What the FUCK IS GOING ON?" Maggie shouted at the wall, feeling a sudden pinch of panic. She feared the worst, that she was locked out of the portal, never to see her family again.

"Is someone there? SOMEONE, ANYONE, PLEASE!"

"HEY, MISS, ARE YOU ALRIGHT?" a male called out from a distance.

Maggie swiftly turned her attention to see an older fellow standing ten feet away from her at the entrance of the alley. He seemed concerned but also could have just been a nosey pedestrian. She quickly pulled her smartphone from her pocket and waved it around.

"Yes, I'm just on my phone."

The man nodded and walked away not before muttering "Crazy kids," under his breath.

That was close, said the Right voice.

"Yeah, very close," acknowledged Maggie.

Maggie stared at the wall for what felt like hours, but in reality, only two minutes passed before she heard proof of life from the other side.

"Magdalena, is that you?" questioned the woman from the other side of the wall.

"YES! YES! It's me, the protection shield is not letting me through."

"What do you mean? Just walk through," stated the woman, sounding slightly irritated.

"The damn thing just shocked me. Is this some sort of cruel joke, Keiko?"

Before Maggie could say another word, a slender arm reached through the wall, yanked the top of her leather jacket, and forced her through the other side. The magic aurora disappeared immediately.

The sun above radiated a summer's heat causing Maggie to remove her leather jacket. The sweet-smelling aroma of fresh flowers, combined with the lack of humidity, made her feel less tense, although she couldn't stop wondering why the portal initially denied her entry.

Maggie walked along a trail in an open field following the crunch, crunch of Kieko's footsteps on the unpaved ground. Keiko was Master Anu's loyal advisor, his most dangerous soldier, and his adopted daughter. She'd known Maggie since she was a child and held a special place in her heart for her. Protecting Magdelena was always her number one priority.

She quickened her pace to keep up with Keiko while trying to make conversation.

"Hey, what was up with me not being able to walk through the portal?"

"I don't know." Keiko retorted in her usual taciturn manner.

"Are you guarding the portal now?"

"NO!"

"So, what were you doing out here?"

Keiko stopped short and eyed Maggie with obvious irritation. She folded her arms tightly across her chest, revving up to give her the business. Today was surely a "snap at Maggie" kind of day. Keiko had never gotten as frustrated with Maggie before. She generally adored her, ever since she was young. However, grown-up Maggie was a handful that no one could tame. She was reckless and immature.

In the summer's heat, Keiko didn't break a sweat in her ensemble of black-on-black. Her dark, fitted shirt with sheer sleeves clung to her black spandex tights. Her shapely, muscled gams and thighs tapered down to her high boots. Her ponytail stood on the top of her head and swayed with the breeze. Staring at her was like looking at the perfect picture of a Japanese model fiercely owning the camera. Maybe that's something she could have been if she weren't so dangerous.

"Why do you do that?" Keiko questioned, her tone annoyed. Since Maggie has been home, she has never been one to involve herself in her family drama. But the look on her face told the story of someone who was growing tired of the bullshit, especially since she couldn't hide the fact that it was stressing her out.

"Do what?" Maggie averted her eyes.

"Stay out all night, knowing we are supposed to be in hiding. We are not ready to face the evil that is following us. I understand you want to live your life, hell, we all do, but not like this, not recklessly."

"I'm getting tired of running, Keiko. I'm just over it. I've been running my entire childhood and half of my adult life with my father. And I'm still running with my mother. When does it all end?" Maggie couldn't help the high-pitched tone in her voice.

"Well, get over yourself. Because it's not just all about you. You are putting everyone at risk—me, my father, the other angels, and the Vs. Everyone! So, STOP thinking about yourself for once, Maggie. We will stop running when time is on our side."

Maggie never once stopped to think about all the harm she was doing. When she pictured the demon fight in her head, it was her against them. There was no Keiko, or mother, just her and the demons. *How could you be so senseless?* questioned the Right voice.

"Understood," was all Maggie could mutter.

Master Anu Du'Shun's newly-owned property was situated in a remote location off the coast of Ireland. Its locality was cloaked, unlisted, and undetectable via satellite. It was untraceable by any humans or supernatural beings as he made sure to fully secure and protect his whereabouts. He kept his location such a secret that not even his top advisors or his counter-partner, Master Andrew, knew his whereabouts. It was better that way; not disclosing that information safeguarded his people, as well.

Master Anu was extremely careful. He meticulously planned so as not to repeat the destruction of this property as in his previous estate. His last home had been demolished by his former Vampire leaders. Every human servant was wiped out, and almost every Vamp guard was left for dead. However, losing everything during that fight only reborned him into who he is today. The new Leader of the Vampire species.

The only transport on and off the island was through a portal that was designed by his most trusted witches to keep out evil demons. The portal became the gateway to New York City because it gave him access to conduct business there whenever needed. All of his subordinates and his partner lived in the city. New York was a breeding ground for Vs. Many of the other species called it Vamp City.

The three-story home Master Anu owned, arched in a U-shape, and sat on the top of the cliffs overlooking the crisp, clear, blue sea. It was equipped with thirty-two rooms and thirty-three bathrooms. There were several small cottages built around the property that were reserved for the Vampire guards and other species that worked for him. The layout of his new home was much bigger than his last estate and over-the-top luxurious. The emerald lawn was neatly manicured, and the cherry blossom trees were freshly trimmed. It was as if Master Anu was replicating his version of Eden for his wife.

The estate rested on an open field with no fence guarding the home, just three huge wolves and two silky, midnight panthers roaming freely. The five beasts strolled toward Keiko like obedient lapdogs as she approached. One of the wolves glared at Maggie, giving a low, slow growl, not recognizing her.

"Stand down, you five. This is Magdalena, Queen Angel's daughter. She's to be protected like everyone else," Keiko said authoritatively.

The beasts stood at attention three feet away from Maggie, observing her as if she were a foreign object. The panthers seemed as if they wanted to devour her like a freshly-marinated T-bone steak. Maggie felt a bit uneasy, not sure why Master Anu decided to hire more help.

"Wolves, go guard the portal. Panthers, stick around and protect the property," ordered Keiko. The three wolves hurried off without question.

"Why do we have animals guarding a portal now?"

"They're not animals. They're shifters. Father hired them yesterday to guard the portal since many of the Vs can't stand the heat for long periods. They will guard during the day and the Vs at night. Besides, guarding is a shifter's job anyway, since they love a good fight."

"Wow! Shifters? Here? I've heard of them but have never personally seen one up close."

"Don't get too close," ordered Keiko ominously without further explanation.

Keiko and Maggie were greeted at the entrance by a female human servant. Her black pencil skirt hit a bit past the knees, and her short-sleeved, fitted blouse hugged her perfectly. It was the uniform attire of all the servants in the house. Black-on-black and fitted with neatly kept updos or buns for the ladies, clean-shaven men, and a golden "A" red-lettered pin cinched on the left breast of the uniform. The A represented Master Anu's line. His workers either had the letter A permanently inked on their inner left wrist or sported the pin proudly. Since many were loyal to Master Anu, several of the servants were permanently inked.

"Welcome home," greeted the servant, giving a pearly smile. She laid her baby-blue eyes on Maggie and kindly removed the leather jacket from Maggie's sweaty hands.

"Thank you. Where is everyone?" responded Keiko.

"In the sitting area, Madam Keiko. There is breakfast served if you two desire."

Maggie followed Keiko across the white marble floor. The arched windows were wide open, letting in the cool ocean breeze. The interior of the home was beyond any millionaire's imagination. It was brimming with high-end fixtures, vaulted ceilings, and a grand marble spiral staircase that appeared to loop endlessly. Each piece of furniture was imported from an exotic place around the world—leather couches from Italy, area rugs from Morocco, the list continued. At times, Maggie was afraid to sit her ass anywhere for fear of damaging anything. The house was just another constant reminder of how damn rich and powerful the Vs were.

Servants shuffled around the house cleaning, preparing feasts, and handling the daily tasks. Maggie and Keiko walked through a brightly-lit corridor, passing a few rooms en route. Pierre and Gia sat quietly in a study examining a thick, ancient book. The clicking of Maggie's heels must have drawn their attention as she walked past; they were already staring at the doorway waiting to see who was behind the click-clacking. Maggie and Gia locked eyes. Gia appeared unmoved and stared directly at Maggie without flinching. Maggie took the opportunity to sardonically salute her as she strolled by.

As they reached the sitting area, Angel, Maggie's mother, and Master Anu cut their conversation short to acknowledge Maggie.

The large arched windows in the circular sitting room allowed natural light to filter through the area. Angel preferred to welcome the sunlight into her home, especially since it did not negatively affect Master Anu in the slightest. Ever since he drank Angel's blood, he'd been almost human-like, minus the beating heart and his thirst for blood.

There was a delightful breakfast laid out on the coffee table. Maggie was internally salivating over it. Before she could make her way toward the food, Angel rose from the plush, cream-colored sofa and stood between Maggie and the pastries. Her hair was tied up in a neat updo showing off the length of her sleek neck. She and Maggie appeared almost identical, nearly passing for sisters, except Maggie stood three inches taller.

Angel pressed the creases down on her white satin pants before squeezing Maggie into a bear hug.

"Oh, goodness, Magdalena, you had me worried sick," Angel fussed.

"Mom, I'm fine."

"I never seem to understand you. Never!"

Here she goes again, said the Left voice. *This is the part where we tune her out.* Maggie's attention wandered as Angel gave her the usual daunting lecture.

It was the same scolding she received almost every other day. *Stop staying out overnight. Try calling. We spent ten years finding you; we don't want to spend another ten looking for you. We want you to quit the band, but it's like asking hell to freeze over. Educate yourself more on your celestial culture. Maggie, just stay put. Maggie, you're too reckless. Maggie, it's too dangerous. Maggie. Maggie. Maggie. Maggie...* It was the last thing she heard before she completely tuned out her mother and began mentally summoning a strawberry pastry from the coffee table. Angel yanked the floating pastry before it reached Maggie's eager fingers.

"Whoops, I guess eating during this meeting is out of the question?" asked Maggie, not realizing her actions were disrespectful.

"Not when I am speaking to you, Magdalena." Angel furrowed her eyebrows and crushed the pastry in her hand, sending flakes of crust and powdered sugar snowing to the polished marble floor.

Maggie wanted nothing more than to re-establish the bond she used to have with her mother, but she couldn't go back to her childhood life. She was eight years old when she was snatched by her demon father and lived on the run with him and his witch girlfriend, Ruby Jane. Ruby Jane was the only mother she'd ever known as she thought her biological mother was dead, but that changed when Angel found her ten years later living in Australia. Everything she thought to be true was a lie. Her father, Jack, knew Angel was still living and searching for Maggie. Yet he continued to run because he was being hunted by the Underworld. His way of not hurting Angel or Maggie was to keep up the good run. However, after Angel retrieved Maggie, running was no longer an option. They decided to remain in hiding until the "adults" could come up with an extravagant plan to defeat the Underworld. It was a plan that was taking them three years too long to implement.

Angel cut her lecturing and silently stared at Maggie as her light brown eyes slowly turned greyish-green in attempting, for the umpteenth time, to figure her out. Maggie interpreted her mother's expression all too well; she was breaking the shields inside of her head to flash into her memories.

"I suggest you don't do that, mom," shot Maggie. She tried to force her out, but her mother's energy was too powerful.

Maggie gave a look of despair as she watched herself through her mother's eyes. Angel was flipping through Maggie's memories as if she were flicking through unwanted television channels. Techno dancing, body shots, lip-locking in a dark corner, and images of her laughing hysterically with a male human shot into a clear vision. Flashes of swaying, white, cotton sheets, hands reaching for pleasure, and erotic moans danced in site. Angel jumped forward in the memory to see Maggie arriving in Brooklyn. She was ready to cross the street before she hesitated and held her head in her hands. The vision became distorted as the colors faded into darkness and the people around them turned to charcoal ash and cinnamon dust. Angel looked around the memory appearing confused until she snapped her eyes shut and dropped to her knees as if she'd been heavily kicked. She held her head between the palms of her hands and squeezed as she tried to hold in the wails of agony that was itching to escape between her rapid panting. It became clear as day, Angel felt Maggie's pain.

Their suffering in the vision materialized in real-time. Painful punches to the temple manifested inside Maggie's head, throbbing and pounding away. She buckled and dropped to her knees, holding her head in her hands, screaming in agony.

"FUCK!! GET OUT! Get OUT OF MY FUCKING HEAD!"

Keiko quickly bent down to help Maggie, seeming confused and silently seeking answers. Angel promptly snapped herself out of Maggie's head. She held her forehead in a drunken state desperately trying to regain focus. She stumbled backwards and nearly succumbed to being one with the floor. However, she was rescued inches before she hit the ground; all thanks to Master Anu's lightning speed.

"Are you alright, my darling?" asked Master Anu in a worried tone.

Angel shot her eyes open and spoke hurriedly.

"No! No! This can't be true."

She hurried over to a sobbing Maggie who was still holding her head tightly between her hands in excruciating pain. Keiko kept her arms wrapped around her in comfort as Angel knelt beside her and began frantically parting Maggie's hair from the top of her scalp until she felt and saw what she had dreaded finding. Sitting on her scalp near her hairline, camouflaged by her dark curls, were two small, newly-forming HORNS!

CHAPTER 3
THE DEMON INSIDE

Was it just her inner and currently off-kilter instincts or did the night just fall in a blink of an eye? Maggie slowly fluttered her eyes out of her meditative serenity zone and took in the darkened scene. Gone were the usual glorious and righteous colors of sunset. They were suffocatingly replaced with an ink-black sky that fought against the valiant little stars that tried to shine forth. The hairs on her arms stood eerily at attention as the chilled ocean breeze persuaded her that it was time to find warmth.

Maggie sighed as she gave up on enjoying a few moments alone on the cement steps at the front of her house. What was the point? A part of her was conspiring to leave her problems behind and find an unsanctioned speakeasy, a well-frequented burlesque club, or just hang around at a boisterous nightclub where she could pretend to be normal. Even if normal meant living with baby horns on the top of her head. However, a part of her was also relieved to be home.

Maggie strolled toward the rear of the house, hoping to find her brother Jesse working late inside the research lab. Master Anu had built the lab under the estate to safely continue his work as a researcher of the supernatural. Jesse was constantly working on experiments, writing articles, and keeping journals of his studies of the unknown. Because of his passion in learning about the celestial culture, he became Master Anu's apprentice.

Jesse researched and studied the worlds of Eden, Hell, and Earth. He cultivated and fed an insatiable hunger for learning any and everything he could get his hands on regarding Lucifer's downfall, the decisions of the divine right, and the reasons why angels roamed the Earth. He traveled the world seeking out demon sightings and portents. On most days, when he was not documenting his travels or picking Angel's memories about Eden, he was researching the history of his biological parents. He'd always known that he was adopted and was left in Angel's custody at the age of five. But as Jesse learned more about himself and his supernatural gifts, he couldn't help but feed the curious cat within.

The ever-growing questions of what truly happened to his parents ate away at him on several occasions. It was a conversation he constantly rehashed with Maggie, probably ad nauseam. The mystery of his mother's disappearance along with the struggle of finding his father's identity was weighing down on him. Jesse was generally good at finding answers to everything he researched and he absorbed information like a wet sponge. However, finding clues that were directly linked to his parents became like searching for the world's smallest needle in the tallest haystack.

Maggie pressed the buzzer on the steel door and scanned the oppressive darkness making sure that not even the shifters were around or hiding out of sight. The motion sensor lit up in silent alarm; Maggie's eyes glanced to the small dome camera above her head. She stuck out her tongue and raised her right hand giving her best "rock & roll" gesture while shaking her head back and forth as if rocking out to her favorite Guns-N-Roses song. Within seconds, the door buzzed and unlocked.

Jesse greeted Maggie at the bottom of the stairwell still chuckling at her silly antics on the camera.

"You are ridiculous sometimes," he joshed as he pulled his little sister in for a hug.

"I have to be. Someone around here has to help you lighten up."

Maggie squeezed her brother tightly in a bear hug, displaying just how much she had missed him. She hated seeing him consumed by his work and drowning himself in research that may never give him an answer.

"So, what's keeping you up this late, big brother?" Maggie walked around the fluorescent-lit lab touching ancient artifacts and sneaking peeks through several microscopes. The room felt cooler than usual. She slightly shivered and grabbed one of the lab coats hanging on a chair and casually slipped it on as she sat on a stool behind a high-top desk. The lab was filled with state-of-the-art equipment. Master Anu spent millions of dollars securing the best-computerized merchandise possible for the sort of delicate research he conducted. The computers around her made small humming noises, and the room smelled of freshly-opened plastic packaging, suggesting that much of the equipment was brand new.

"You're keeping me up," Jesse responded as he sat across the table from Maggie, adjusting his black-rimmed glasses.

"I heard mom finally found out about the horns forming. I told you that you weren't going to be able to hide them forever."

"Well, it was worth a try. I just didn't want her to freak out, and that's exactly what happened. You know how dramatic mom gets." Maggie's eyes rolled, she then drew her attention to a set of scattered papers on the table. "Have you found a way to fix me yet?" she asked curiously, fumbling through the documents.

"I can't fix your demon DNA. Unfortunately, you're stuck with it. And these papers are not part of my research on you." Jesse reached for the papers she was reading and quickly secured them in a draw.

"So whose Camila Del Rio?" Maggie questioned, remembering the last sentence she read at the bottom of the page. "Please tell me it's a woman you're dating. Or someone you're interested in?" Maggie often worried about her brother. Not only was he burning himself out with work, but he also had a non-existent love life. She got more action than he did on any given Sunday.

"No, She's my biological mother," stated Jesse without thinking, seeming tense at her unexpected intrusion. He reached for a folder labeled "Maggie" sitting in a file organizer as if she were one of his experimental specimens.

"You found her real last name? That's great news! What else did you learn about her?"

"We have plenty of time to talk about her later; let's talk about you." He nimbly sidestepped her curiosity trap.

"Well..." Maggie chuckled and nonchalantly shrugged. "You know me, I'm just your average young adult growing horns out of her skull."

Jesse walked over to Maggie with a small flashlight and began feeling around the top of her scalp for the two forming lumps.

"Here these babies are," he said, referring to the lumps. "Have the headaches gotten worse?"

"Yes, And the voices have gotten louder."

Jesse flashed the light into Maggie's eyes, examining her dilating pupils. He noticed the veins in her eyes were turning into slightly dark and ash-colored micro tracks.

"It appears the demon inside you is getting much stronger," he stated in a somber tone as in a doctor delivering a deadly diagnosis to his patient.

Maggie's heart dropped ten notches and settled uncomfortably in her queasy stomach. "What do you mean? Am I becoming one of them? Jesse..." She grabbed the collar of his lab coat, pleading with him. "You can't let me turn into that thing. I have a date on Friday night."

Jesse raised his right eyebrow and seemed to repress a ridiculous twitch at the corner of his mouth. Her complete inability to not appear overly dramatic seemed to amuse him. His raised eyebrow was a common gesture Master Anu usually did when he was intrigued or fascinated by someone's response. It was clear the pair were spending way too much time together.

"The entire Underworld is ready to flip Earth upside down looking for you, and all you can think about is your date on Friday night? I thought you didn't date?"

Maggie released and smoothed out the wrinkles she had caused on Jesse's collar before she allowed herself to sink regretfully back down onto her seat. This was neither the time nor the place for her humor to kick in. She should be prostrated with fear of the unknown. Her next words were spoken with sincerity.

"I don't date. But in all seriousness, Jess, I don't know what to do. The headaches, the voices, and the constant inner battle—it's exhausting. And it scares the hell out of me. I try so hard to remain calm and to channel my celestial side more. But it's as if my will is slowly failing me."

Jesse stared at the glimmer of worry that drifted and settled into the depths of Maggie's soft brown eyes. He removed his glasses and rubbed his hand over his shaggy blond hair. He was long overdue for a haircut, and his five o'clock shadow was evidence that he was overdue for a shave, as well. He quickly walked over to a small refrigerator and shuffled between a few vials before coming back with a small ampoule and a syringe filled with a green substance that seemed to glow ominously.

"What is that?" Maggie curiously questioned, her voice a bit above a whisper.

"Master Anu designed this. It's a power-suppressing chemical. It's what he gives Keiko to help her not lose her shit. It works by repressing her most dangerous powers on the inside. She's half-demon and I'm sure her demon DNA is less powerful than yours. I'm not so sure if this will even work on you, but I know for a fact that it won't kill you."

"How are you so sure it won't kill me?" Maggie nibbled nervously at the right corner of her lip. She was two bad news sentences away from curling up in the fetal position with her thumb in her mouth.

"I have faith that your celestial side won't let you die." The confidence in Jesse's tone made Maggie wonder if he was secretly crossing his toes inside his tennis shoes. So much of science was accidental discoveries.

"I don't know about this, Jess." Maggie second-guessed this path as the gateway to her freedom or her death.

"I won't let you die. We have to try, Maggie. It's the only option I have at the moment. If we don't try, your horns will grow, your eyes will go completely dark and demon dilated, and Lord knows what else. You may not want to admit it, but you are something of uncharted territory. I don't know how much more time you have before that happens. At least with this, if it works, we could borrow time until Master Anu and I figure something out."

Jesse was holding the green glowing vial as if it were an inviting shot glass at a party.

Maggie inhaled, gathered her courage, and stared into Jesse's once blue eyes now reflecting the emerald, menacing glow. As the magic inside him grew, it changed the shade of his iris. She often missed his pale blue eyes, reminding her of a cloudless summer sky where she easily lost herself. Now, all she stared into were tired and worried green eyes.

"Okay, let's do it!" She finally stated.

Maggie removed her lab coat and readied her right arm. Jesse disinfected the top middle area of her arm with alcohol-soaked gauze. He reached for the syringe and injected the hypodermic needle into Maggie's arm without a warning. She didn't flinch as she felt the warm substance flowing under her skin.

The needle was quickly removed as Jesse massaged the area.

"All done," he reassured.

What the fuck is happening, said the Left side of Maggie's voice, sounding extremely distant.

Maggie blinked a few times, not exactly sure of what was supposed to transpire or what she could reasonably expect as a side effect.

"How do you feel?" Jesse asked, taking caution for any negative reactions.

Maggie stood up and stretched her arms toward the ceiling. She stumbled a bit as her head spun for two seconds. However, she swiftly regained her composure and felt normal.

"I feel great!" she answered as she took a few more steps forward and collapsed like a sack of potatoes without warning.

"This is why you're the apprentice, Jesse. Your job is to watch and learn, not take matters into your own hands," scolded Master Anu as he, Jesse, and Angel waited patiently for Maggie to regain consciousness.

"I know, I should have consulted with you first. But I was so positive it wouldn't harm her," Jesse's voice quivered with regret and disappointment.

"It was absolutely careless, Jesse," interjected Angel. Her nose and eyes were red from a brief but tear-filled emotional indulgence. "My healing abilities are not even working on her, and that's concerning me the most."

"I'm sorry," was all Jesse could mutter.

After Maggie's collapse, Jesse carried her over to the gurney inside one of the examining rooms in the lab. Before he could call Master Anu, his footsteps were already heard thumping down the stairs.

Late-night research and business calls were not uncommon for Master Anu. However, they were duties he usually handled inside his study, not the lab. Jesse was not expecting him, nor was he anticipating Angel to be tagging along behind him. The scene was set up for more of Angel's dramatic crying, especially when she couldn't heal her own daughter.

Master Anu drew blood from Maggie and continued monitoring her vitals. If she were human, it would have been so easy to care for her. Angel could have revived her. But with her half-demon, half-celestial species, it was difficult to detect how long it would take her to fully recover.

Hours passed as the clock inside the lab indicated 7:00 a.m. There were no windows in the underground lab and zero natural lighting to make the atmosphere feel inviting.

Angel sat silently watching Maggie while Jesse slept on the gurney in the examining room next door. Anu worked tirelessly throughout the dark morning hours putting together a chemical combination that would counteract the suppressing concoction. He walked inside the examination room and placed one strong, reassuring, hand on Angel's shoulder. She leaned into his touch, hoping this was the beginning of good news.

"I think this may work," Master Anu stated in a soothing voice.

Angel started at the blue-filled syringe and walked over to Maggie. She ran her fingers over her daughter's scalp, feeling around for the horns.

"The lumps are gone."

Master Anu remained silent.

As Angel continued, "I'm losing my child. Even after I've found her, I've already lost her." Tears began to form in the corner of Angel's eyes.

"We haven't lost her yet, my darling." Master Anu placed the syringe inside his lab coat pocket and wrapped his comforting arm around Angel. She sank into his embrace, resting her head on his shoulder and snuggling into his silky dark, shoulder-length, hair.

"Eventually, she is going to get stronger, and I won't know what to do with her. I'm afraid that one day I will have to go against my own daughter. I've been praying to Eden, begging them to have her celestial side overcome her deviant one, but I'm afraid my pleading is going to remain unanswered." Angel's words were filled with hurt, dread, and resentment. The reality of a mother having to end her child was the most difficult decision she would have to make if it came down to it.

Master Anu rubbed her shoulder and consoled her as much as he could. "Let's not think like that. I will exhaust all my resources before we let Maggie get taken over by the demon world. Whatever it takes, we will stop this one way or another. Now, let's see if my new elixir works."

Angel nodded and stood back to watch Master Anu work his brand of magic. As he began disinfecting the area on Maggie's arm, Maggie quickly shot up, pulling her arm back and yelping in the process. Angel gave a startled shriek as Master Anu dropped the gauze, trying to calm everyone in the room, including himself.

"MOM!" Jesse appeared inside the room like the Flash.

"Maggie, are you alright?" Jesse and Angel questioned in unison.

"She's fine. Calm down, everyone, and give her a moment," suggested Master Anu.

"Jesse, grab her a bottle of water, please."

Jesse did what he was told by Master Anu without question.

Maggie looked around the room, confused, trying to focus on her environment and the people surrounding her. Her thoughts were moving faster than she could comprehend. The two voices inside her head were bickering back and forth, and she couldn't shut them up.

What took you so long to wake me up, said the Left.

It was finally so peaceful not having you around, retorted the Right.

How fucking dare you? Maggie needs me.

No, Maggie needs, ME! You're nothing but a disease that won't go away, declared the Right.

You're so weak. Do you think one ounce of green bullshit is going to make me go away? Well, you have something else coming to you.

Maggie brought her knees to her chest, held her head between her hands in an effort to dilute the voices, and rocked back and forth. Tears formed in her eyes and rolled unheeded down her cheeks.

"Shut-up, shut-up, shut-up!" she whispered while slapping her forehead with the palm of her hand.

"The voices are battling inside her head. She won't be able to focus on you two until she gets those two to comply," Jesse explained as Angel and Master Anu watched the mental breakdown slowly unfolding before their eyes.

"Voices? How do you know all this?" Angel quizzed.

"Because she's been confiding in me," Jesse reluctantly gave up his sister.

"Voices?" Is it two voices?" asked Master Anu, assuring he had heard correctly.

Jesse nodded, giving confirmation, unable to meet their eyes.

"The two voices of Good and Evil. Of course! Makes perfect sense." Master Anu exclaimed with a sense of eureka. He had dealt with a situation similar to this before with Keiko. He ran over to his fridge again and pulled out a small vial with a clear substance.

"I know exactly how to get those voices to power down, at least for a few days. Hold her arm, Jesse." Master Anu rapidly filled a new syringe. Maggie struggled and cussed at them to let her go. She violently kicked with all her might, trying to fend them off, but she was no match for her mother. Angel placed her hand on Maggie's leg and mentally paralyzed her. The voices inside Maggie's head were screaming louder than she'd ever heard them, causing her temples to ripple like a series of swiftly-moving waves of molten hot lava.

Anu jabbed the needle into Maggie's arm and pressed firmly on the syringe, shooting the entire tincture into her bloodstream. Maggie was suddenly still as Angel gingerly let go of her mental paralysis and set her daughter free.

They all watched as Maggie fell silent, seemingly catatonic but staring at the high ceiling. She closed her eyes tightly, every cell in her body straining to listen for an ounce of bickering voices, but it was as quiet as the hour of the jackal in the desert.

"They're gone. I can't hear them. They're gone." Maggie held her hands to her face, sobbing with relief.

Angel moved closer and embraced Maggie, allowing her to pour out her emotions on her silk, floral robe.

"As I stated before, my darling. We do whatever it takes," Master Anu whispered for Angel's ears only.

CHAPTER 4
THE DEVIL'S PIT

Lucifer stood motionless, deep in thought, as tableau after tableau of horrific mosaics played in his mind of the oppressed withering in agony as the demons worked their evil tricks. He never once blinked as his eyes remained fixated on the floating, golden-rimmed mirrors displaying the gruesome scenes. The desperate sounds of wailing, gnashing of teeth, pleas, and cries for mercy were usually soothing to Lucifer. However, today, not even the sight of a much-anticipated damned soul could pull him out of his doldrums. It was a shame. He was looking forward to several religious hypocrites, murderous drug dealers, and bigoted politicians to enter through the fiery gates of the Underworld.

The various toys, gadgets, and sight-enhancing mirrors could not slow the anger that coursed through his veins as he replayed yesterday's incident in his mind like a really bad movie loop. He continued to overthink and play out scenarios on how he could have done things differently while monitoring Maggie's movements. He practically could have snatched her off the streets if he wanted to, but Maggie was not his priority.

Witnessing Gia dive from the skies like some sort of Invincible Savior, all glittering with light and peace, changed the dynamics of his plan and completely maddened him.

Three loud knocks on the door brought the Master of the Underworld out of his irritated musings. Woe betide that messenger!

"WHO'S THERE?!" His question had been voiced in a menacing growl—every word punctuating the fact that, although he was asking, he definitely did not want to be disturbed.

"It's Camila and Tommy. May we please enter, Sire?"

The cringing, fawning sound of No-Nose Tommy brought back some equanimity. He was the closest demon he had to a Court Jester at this point. Besides, it amused him that Tommy had offered up Camila's name first. Lucifer thought to dismiss his minions but decided to hear them out.

"ENTER!" he commanded, never turning his devil face away from the constantly shifting mirrors.

Camila entered the lair with No-Nose Tommy in tow. She removed her wool, brown hood, allowing her long, dark hair to breathe freely. She glanced around at the torture games on the large mirrors; the demons were showing no mercy and having a gruesome and fabulously grand time.

Most of the floating torches remained unlit, leaving the room more shadowy than usual. Lucifer, the Morning Star, preferred the darker corners of Hell. It helped him think when he was most troubled. But even in the murkiness of the nearly-dark lair, Camila noticed her master's unusually large skull. It sat on his shoulders like a massive, heavy bowling ball. She paused, assessing the situation.

Exposing his demon face for a long period was something Lucifer never did. His servants were reluctant to talk to him, and many hid from his presence unless they were summoned. Camila, on the other hand, refused to let her master soak in his thoughts. If something was bothering him, she would be the first to handle the situation.

"Sire, I do not wish to overstep, but I need to know what happened on Earth. How can we help you?" Her voice slightly quivered. One wrong move and Lucifer would rage, stomp his feet, and then burn them all into the void. It was a risk they were willing to take.

"Tommy, I want you to go," Lucifer ordered, still refusing to tear his fixed gaze from the action that was reflected in the torture mirrors.

No-Nose Tommy stared at Camila, not moving from her side as if he had gone deaf. If she were going to burn, then they needed to disintegrate together. Besides, he was the one who told Camila of their retreat once the angels appeared. But it was Camila's bright idea to get to the bottom of it.

"I SAID LEAVE!" Lucifer slammed his hand against the mirror, shattering it into a thousand pieces. The blow to the mirror sent a powerful gust of wind towards Tommy's direction and forcefully shoved him out of sight faster than his demonic powers could muster. The backdraft closed the door behind him.

Camila waited anxiously as sweat beads dripped from her forehead. She hadn't been afraid of her sire since the day she first arrived in the Underworld. She worshiped the gravel he walked on, but at this very moment, her lips noticeably twitched; and she fidgeted with her fingers, giving off a sense of uneasiness. She tried to hold a hard expression, but Lucifer could see past her fearlessness without even looking directly at her.

"I'm going to speak freely with you, Camila. You're honestly the only person I trust in this shit hole."

Lucifer slowly turned to face her, morphing his face back to normal. His piercing, sea-green eyes pondered her from beneath his stormy, dark brows. Irritation weighed heavily on his shoulders, the same shoulders that had held the line in Hell for a millennium. With a tiny, well-placed sigh from his minion before him, he felt infinitesimally lighter.

"Yes, Sire?" Camila lowered her head in compliance.

"Do you love my nephew, Castus?"

Camila's eyes grew wide, and her posture stiffened as the question drew a surprising reaction she couldn't hide if she tried.

"I'm sorry, Sire, que?"

She couldn't hold her Spanish from slipping. It was as if she was being tested.

"Do you love Castus?"

Lucifer glared at her, awaiting her response.

"I love him because he is the father of my son. Because he is…I mean, *was* someone I trusted. But I am not *IN* love with him, and I am quite satisfied that he is confined to the void."

Camila paused, waiting to see if her responses were to her master's satisfaction.

"It's a shame. Angels have this angelic energy that makes loving them so easy, even at their worst. I figured since you were still human, my nephew would still warrant that effect on you. But looking into those icy blue eyes of yours, you're as cold inside as you are out. I LOVE IT!"

Lucifer lightened the mood as he grinned at Camila and lifted her chin to get a better look. She didn't smile back. Instead, she stared at him intently.

The Prince of Darkness turned on his heels and paced over the shattered glass. With an absentminded wave of his hand, the mirror reconstituted itself and probably got an upgrade in the bargain.

"The angel that I saw on Earth was someone with whom I've had a bit of history." The words tripped over themselves as they forced their way up from the cavity that once might have cradled a heart.

"An enemy?" Camila quickly questioned as still as a deer enjoying the forest but aware that danger was close by.

"Far from it. Gia was my companion…my dearest love." Lucifer stopped his pacing and gazed in Camila's direction. "Someone who I'd thought would be by my side till the very end. Of course, that all failed once I was thrown out of Eden."

He rubbed his hands together as if trying to keep them warm, even though the temperature inside his lair was over one hundred and ten degrees. In reality, he was rubbing his palms together suppressing his anger and calming the inner demon inside of him that wanted to raise its horns and wreak havoc, carnage, and destruction.

Camila walked over to her master and placed her gentle hands on top of his, conveying her understanding of his struggles. Her crystal blue eyes filled with compassion as he wondered if those were the same empathetic eyes that manipulated his nephew Castus. When she spoke in her hypnotic Spanish accent, it was as if he was seeing her for the first time.

"Sire, past lovers are to be kept in the past."

Those were the words that passed her lips. But those words sounded as if they meant something else, or as if it were left waiting for the proverbial shoe to drop.

Lucifer slowly brought his hands down and stepped back, taking a hard look at his surroundings. Camila's words struck him like the hard slap his sister gave him the day she blamed him for her children's misfortune. It was the slap heard around the universe, the cold hard smack that brought him back to reality. *Past lovers are to be kept in the past,* he pondered that statement for a few seconds, agreeing with every syllable, but also questioning why he couldn't let it go.

The Lord of the Underworld was in pain and, as always, Camila was willing to do anything to wipe away the troubles eating away at what was left of his heart. She placed her delicate hands on the side of his face, cradling it while ignoring the rough, stubble of his beard on her fingertips. Her expression remained stony as she made sure that she could see her reflection in his eyes.

"You have me, Sire. I will never betray you. If this world freezes over, then I will freeze over with it, standing by your side."

Lucifer could feel the sincerity, loyalty, and love in Camila's words. It was as if some form of energy was washing away his fears and anxiety and replacing them with the truth. Her words were what he longed to hear from his ex-lover, Gia, but she chose to walk away when she declared *his* actions were insufferable. It destroyed him when the glue to their bond wasn't enough to hold them together. He needed unconditional commitment and devotion. He desired what Camila was offering, something that Gia never gave him, and still couldn't give to him.

Deep down, he knew he could never take her as a lover. He would burn the world down for her; her loyalty meant everything. However, becoming lovers is not what his heart desired. He held her to a higher standard above his other demons and servants, for she proved her worth more than he cared to acknowledge. Even when she was kidnapped from the Underworld and was given the opportunity at a second chance at life, she left it all behind to return to Lucifer. He never punished her for the actions of another, which was not the case with the other demons. He knew that the guilt she carried for leaving behind a piece of herself manifested and ate her up inside like cancer. That agony was punishment enough.

Lucifer brought her smooth hands to his lips and kissed them gently, almost reverently. He rubbed the softness of her knuckles, sending tingles of relaxation down her arms and up her spine. Even for a fallen angel, he still held on to most of his angelic magic. The energy of relaxation was one of them.

"Darling, it appears we will be two frozen fools then," he slyly grinned.

"Then my second death will be a happy one," she returned the grin, hoping for more to come out of it. However, Lucifer gently dropped her hands, faced the torture mirrors, and continued their conversation nonchalantly.

"I wanted nothing more than to crush Gia and her bloke with one stomp of my leather loafers, but doing so would have severely affected my long game. I have no desire to start a fight that I know would doom the Underworld. That is the reason why I left so suddenly."

Lucifer walked over to Camila and left a short distance between them.

"My ex-lover would have driven me to do something stupid. And since I was with bullheaded No-Nose Tommy, he would have only followed me into battle and not talked sense into me."

"Then, from now on, I will follow you to Earth. It's best. For the both of us."

"Are you certain?" Lucifer questioned, needing confirmation that she was ready to step foot into Earth again.

"Yes, besides, all of this tracking is to find Angel and to get my son back. I should be the one bringing him home."

The lair's steel door swung open without warning as if cops were barging through without a warrant. A startled Camila quickly rose from the red velvet chair to stand beside her master, who cut his babbling short to address the commotion in the room.

No-Nose Tommy was running behind a six-foot-three-inch angel with wings as white as clouds, demanding for him to stop. Out of breath, he promptly drew his attention to Lucifer.

"Master, please FORGIVE ME. Forgive us. We tried to stop him, but he wouldn't obey…"

Tommy's sentence was cut short by the strong hand that grabbed the back of his neck, squeezing the air out of his lungs. He was raised inches from the ground and was about to get thrown until Camila intervened. She swiftly approached the angel, kicking him and pummeled his chest, screaming for him to let go of Tommy. The tall angel found nothing but humor in the situation and began chuckling.

"This has to be some sort of sick joke, Lucifer," The angel's deep baritone voice ridiculed.

"Mendulous, what a pleasant surprise. I wish you would have called before visiting. I would have thrown you a party," sneered Lucifer through clenched teeth. Mendulous, the loyal hand of Father, arriving brazenly in the Underworld, unannounced and uninvited, boiled Lucifer's demon blood.

Mendulous discarded No-Nose Tommy to the side as if he were yesterday's trash. He grabbed Camila's small-framed face with one palm of his strong hand and forcefully shoved her to the side, keeping his charcoal-flaming eyes fixed on Lucifer. Camila landed hard on her ass and an echoing crack was heard, followed by her loud cry. Her tailbone broke on impact.

Her misfortune ignited a dark fury inside Lucifer. He instantly morphed into his devil face and grabbed Mendulous by his broad shoulders. The two magical beings struggled and wrestled with each other, trying desperately to knock one another to the ground.

Mendulous broke free from Lucifer's grip and punched him directly on the right side of his devil jaw. It seemed as if a shock wave reverberated throughout the circles of Hell. Lucifer never flinched; he took the pain like a champ and stared into Mendulous' eyes before sending him a powerful sucker punch to the gut.

Mendulous huddled over, holding his stomach, heaving like the little bitch Lucifer knew him to be. He could tell his dear old friend was trying to repress the urge to vomit, something he probably hadn't done since dinosaurs roamed the Earth.

"This has got to STOP!" Lucifer demanded, breathing heavily. He changed back into his human face, giving Mendulous a few seconds to heal himself, and issued a few house rules.

"The pain hurts more in the Underworld. After all, this is a place of torture." Lucifer raised his arms as if giving a brief tour with his gestures.

Mendulous continued breathing rapidly until his celestial energy enveloped him in a glowing aura and healed him. His angelic energy radiated the lair, nearly blinding the demons who surrounded him.

Camila's eyes widened, nearly bulging out of their sockets. Even in her agony, she couldn't wrap her head around the fact that an angel, a real-life angel of Eden, was standing in the trenches of the Underworld.

No-Nose Tommy regained consciousness and ran to Camila's aid. He tried to lift her but decided to be guided by the sounds of her shrieks. Her pain was unbearable.

Now that his surroundings had settled, Lucifer assessed his situation. Mendulous was alone. If he wanted to turn the tables, he could easily summon his demons in the blink of an eye and make the predicament worse for his celestial old friend. Instead, he decided to get to the bottom as to why or how he was in the Underworld.

"Mendulous, let's settle this like gentlemen. I have no quarrels with you. Why are you here, old chap?"

Mendulous straightened himself to full height and adjusted his fitted leather jacket. He retracted his silky white wings and glanced over at Camila.

"She's human?"

"Yes, and you nearly shattered her. Did you think she was a scary demon? Not everyone down here is a purebred demon; she's a branded demon. It doesn't give her special abilities. Now, answer the question. How did you get here and why?"

Ignoring Lucifer's curiosity, Mendulous casually kneeled in front of Camila and placed his strong hands on her back. She curled into No-Nose Tommy's chocolate cloak, afraid of what was to come.

"Hey, buddy, she's had enough," interjected Tommy, raising his hand and slightly shoving Medulous away.

"It's alright, Tommy. He's going to heal her. It's what angels do best." Lucifer mocked, waving his hands like a magician.

The golden, shimmering glow from Mendulous' hands sent a quick, illuminating flash inside the lair. Within seconds Camila's tailbone was mended and her pain diminished. She slightly tilted her head toward Mendulous as he half-smiled. She quickly buried her head back into Tommy's cloak and remained silent as No-Nose Tommy helped her up.

"Tommy, take Camila outside. I will take it from here."

"Yes, Sire," complied Tommy.

"No, wait! I want to stay, Master. I won't leave you alone with him," Camila dashed toward Lucifer, grabbing his hand.

Mendulous crossed his arms tightly and stared intently at their interaction.

Lucifer gently kissed Camila's hands, again reassuring her that everything would be alright.

"I admire your bravery, but I will be just fine. Trust me." he winked saucily.

Camila took the hint and slowly backed away, not once looking in Mendulous' direction. She pulled her hood over her head and walked into No-Nose Tommy's arms. He rested one arm around her shoulder and walked her out, shutting the door behind them.

"Lover?" questioned Mendulous, peering sharply with his arms crossed over his chest.

"Heavens no! But what's it to you?"

Lucifer grinned at the thought of that rumor. However, the grin covered up the fact that he was indeed impatient and needed answers.

"What do you want, and again, how did you get here?"

"I'm here to collect Castus, as well as our slain angels. And how do you think I got here? Father, of course."

Lucifer stiffened at the sound of his nephew's name, then huffed a chuckle under his breath until he burst into full-blown laughter. His chuckles echoed within his lair and vibrated throughout the halls.

"Why do you laugh?" Mendulous appeared agitated by his old friend's stalling.

"Now this has got to be a cruel joke! Are you sure you can get back home, Medulous?"

"What do you mean?"

"Father has sent you *here* to 'collect' the angels, alone? With no army? Why?

"I am the Hand, I DO NOT need an army. This is not a war."

Lucifer smirked convincingly, trying to turn the wheels inside Mendulous' head.

"Have you forgotten the laws? Once an angel enters through the gates of Hell, they automatically belong to *me*. There is no 'collecting' them. You just walked through my gates. Are you not one of us now, Mendulous? Has Father sent you here as punishment for what you have done to his precious Angelina?"

A growl crept from Mendulous' throat. Hell was the master realm of manipulation; one could easily let the demons conquer their thoughts. It was a place where only the toughest minds would survive.

"Angelina?!" huffed Mendulous. "I haven't heard you call her that since she was a mere infant. But since you must know, I was never punished for eliminating Angel's memories."

"Is that so?" questioned an intrigued Lucifer.

"That is so. Father agreed with me that eliminating her memory was the right thing to do. She is right where she is supposed to be."

"AHAAHAHAHAHAHA!" Lucifer couldn't suppress the roar of laughter that escaped his mouth. Mendulous had turned into a stand-up comedian before his very eyes. He desperately gasped for air before responding.

"She's knee-deep in vampire and demon drama. She spends the majority of her time hiding from me, and Father says she is right where she is supposed to be? What a load of rubbish! HAHA!"

Mendulous drew closer to Lucifer. The laughter stopped abruptly as Mendulous gripped Lucifer's collar and tightened it as if reprimanding a dog on a leash. Furiously, he slid his next sentence through a clenched jaw.

"Don't ever question Father."

"I would highly advise you to remove your hands, ol' friend, before this turns ugly very quickly."

The silence between them grew tense. Mendulous removed his hands and took two steps back, realizing Lucifer was finally right about one thing. He was alone in Hell with no army to have his back.

As Lucifer straightened his collar and brushed the wrinkles from his suit, he couldn't help but feel empowered. After all, this was *his* world. He was the ruler, not Father.

"Concerning Castus, if you wanted him so badly, you should have saved him before he got down here. It's too late for him. His brand will never allow him to walk through the gates of Eden."

Mendulous rolled up his sleeves and revealed his darkened, smooth wrists. Even after passing through the gates of the Underworld, they were clean, with zero signs of the demon barcode and 666 numbers branded into them.

"Father has found a way to reverse the brand. We can bring Castus back to Eden."

Lucifer stood toe to toe with Mendulous, appearing like two fearless warriors. He clenched his teeth in annoyance. "Well, look at that. Father really outdid himself." Lucifer thought for a moment before the lightbulb above his head illuminated. "Here is what I will do for you, mate. I will release all of the angels in and out of the void, except for Castus."

"HAVE YOU GONE MAD!" Mendulous couldn't hide his emotions from the bombshell being thrown at him. The baritone in his voice went up a notch, shaking the gravel under him.

"YES!! I HAVE!"

"Father and Helena will never let you get away with it," Mendulous threatened.

"My dear sister, Helena, will have no choice. I need Castus."

"For what?!"

"Collateral!" shouted Lucifer, giving a sinister grin and walking toward the steel door.

Mendulous remained silent, not comprehending the goal behind Lucifer's thought process.

"Now that Angel has her memory back, no thanks to you, by the way, she has something I need. The trade-off will work for both the Underworld, Earth, and the entire mighty Paradise."

Mendulous crossed his arms over his chest even tighter. His

smooth, midnight skin appeared darker under the dimmed lighting. He swiftly motioned with his hands, lighting all of the floating torches and making the lair brighter than what Lucifer was accustomed to. He needed to get a better look at the manipulative face of his old acquaintance.

"I'm listening," he stated, seeming intrigued as he took a seat on the red velvet chair and crossed one leg over the other.

CHAPTER 5
REFLECTING

Maggie sat at her desk mesmerized by the fun, outrageous party scene shimmering across the YouTube video on her computer screen. The undulating "utz, utz, utz" of hypnotic beats blared from her state-of-the-art sound system with its speakers strewn around the room but out of sight. Her soft brown eyes widened in wonder as she followed every fist pump, nob twist, and record spin that this DJ used to keep the energy of the party going. She marveled as he knew when to amp up the crowd with a music switch.

Every sonic beat, every sweat, and every time the camera caught his eyes gazing intently into the crowd, it seemed as if he was looking straight at her. Maggie's eyes remained glued and barely blinking, like a drooling groupie who just got a backstage pass to a Bruno Mars concert. The DJ was hyping up the crowd of insane partygoers as if it was their last night on Earth. The scene constantly shifted between the crowd of amateur dancers who were gyrating to the charismatic, spellbinding music and the disc jockey.

Maggie couldn't help but smile as she felt the tickle of butterflies fluttering inside her belly as the camera zoomed into the chocolate eyes and blemish-free face of her lover, Dom. He wore his navy baseball cap backward on his head and winked into the camera as if he knew she was watching. He pouted his full, appealing lips and kissed the air for his fans. He held his Beats headphones with one hand and skillfully spun records and twiddled with the DJ mixer with the other.

Watching Dom enjoy the musical mischief he was creating was like Christmas in July for Maggie. Although she mentally chastised herself for getting close to anyone, she seemed to have developed a soft spot for him that would take the powers of Zeus himself to suppress.

The breeze that swirled through the huge open windows in Maggie's bedroom nearly blew out the sandalwood candles she had lit. Their scent reminded her pleasantly of her days on the run with her father, Jack, and his lover, Ruby Jane. It was a time in her life that was dark and excruciatingly melodramatic for her mother, but a cherished and valuable learning experience for herself. Though arduous and sometimes dangerous, it was an experience she would not have avoided even for a king's ransom. Those were the days of her greatest taste of freedom. It was those experiences of spells, realms, and magical beings that enabled her to learn as much as she could through the teachings of a witch. But Ruby Jane was not just any witch. She was the venerable and powerful Ultra of her coven. A force never to be reckoned with—unless it was a last resort—and a lady who had done more dealings with Vs than anyone could count.

As Maggie's powers increased during her teenage years, it was Ruby Jane who taught her how to control her energy and channel it for good while making sure she was not giving in to *any* temptations. She filled the void of an absent mother and loved Maggie as the flesh of her flesh until the day she disappeared without a trace.

Jack, her demon father, was known for his charming if somewhat scheming and selfish habits. However, to the outside world he was simply a man taking care of his daughter.

The father Maggie knew loved and protected her until the day

Angel tracked them down. Her parents' reunion wasn't pleasant. In fact, Jack took several blows to the face by Angel's hands for kidnapping their daughter. It was an infliction of pain that he very well deserved. Angel wanted nothing more than to end his demon life and send him back to the Underworld with his horns in hand. But, for Maggie's sake, she offered Jack sanctuary instead. It was an offer he gladly accepted, then double-back and declined after spending a week in hiding with them. Now that Maggie was safely secured by her mother and her new reign of soldiers, he ventured off in search of Ruby Jane.

As Maggie continued to watch Dom's set on her computer, she wondered if she would ever be cursed to travel the Earth— peeking under every crack and crevice— in search of someone she was madly in love with. Her mother did just *that* for Master Anu, and now her father was doing the same for Ruby Jane. She brushed the images away quickly, not wanting to entertain those thoughts. It would only take one melancholy reverie for it to multiply and manifest into her permanent psyche. It was as if her body had become an antenna, capturing and amplifying negative feelings. *It's the main reason why I refuse to fall in love. I don't ever want to put someone in harm's way,* she thought. *The guilt would kill me.*

Even though she knew she shouldn't, her eyes followed Dom's image closely as he continued to amp up the crowd. She could see the passion in his expression and the determination in his eyes. He loved moving a crowd, gaining their support and fandom, and playing his mixture of techno beats. He, just like Maggie, lived for the applause.

The scent of sandalwood grew stronger inside the spacious bedroom as droplets of hot wax steadily streamed down each candle. The strong aroma swiftly brought her back into reality and triggered another thought—she hadn't heard from her father in weeks. Maggie stealthily reached for a small, hidden compartment under her desk that she generally kept unlocked since no one ever walked into her bedroom uninvited. She pulled out a small, simple gold ring with a ruby stone set in the middle that hung on a delicate, filigree gold chain. Ruby Jane had given her the ring long ago when she was just a child. She had bound a few items with a magical spell so that she could track everyone in case any of them went missing during their time on the run. Jack had the pleasure of sporting a gold timepiece decorated with deep, blood-red rubies that counted the hours. Ruby Jane's talisman was a dignified and ancient ruby necklace whose stone gleamed and glistened as if it had once been the red eye of a fierce Cyclops. A necklace that was left behind on her bed the day she disappeared.

Maggie abruptly stopped Dom's party video and powered down her computer. She swiftly walked over to her windows and stared out into the shrubbery one last time before closing them and pulling the drapes, shutting out the outside world. She sat Indian-style on her queen-sized bed and clasped the ring between her hands in prayer. She inhaled and exhaled, chanting in a whisper the words she was taught as a child.

"Rubies of jewels, Rubies of Isle, show me, show me, my father's miles"
"Rubies of jewels, Rubies of Isle, show me, show me, my father's miles"
"Rubies of jewels, Rubies of Isle, show me, show me, my father's miles"

The stone blew out a cloud of purple, hazy smoke between Maggie's fingers. She continued to chant faster and lower, as Ruby Jane once taught her. She felt the words vibrate in the cavity of her chest and felt the static of the magic building around her. Tiny hairs stood up at attention all over her body.

"Rubies of jewels, Rubies of Isle, show me, show me, my father's miles"
"Rubies of jewels, Rubies of Isle, show me, show me, my father's miles"

The purple smoke turned into light lavender and swirled until a perfect picture was displayed of Jack. The bright sun shone on his forehead as he pretended to read a newspaper outside a cafe.

The face of Jack's timepiece began to steadily fog. As he turned the page of his newspaper, he noticed the hands inside the watch had changed course and that the clock was filling rapidly with purple fog. Jack steadied his breath and slowly blew on the face of his timepiece until a clear image of Maggie, smiling and content, appeared. He surveyed his surroundings, making sure no one was lurking about. For an early morning, the streets were not as busy at his location. He pulled his wrist closer to his lips, discreetly making it seem as if he were going to wipe his goatee.

"Hey, baby girl." he answered casually.

"Dad!" Maggie beamed with excitement. "Where are you?"

Jack folded his newspaper and gently placed it on the cafe table. He reached for his coffee cup and held it by his mouth pretending to sip.

"France. Is everything good with you?"

Maggie paused for what seemed like minutes. She felt compelled to tell him everything. She wanted to alert him that she was becoming more demon day by day and that Master Anu could only band-aid the situation. She wanted to vent about her mother's overprotective ways, Jesse's obsession with finding his mother, Gia's resentment toward her, and her strained relationship with Keiko. Most importantly, she wanted to tell him that Ruby Jane might be dead, and he needed to come home. But she couldn't, and she wouldn't, for that was not something she was prepared to believe.

When it came to Jack, Maggie wanted the best for him. It was as if their roles were reversed and she was the parent and he was the truant child. She wanted to tell him how much she missed him and wanted him back home. Instead, she swallowed her complaints and sucked in her selfishness.

"Oh, you know me, just living the dream here with mom. I haven't heard from you in a while and just wanted to check in. Found anything on Momma Ruby yet?"

"No, just a bunch of dead ends. I swear, every time I get close, I hit a wall."

Maggie silently sighed. "Don't worry, Dad. Wherever she is, or whoever has her, I'm sure you'll find them. I have faith. Besides, you're the best tracker in the world."

"Thanks, baby girl. I needed that motivation. And as long as you're well and safe, it adds less stress to my life." There was a silent pause that seemed as if Jack was distracted. Before Maggie could speak, he broke the quietness that lingered between them.

"Hey, promise me you'll take care of yourself and not worry about me. I'll be around again before you know it."

"I'll try," Maggie fibbed, knowing that she could never stop worrying about her dad.

"It doesn't hurt to try harder," he smiled charmingly. "I better get going. You know how these tracking spells are. If you need me again, you know how to find me. I'll always answer."

"And you know how to find me." Maggie repeated, not wanting the conversation to end but knowing the spell wouldn't last as long as an old-fashioned telephone call. Eventually, their connection would be lost. Electronics were forbidden when speaking to her father; it was easily traceable. The magic system was their best and only way to communicate, especially when protected by Momma Ruby's magic.

"I love you, dad." Maggie was able to get in before the image became obscured by thick, grey smoke.

"Love you more, baby girl." Jack quickly snuck in before he vanished.

Maggie stared into the lingering fog and fought valiantly against tears that filled the corners of her eyes, threatening to spill over onto her flushed cheeks. She kissed the ring, held it to her heart, and closed her eyes tightly, wishing things could be different.

The soft, bell tone of her text messages interrupted her thoughts. Maggie contemplated ignoring any text/calls for the day. Seeing her father again and hearing there were no breakthroughs in finding Momma Ruby dragged her mood way down. She slid her ruby ring back into the secret compartment underneath the desk and glanced at her smartphone resting by her computer.

Dom: *Can't wait to see you tonight at dinner.*

Maggie's heart skipped a beat. She reminded herself of the fun she could have by convincing Dom to skip dinner and go straight to dessert. However, tonight they were playing on his terms, and canceling his ideal date night wouldn't be fair. She could already sense Dom's excitement through his message.

Maggie: *I'll be there. See you at six-thirty.* She responded with a smiley face emoji before her video calling overshadowed her text box.

An image of a young blonde with dark sunglasses, smiling brightly, while holding a dry martini precariously close to her rose-tinted lips popped up as a profile picture. With everything that had happened, Maggie had forgotten to call back her best friend Charlie. She swiftly slid the answer bar on her phone and answered excitedly, cycling through a complete three-sixty in her mood-o-meter.

"Hey, girl! What are you up to?"

"Heyyy, finally, there's life on the other end. I was getting worried about you. I haven't heard from you since your 'lucky night.'"

Charlie grinned from ear to ear and raised her sexy, well-shaped eyebrows up and down in a playful, flirtatious manner. She sported dark, rectangular sunglasses, which were not her normal style and appeared rather larger than usual. They covered half her forehead and slid down with every twitch of her nose and raise of her brows. She constantly adjusted the sunglasses to their rightful position. It was like watching a Hollywood celebrity trying to hide her identity from the paparazzi with little success.

Maggie chuckled at her friend's comical gestures, but it was her clownish sunglasses that were stealing the show. She took note of Charlie's background. The sound of soft music, colorful display of an assortment of glasses, and fluorescent lighting indicated that she was inside a sunglass store, or maybe even at the optometrist. Before Maggie could open up her bag of questions, she was cut off by Charlie's preemptive plea for help.

"Although I still want to hear every slutty detail about your romp the other night, I need your advice first." Charlie's pert lips smiled playfully.

"Okay! Shoot!" Maggie giggled like a naughty schoolgirl. She took a seat on her bed and pulled her purple comforter over her slender shoulders. The aftereffects of her recent use of magic were giving her chills.

"It's these sunglasses. I'm sensing they are all wrong for me. Your chuckling is not giving off a sign of approval but of disapproval, perhaps even ridicule?" An eyebrow was raised ever so slightly in playful caution.

Charlie used her free hand to feel around the rectangular sunglasses. She felt the details of the frame and maneuvered her delicate fingers from the top of the frame to her forehead, then over to her hairline. It was her way of averaging the distance from the frame to her hairline. If Maggie didn't know any better, she could have sworn that at that very moment, Charlie had frowned at her realization of the silliness on her face.

"They look...different." Maggie stated, lightening the mood.

Charlie raised the sunglasses to the top of her honey blonde hair and smirked at the comment. Her cloudy greyish eyes were like staring into an obscured crystal ball.

"Thanks for being honest, but I know they look ridiculous. You tend to forget, my dear best friend, that I'm blind, not dumb."

Maggie sighed at the reminder.

Charlotte, or Charlie, as Maggie called her, was far from a simpleton. She graduated college with a degree in Religious Studies and was pursuing a Master's degree in the same subject. Her dream was to obtain her Ph.D. and become a professor of Cultural and Religious studies like her parents. All subjects for which Maggie had zero interest.

The girls were complete opposites, but that never dissuaded them from gravitating toward each other. They had been childhood friends before Maggie's kidnapping and Charlie's traumatic accident.

Charlie wasn't always blind. At the age of eight, she was traveling to Vermont with her parents for their annual ski trip. The snowy weather had not been in their favor, and they were involved in a six-car pile-up. The accident left both of her parents dead and Charlie permanently blind from the head trauma she received. She was their only child and was extremely fortunate to have survived and been able to continue her parents' legacy. The tragedy left her in the care of her wonderful, loving grandparents with a life insurance entitlement and accident settlement that ensured she would be financially secure for life.

Maggie often felt that it wasn't Charlie's time to go and, just maybe, they were meant to find each other again as if their tragic stories were the threads that wove their lives together. After both of their misfortunes, they managed to find each other through a friend finder app on social media. Maggie didn't have an account of her own, but that never deterred her from constantly surfing the web. It eventually led her to a few profiles under "This Week's Most Popular Photos," thread and sure enough, there was Charlie. She was sipping on a margarita on a sandy, white beach with her black Labrador, Pete, her very protective but sweet guide dog. The comical image showcased her service dog also wearing dark sunglasses with the caption underneath that read, **"We love margaritas!"** One message and a few gatherings later, the girls became inseparable again.

"Charlie, where are you?" Maggie bit down on her nails, a habit she seldom did. Charlie turned her video camera around showing her location. The video was moving as fast as the Blair Witch Project.

"Slow down, you're making me dizzy," Maggie chuckled.

Charlie swiftly switched the camera mode back to her bright face as the oversized sunglasses slid back down over her eyes.

"Whoops," she apologized innocently. "As you couldn't see, I'm standing inside a local sunglasses store. Although the clerk is being very helpful, I kinda think he's trying to take advantage of me."

"How so? Do you need me to go there? I can be there in a flash." Maggie walked over to her closet searching for her leather jacket, preparing herself to come to her friend's aid.

"No, I'm sure I can handle this. But I'm positive the clerk is trying to pull a bait and switch with these sunglasses. I don't mind the cost, but seriously, don't sell me hideous sunglasses because you're trying to make a sale. Pete keeps making weird whimpering noises every time I stare in his direction. He's been disapproving of everything."

Charlie removed the sunglasses and placed them on the glass counter as strands of her honey-blond hair began to fall from her messy bun. She chuckled, reminiscing about her service dog Pete's reaction.

Maggie slapped her forehead playfully, "Charlie, I don't understand. What's wrong with your old sunglasses?"

"Long story," Charlie pulled a satisfied smile, "but let me give you the Cliff Notes. Attended a nerdy, classical music, dinner party last night. Had way too much red wine. Went home with a hot cello player. At least I think it's the cello, it could have been the violin. I'm not sure. Anyway, as I was sneaking out of his place this morning, I forgot them. I was too embarrassed to go back inside, so I cut my losses and left. It sucks, I really liked those glasses."

Maggie couldn't help but laugh hysterically. The thought of her visually-impaired friend doing the walk of shame then leaving her belongings behind proved she was not cut out for the game. However, she thought about her own experience with Dom and how he caught her slipping away. At least Charlie had been able to escape, taking after the great escape artist Dean Gunnarson, whereas she hadn't. She decided that they were both rookies at the game of one-night-stands with hotties.

"Well, my darling, you're going to have to suck it up and call your cello man for your glasses back," suggested Maggie.

"NO!!! I'm not doing that. He was a terrible lay, plus he already texted and called, and I just ghosted him."

"He was probably trying to return your glasses." Maggie was tickled pink because Charlie was always getting on her for being a coward and sneaking out even when the sex was really good.

"Nope! I'm good. He can keep them as a souvenir."

Maggie giggled at the comment as the clerk circled back to the counter and interrupted the call between the two friends.

"Excuse me, ma'am, we have these in stock. These may feel much better on you than the pair you just tried on."

"Thank you!" Charlie slipped on the glasses and raised the phone higher so Maggie could get a better look. Her silky skin glistened under the fluorescent lights as if she had drowned herself in essential oils again.

"What do you think, Mags, yea or nay?"

The glasses were dark with a slight vintage frame and fit Charlie's face perfectly.

"I love those. Much better than the last pair you owned. Most definitely a yea."

"Great! They actually feel a lot lighter than my last pair. I'll take them!" exclaimed Charlie as she returned the sunglasses for purchase.

"I'll wrap these right up for you." stated the clerk, walking away to ring up the glasses.

"Thank you for helping me, Mags. I almost left this place looking foolish."

"Sure, next time just ask me to come along. I don't mind." Maggie offered.

"I didn't want to disturb you. I left so early in the morning. You know how determined I get. I wait for no one when I need things done."

"I get it," answered Maggie softly.

"Anyway, what are you up to tonight? Have a gig? If not, do you want to come over and watch some RomCom?"

Maggie hesitated, "I would love to, but I have a date?"

Charlie gasped into the video call, "A WHAT?!"

CHAPTER 6
THE LITTLE BLACK BOOK

Piles of colorful clothing were heaped haphazardly throughout Maggie's bedroom. There was even a silver-colored bra that seemed to be made of gossamer that was draped over her rolling chair. It seemed as if a whole convention of temperamental clothing designers had gone to war, and her boudoir had been the battlefield.

Maggie only had eyes for her full-body reflection that showed a well-dressed, but a bit nervous, young woman. This was the second time that she was gathering up her dark curls into a high ponytail. The hairstyle complemented the sleekness of her honey-kissed neck when paired with a borrowed wine-colored, spaghetti-strapped dress. The dress had once belonged to her mother. Its color played well against her smooth skin that glowed with youthful vigor. It hugged her sensual curves, flawlessly defining each well-formed glute with every enticing motion of her hips. The saucy panel of black lace that was stitched at the final length of her dress stopped a few inches above her knees. She was already towering at five foot nine inches. Her black, strappy, stiletto sandals added to her height, making her appear like an irresistible Glamazon. She was admiring her runway model legs with awe, mainly because she was usually a jeans and tight tee-shirt type of girl. However, tonight was a special night, and she was banking on it transforming into something extraordinary by the end of the date.

"Come in!" she commanded in response to the slight knock on her door.

She watched from the mirror as Keiko entered her room.

She folded her arms across her chest, examining Maggie from head to toe while ignoring the mess of clothes that cluttered her room.

Maggie noticed the disapproving expression on Keiko's face and reluctantly refrained from styling her fashionable updo. She turned to acknowledge the woman she admired and loved as a child, feelings that she still had to this very day.

"Something wrong?" Maggie pressed her lips together, easily knowing the answer to her own question.

"I told your mother that I forbid you to go on this date. It was a battle that I lost, miserably."

The fact that Keiko had moved against her liberty, and was shot down at the mere mention of restricting her, was too funny to beef about.

Maggie silently chuckled and strolled past Keiko, reaching for her leather jacket inside her walk-in closet, expertly sidestepping the usual bullshit.

"I still don't understand why you do not take any of this seriously, Magdalena." Keiko's eyes narrowed in rebuke.

Maggie remained silent as she slid on her short, leather jacket and gave her reflection in the mirror a final once-over. The jacket wasn't the best outerwear to drape over her skimpy dress, but it gave her an edginess that suited her personality. She looked damn good and she knew it. She turned to Keiko with a sobering glance, no longer finding humor in their light chit-chat.

"I am taking this seriously, more than you will ever know. But before I turn into one of them for good, I need one night of normalcy," Maggie stated stoically.

"We will never be normal." Keiko's voice was riddled with frustration.

"Don't you think I know this already."

Maggie could feel her blood rushing through her veins and her pulse thumping rapidly as if it would beat outside of her wrist. She was annoyed almost to overload. She tightly closed her eyes and inhaled, internally practicing her yoga breaths.

Keiko stared intently at Maggie as if waiting for some sort of magical force to push her away. Her arms never uncrossed from her chest. However, whatever she was expecting never came, and Maggie continued to gather the last of her belongings hoping that Keiko would take the hint and leave on her own accord. But that was only wishful thinking.

Keiko took one last hard look at Maggie, appreciating her ensemble. "The last time I saw that dress was on your mother. Father had chased her to a nightclub, declaring his love for her. Since you want normal, I hope the attire does the same for you."

Maggie paused, her memory drifting to the story her mother once told her about Master Anu blindsiding her at a nightclub in Puerto Rico. A place she went to forget about him. She wondered how she would react if she were in her mother's shoes. It was a constant battle not to buy into the thought of Dom falling head over heels for her and professing his love. It would never work. How could it? She was conflicted, and although she wanted to hear the words "I love you" from someone she admired, she also dreaded it more than she would ever admit out loud. She preferred entertainment with no strings.

"I really hope it doesn't." Maggie retorted, ignoring the slight excited tremor that ran through her at the very thought.

Keiko finally unfolded her arms, placed her slender hands on Maggie's shoulders, and gazed steadily into her soft brown eyes. "If anything happens, promise me that I will be the first person you call."

For the first time, Maggie could recognize the raw fear in Keiko's eyes. It was the fear of a mother losing a child. The same fear she saw in her own mother's eyes several times before. That heartbreaking fear she's ignored time and time again.

"I promise," Maggie confessed with absolute sincerity.

Keiko gently brought Maggie's forehead toward her rose-colored lips. This was Keiko's blessing, her silent way of connection.

Maggie slowly stared into Keiko's dark eyes as she wiped the red-stained lip marker off her forehead. She held her hands and gave her longtime friend and protector a reassuring look.

"Hey, nothing will happen. I promise to be careful."

Keiko released herself from Maggie's grip and took two steps backward, ready to turn on her heels.

"I hope so, Magdalena. I hope so." was her last resigned comment before she exited the bedroom leaving an eerie feeling behind.

Angel walked into the backyard and headed toward the pool area. She glanced at the two enormous, silky-coated panthers lying on the opposite side of the pool. They rolled lazily, enjoying the coolness of the brown flagstone underneath their skin as they took in the night's breeze. Colorful LED lights illuminated the lavish stone, Mediterranean-blue waterfall that swished down to the aqua pool below. Its heavy stream cascaded in a soothing flow as if listening to the calming melodies in a high-end spa.

Angel silently watched the group as she approached. Master Anu sat in the blue and cream-colored sectional in front of their magically-lit fire pit. His long, dark, sleek hair rested calmly on his shoulders as he pulled one side of it behind his ear. He was engaged in what appeared to be an intense conversation with

Keiko, Jesse, and Gia. Each movement he made with his hands as he spoke seemed serious. She loved watching him in business mode. Aside from his chestnut smooth skin and full lips that she drowned herself in, his intelligence and wordsmith were the icings on the cake. After all, he didn't become the leader of his species by being a big dummy. It took more wits and power than most Vs possessed.

The three of them passed around sheets, scrolls, and a little black leather book wrapped in a golden string. As Angel neared, she instantly reached for the book once it was put down.

"Where did you find this?" she questioned in fascination, unable to believe that the book her Uncle Lucifer gifted her years ago had finally made it back into her hands. She ran her fingers over the golden string, admiring its detail. She brought the book to her nose and carefully sniffed it, inhaling the scent of genuine leather.

Master Anu was the first to speak, realizing Angel's attachment to the book.

"Jesse located it during his travels to Egypt."

Angel, trying to suppress her bewilderment, directed her questions to Jesse. "Egypt? I don't understand. How did you find this book?"

"It wasn't hard," Jesse easily responded as if he landed on something golden. "During my research on the web, I came across a whack job with the code name, 'Badr the Seer.' He blogged about a book that possessed all of the secrets to Eden and the Underworld. At first, I thought he was full of shit; but what made me believe he was the real deal was when he wrote about you, mom."

"ME!" Angel couldn't believe her ears. With all the precautions she was taking to protect herself and her people, she was nearly exposed by a mentally-unstable human.

"Yes, Mom, you! He practically exposed the existence of angels on Earth." Jesse confirmed. "So I reached out and arranged a visit. He sold me the leather book—for an insane amount—and in return, he shut down his site and handed me all his research."

Angel took a seat, relieving her shaky legs. Her face flushed and then quickly drained of color—becoming dangerously pale.

"Are you alright, my love?" Master Anu asked as he wrapped his arm around her chilled shoulders.

"Yes, I'll be fine," assured Angel. "Jesse, what did this human post?"

"At first, he just wrote the standard stuff. The Guardian of Eden will be placed on Earth to protect mankind. The Guardian was chosen not by the Father of all creation but by the powers of the Divine Right. Earth is a jungle and humans are prey to the evil beings that live among them. But it's what he wrote after where things became unclear. It was as if he were talking gibberish. He had stories of how Eden and Hell may face a common enemy. And that unknown realms will open, releasing creatures on Earth that not even the Underworld wants."

Angel's body stiffened and her palms grew sweaty. What Jesse believed to be gibberish seemed to have raised her anxiety level. Gates opening to unknown realms is something she didn't want to rule out as a false prophecy.

If Vs, angels, demons, and shifters already roamed the Earth, what else could be locked away beyond the darkness? Maybe if she had finished reading her uncle's little black book, it would have eased her misgivings.

Master Anu plucked the book from Angel's grip and cautiously flipped through the pages. His fingers perused the script as if deciphering its words through his fingertips.

"Fascinating! I remember this book. I had it in my possession once. It's what assisted me in knowing more about you, Angel."

"I'm sure that book has been in many hands," Angel regarded the book as if it were the proverbial snake in the grass. "This used to belong to me. My uncle gave it to me as a child. I sneaked it out of Eden when I was first sent to Earth and then lost it during one of my journeys. I never got the opportunity to read it entirely. I can't confirm nor deny what's in here."

"I never finished reading it, either," Master Anu confessed. "It was as if the book only wanted me to read a certain section and once I learned it, it disappeared."

Angel's bottom lip twitched with worry as she contemplated the sudden appearance of the very book back into their lives.

"Can I see it?" Gia pressed the leather book bindings to her nose and took a small sniff. She scanned the first couple of pages as if absorbing information like Data from *Star Trek*.

"Lucifer," The name passed through her lips like a burning whisper.

All eyes were on Gia who was now gripping the book as if she had been petrified at the supernatural sighting of a ghost.

Keiko hastily snatched the book from her and was almost sent off balance when she tried to straighten her posture. The surprising counterweight provided by such a tiny book felt equal to a hardcover set of the *Encyclopedia Britannica*.

"What's so special about this book?" she asked as she surveyed it suspiciously. "Is it going to tell us anything about Maggie's condition or how to defeat the Underworld? If not, this book is as useless as we are just sitting here waiting for things to happen."

Jesse stood up and grabbed the book as if wanting to do his part in this game of hot potato. "This book may just hold the answers to the connections between Eden, the Underworld, and the Unknown worlds. It could possess secrets about other realms or other species. If that's true, I need time to research and study it. And who knows, maybe I'll get lucky and it may disclose information about my parents."

The hope in Jesse's voice was heart wrenching.

Angel sighed, "Do what you wish, Jesse. Let me know what you come up with. But Keiko is right. We can't be distracted. Our main concern now is Maggie."

Gia never took her frosty, dispassionate gaze away from the book.

Angel could sense her displeasure in both the book and Maggie. "Gia, is something wrong?"

"With all due respect, My Queen, if Maggie disappears again on her own, I decline to help search for her. It is my duty to protect the humans, not run around the city playing as a personal babysitter."

"Your duty is whatever mission I give you," Angel scolded as if speaking to a child.

Gia's lips retracted into a thin angry line, her face flushed and her brows contracted to mirror the grim line of her lips.

"We don't need Gia's help. It's obvious she doesn't care about this family," interrupted Keiko while crossing her arms tightly across her chest. It was a common gesture she made to express her anger or annoyance.

"How dare you! That is not TRUE!" Gia stepped closer towards Keiko, getting in her face and pointing her finger aggressively at her chest. "I've traveled around the bowels of Earth, just like you, for ten years to help find that child. Years I could have productively spent with Desmond before he was summoned back to Eden. Instead, we spent it working tirelessly for this family, OUR family!" Gia's voice shook with despair in mentioning her husband's name.

Desmond was one of Angel's most loyal soldiers who stood by her side until the day he was called to return to Eden. It was a bittersweet moment. Although his mission ended with a happy ending and he was able to go home, his wife could not. She was ordered to remain on Earth and continue her allegiance with Angel. It was an order that heavily left a bad taste in her mouth.

"If you ever want to use that finger again, I suggest you remove it before I cleave it from your corpse," Keiko stated through clenched teeth. She was leaning so close to Gia's finger that it was hard to decipher which of them were the true aggressor. Keiko looked like every muscle in her body could be a weapon—if necessary.

Gia lowered her hand and took a few steps back. The air remained unsettled, and the group became as reticent as the night. The panthers raised their heads as their ears perked up with curiosity. The tension in the air had telegraphed itself to them almost as if they could taste the agitation and loss of tranquility.

"Go home, Gia." Angel softly commanded, her voice filled with regret and disappointment.

"My queen..."

"That IS AN ORDER!" Angel's vitriolic words cut through the air like white lightning.

Gia stormed off like a passionate tornado, heavily shoulder-bumping Keiko on her way out. Her heels clicked loudly each time her furious steps made contact with the floor tiles.

"I better go check on her," Jesse announced as he jogged after Gia.

The tingling within Keiko's fingertips grew and pulsated with electric current ready to freeze Gia as she retreated. There was no way she was letting that bump slide.

However, Master Anu quickly slapped Keiko's hand down, avoiding further drama.

"Let it go, Keiko. She needs to cool off. Let's just continue as planned," He distractedly began rearranging the sheets of paper they were reading.

Keiko gazed at the moonlit sky as if she were looking for answers through a silent prayer.

The panthers kept their focus on the group, a fire glowing within their eyes, a look of anticipation in their glare. They could sense that something was up.

"I'm going to follow Maggie," Keiko finally stated, breaking the awkward silence.

"NO!" spat Angel.

"Why not?!"

"Because I promised her that I wouldn't ruin this date for her. I want to protect her just as much as you do. But she's made it clear on several occasions that she doesn't want me hovering over her like an overprotective lioness. She will come home; she always does. I have to keep my word this time."

Keiko shook her head in disagreement and balled her fist in frustration. "You two have no idea what you've done to her," Keiko's words slapped Angel coldly in the face.

"What do you mean?" Angel's voice quivered.

"The serum suppresses Maggie's powers. Since her dark side is slowly taking over, which side do you think has been doing all the magic?"

Master Anu raised his dark right eyebrow.

Before anyone could speak, Keiko cut them off. "She's a sitting duck out there. Coco, Pearl, let's go!" The two panthers darted on her command as they followed her out of the poolside area.

Master Anu ran his fingers through his dark hair. His black button-down shirt clung to his chest as he paced toward Angel. "I'll round up some Vs. We will all go."

"No! You all stay here. I'll go with Keiko and deal with this. Jesse needs to decipher the book, and I want you to help him."

"My love, the book can wait…"

Angel placed her delicate index finger on Master Anu's smooth lips, interrupting his words. "I got this, trust me." Her eyes darkened as she gazed into the eyes of her beloved.

Master Anu took her hands in his and hungrily pressed them against his lips, never breaking their gaze. After all these years, she could not stop the smile that crossed her face like a giddy teenager with each peck of his sensual lips that landed on the back of her hands.

"You know what to do if you need me," he whispered.

CHAPTER 7
DATE NIGHT WITH A DEMON

Clinking wine glasses and the tantalizing aroma from a freshly-cooked porterhouse only enticed the mouth to water. Maggie watched closely as a well-pleased patron received their deliciously-juicy grilled steak, plump roasted potatoes, and asparagus. *I know what I'm ordering*, she thought, making a mental note to herself to order her steak medium-rare.

The ambiance was enhanced by the discreetly-lit alcoves that decorated its walls. The warm glow was shared by the patrons mingling near the bar, as well as the lucky diners already seated. Women draped in silk blouses and jewels chatted with men in their designer suits and casual fitted blazers, apparently very comfortable in this element. It nearly felt as if she had been magically transported back in time where it could have easily been the roaring, decadent 1920s.

Maggie scanned the restaurant feeling like a fish out of water. She had an idea the place was upscale. It had plenty of media buzz for its celebrity sightings and temperamental head chef. She had walked past the restaurant on numerous occasions but never had the desire to step inside.

Maggie lightly bit down on her bottom lip, trying to get her nerves in check. She continued reminding herself that it was just a date, her very first date, and possibly her last.

"Hello, welcome to Allen's Steakhouse. Do you have a reservation?"

The almost childlike voice took Maggie off guard. Her eyes quickly dropped toward a cheery little person who was glowing with positivity, holding an iPad two sizes too big for her small framed hands. The hostess bent her neck as far back as it could reach as she admired the beauty of the Glamazon towering before her.

"Hello! Yes, reservation under Dominique Kim." Maggie grinned, thinking how efficient the little person appeared as she scrolled through the iPad with her tiny fingers.

"Mr. Kim has already checked in. Follow me, please. I'll bring you to your table."

Maggie followed the hostess feeling a bit self-conscious with every step of her heels. Maybe wearing her mother's sexy red dress was a bad idea, she mused. She felt as if all eyes were on her as people sipped on their cocktails and took bites of their meals. "This dress is definitely a bit too much for this place," she said under her breath.

All of her doubts vanished as she locked eyes with Dom who quickly, and somewhat nervously, stood up to greet his gorgeous date.

Dom took Maggie into his strong arms and embraced her as if it were the banks of an oasis and he was a man lost in a desert and given this lifeline. The scent of her flowery fragrance lingered just enough to tease his senses and elicit an aroused response from him. He swiftly stepped back to admire her ensemble and to disguise his embarrassment at the strength of his reaction.

"You look absolutely beautiful," he gushed like a starstruck teenager.

Maggie's cheeks instantly flushed red. "Thank you! You don't look too bad yourself," she complimented, admiring his dark blazer and slacks.

"I love your bowtie," Maggie playfully centered his plaid bowtie.

Dom gently took her hands in his and reverently brought them to his lips, seeming to silently revel in her smooth-as-silk fingers.

He helped Maggie remove her jacket and pulled out the leather chair for her to sit. She gladly accepted his gentlemanly gestures and gushed over his thoughtful actions.

After the two were done with their pleasantries, their male waiter arrived just in time to hand them menus and proceed with his welcoming schtick. In a slightly highbrow tone, he addressed the pair as he had the fifty patrons before them.

"Welcome to Allen's Steakhouse. Would either of you like to start your evening off with a drink? Or just stick with the sparkling water for now?"

"Sparkling is fine," answered Maggie.

"Sparkling, it is then." The waiter quickly tapped on his mini pad then flashed his dark eyes toward Maggie and smiled since she had been the first to speak up.

"Do you mind if I order us a bottle of wine?" Dom chimed in enthusiastically.

"By all means." Maggie concurred.

"White or red?" inquired the waiter.

"White!" exclaimed Maggie. Unfortunately, it was at the same time that Dom declared his desire for red.

The two giggled at their indecisiveness.

"Why don't I give you two a few moments to decide," offered the waiter.

"No need, sir, please bring us your most expensive bottle of white wine." Dom kept his eyes on Maggie, seeing if his boldness sparked a reaction out of her. She simply smiled, not seeming impressed, but also not appearing annoyed.

"Good choice!" praised the waiter, not only on Dom's choice of beverage but also on his decision to appease his lovely lady with fine wine.

"I'll be back with your bottle and to take your orders," the waiter genuinely smiled as he excused himself.

Every move Dom made was natural. He reached for Maggie's hands across the table and held them firmly.

"The waiter is right, this is a good choice. I'm so happy you're here."

"Me too," blushed Maggie, feeling her heart skip a beat with each rub of Dom's fingers.

The tower of shrimp cocktail was carefully placed on the center of the table like an extravagant centerpiece for all to see. It was accompanied by a spiral vase spilling with blood-red wine as if the grapes were plucked from the vineyards of Eden. Lucifer adjusted his crystal cufflinks before taking a sip of his sweet wine. He took one whiff of the raw shrimp and cringed his nose.

"How do these sorry humans eat this mess? Goodness, Camila."

"Sire, it's actually very tasty. Better than the stuff we serve in the Underworld," she replied convincingly as she sampled another shrimp and contentedly added "yum" as she savored the flavor.

Lucifer wasn't moved.

"Unfortunately, for you, the chef isn't scheduled to expire for another ten years, and he's going to Eden. However, his idiot apprentice will be with us. Are you okay with getting second best?" Lucifer smiled slyly, knowingly shattering Camila's hopes of having a great chef in the Underworld.

Camila plucked another shrimp and dipped it into the heavy marinara sauce. "As the humans say, "sometimes you have to be second to be first. So it works for me!" She bit into the shrimp seductively, placing its tail on her plate.

Lucifer raised his eyebrows and darted his emerald eyes toward

Maggie's table, watching her every move closely. He rubbed his beard and unbuttoned the one button on his black suit jacket.

Camila slightly turned her chair to get a better visual of Maggie and her date. Her fingers ran across her jet-black, straight hair and fidgeted with the diamond choker around her thin neck. Her hair kept getting caught in the clasp. As annoying as the choker was, she was determined to wear it. It was a gift from her master for this particular night. She smoothed the wrinkles from her satin, midnight gown as she crossed her legs, revealing her silk thighs through the sides of her slits. Her exposed cleavage didn't leave much to one's imagination.

Lucifer, trying to ignore Camila's thin, flawless, legs, leaned his back against the leather chair and made himself as comfortable as possible. Although they sat three tables away from Maggie, he was still able to hear and see her clearly. Besides, it wasn't as if she knew what he looked like.

"If I didn't mention it before, you look rather exquisite tonight, Camila."

Camila held her wine glass close to her chest and stared at Lucifer, his eyes never leaving Maggie's direction. "Is that a compliment, Sire?"

"You take it as you wish. I'm just stating the facts," Lucifer replied in a serious yet stern manner.

"Then, I'll take it as a compliment," Camila accepted.

Lucifer abruptly sighed, quickly switching the subject to Maggie. "I don't understand what she sees in this bloody wanker. He makes me want to gouge his eyes out. Look at him. Feeding her steak and flashing her the most ridiculous googly eyes in the history of googly eyes."

Camila smirked, "He's just being nice. I think it's rather sweet that he really loves her. It must give her a sense of...normalcy. I can understand that feeling." She confessed, "Castus made me feel normal. His golden heart always made me feel more like a lady than a demon."

"Normal? Oh, bullshit! She will never be normal. Just like *you* will never be normal. That right there," Lucifer pointed somewhat angrily toward a love-sick Maggie, "is more of a monster than her father."

Camila placed her wine glass down and patted her rose-colored lips with her napkin. Maggie's father, Jack, was a monster. Heck, they all were. But she wasn't ready to call the kettle black. She glanced over at Maggie and her date who were now sitting close together, giggling and whispering in each other's ears seductively like two entangled, lovestruck birds.

"She seems harmless," Camila shrugged her slender shoulders, "besides we're only here to follow her back to her home. Once we get what we came for, we'll be done with it all."

"Done?" Lucifer's eyebrows furrowed and his face hardened.

Camila straightened in her chair. "We are nowhere near done, darling. The dynamics have completely changed," Lucifer stated, bending the rules to his own game.

The coldness in Camila's orbs transformed into confusion. She couldn't help to question her master. "What do you mean?"

"Jesse is not our only focus anymore," Lucifer confessed.

"Am I not getting my son back?" The worry in her voice couldn't be drowned out by the hundred chatting voices in the restaurant.

"I made you a promise. You will get your boy back. But not before he gives up my little black book."

"Your little black book? Camila repeated, seeming more confused and filled with dying curiosity. "I don't understand. What is this book you speak of?"

Lucifer leaned in closer and spoke in a low whisper for just Camila's ears. "Jesse has managed to find my journal that not only contains documentation and reports of Eden and my travels to Earth, but also dangerous, secret, coded symbols."

"Coded symbols? What symbols? I don't think I'm following," Camila whispered back.

Lucifer leaned in closer and revealed the secrets he had been harboring inside for days. It was like opening Pandora's box.

"There are unknown forces that lie beyond Eden and our world that harbor extremely dangerous power. These forces were pushed into a state of confinement centuries ago by the hands of ancient powerful witches. They used symbols to secure and suppress the creatures behind what they called the Unknown Realms. If the Unknown is unleashed it could be strong enough to destroy Earth, and the existing realms outside of this world, that is including Eden and the Underworld."

Camila remained silent, hanging on Lucifer's every word, trying to absorb every piece of information like a sponge.

Lucifer continued, "If my book falls into the wrong hands, we will all be ashes fluttering in the wind. These realms are capable of nothing more than death and destruction. It will be worse than Armageddon. We need to get to Jesse before any other creatures find him."

"How do you know he has this book? Maybe someone else has it." Camila couldn't hide the "mother's worry" in her tone.

Their half-empty wine glasses were promptly refilled by their waitress. Lucifer carefully leaned back in his chair glancing over at Camila's diamond choker, taking note that it brought out the sparkles that danced in her pupils.

As the waitress proceeded to ask if they needed anything else, Lucifer shooed her away like an annoying fly landing on the last piece of cake. The waitress's mouth bolted tight as she walked away in a zombified manner.

"I've been looking for my book for quite some time. My 'Eyes' finally tracked it in Egypt. When they approached the bloke who had it, it was already too late. He had sold it. Take a wild gander on who was the lucky customer," he stated sarcastically as he reiterated the details that were given to him by his demons.

Lucifer received all his information from his trusty demon trackers called "Lucifer's Eyes." It was the only way he was able to get the latest news from all corners of the Earth without actually having to step foot outside of his lair.

"Jesse?" replied Camila trying not to sound surprised.

"Ding, ding, ding!" remarked Lucifer, pretending as if she had just answered the bonus question on *Jeopardy* correctly. "If it were just Eden and Earth burning, I would have embraced it. But the Underworld is my kingdom, and I will not let anything destroy what is mine."

Gulping noises were heard as Camila guzzled the remainder of her wine. She was making it known that she needed the effects of the alcohol to help her process a situation that had gotten bigger than her. She eased closer toward her master, spilling out a series of questions. By the tone of her voice she seemed desperate to stay in the know.

"How did you get the symbols? And how could something so powerful end up here on Earth?"

"I was originally sent to find the symbols by my father. He knew there was a possibility that something out there could compromise Eden. I was supposed to dispose of them, but me, being the 'good son' that I am, brought the symbols back to Eden, instead, for safekeeping."

Camila huffed under her breath. If he would have done what he had been ordered, they wouldn't be in this mess; but this is the Prince of Darkness, and listening to others has never been in his best interest.

Lucifer continued glancing between Camila and Maggie, making sure he remained vigilant while finishing his story.

"I lent the book to my darling niece before she was sent to Earth. The thoughtless child must have snuck the book out of Eden."

Three glasses of wine disappeared in an instant. Before Camila could reach for the vase to pour herself another drink, the waitress reappeared, casually replenishing her glass from a bottle she was already holding.

"Be a dear and get me a shot of your best-aged brandy," Lucifer commanded. The waitress nodded and mechanically walked away in silence, obeying his demand.

The red wine was slowly creeping up on Camila. She was becoming more inquisitive and talkative than usual, something Lucifer didn't mind. It wasn't every day he got to play date night with his trusted demon.

Lucifer slightly sniffed the brandy and swirled it around before pressing his full lips to the glass and downing its contents in one gulp. The heat of the brandy soothed his throat as he signaled the waitress for another one. He slammed down the empty, crystal snifter, ready to move on to the next topic of conversation.

"I'm bored! Now, let's see what this little monster can do," Lucifer grinned slyly.

Camila sat back to observe the ridiculousness that had transpired. With one wave of his devilish hand, Lucifer managed to knock over the bottle of wine sitting on Maggie's table. Alcohol flowed all over her tight red dress. She and Dom stood up simultaneously to dry her off. However, in Dom's haste, he absentmindedly knocked over the passing waiter who was holding a tray filled with bowls of soup, sending everything shattering to the floor and leaving Maggie's black, stiletto shoes soaked with chicken broth.

In all the commotion, the restaurant manager rushed over to assist but slipped on the wet floor as if diving for third base in a baseball game. He collided into Maggie so forcefully that it sent her crashing into the next table of patrons who were trying to enjoy their steaks. As she toppled over, her dress lifted above her rump displaying her sexy lace thong and bare, smooth ass. Embarrassed for her, Dom quickly pulled Maggie's dress down and tried to stand her up. The guests at the table tried their best to gather what was left of their drinks and brush off their ruined clothes. More than ten restaurant employees, including the kitchen staff, dashed over to inquire and assist with the mayhem.

Dom removed his blazer and draped it over Maggie's shoulders while holding her stained leather jacket in the other hand. Maggie kept her head low, lower than she normally would during a walk of shame, as they exited the dining area trying to regain some dignity from their complete and ultimate humiliation.

"I think that is enough, Sire. We need to follow them out." Camila rose and slipped her navy, silk shawl over her shoulders.

"Oh, darling, I'm just getting started," Lucifer grinned as he signaled for his zombified waitress one last time. He slipped her a huge clip of cash, something he was sure she wasn't used to, and sent her on her way. He couldn't help to get the gnawing feeling that his work wasn't done yet.

Maggie was never his priority. He only followed her because she was the easiest to track as she enjoyed roaming around free as a bird and as carelessly as a child. Tailing her meant they were getting closer to closing in on Jesse. But like clockwork, every time the demons cornered her, they were two seconds too late. She would disappear in the blink of an eye.

Tonight was the first time Lucifer was in close proximity to Maggie; tonight she was not getting away. He could feel the significant amount of energy she harbored inside. However, her magic felt suppressed and trapped, like a caged animal patiently waiting to be set free. Everything about her now sparked his evil curiosity. He buttoned his suit jacket and quickly followed Camila out of the restaurant.

CHAPTER 8
THE DEMON INSIDE

The traffic was horrendous, a typical Friday night in New York City. Dom and Maggie exited the cab two blocks away from Dom's apartment. If they hadn't decided to walk these couple of blocks, it would have taken them an extra thirty minutes to get there.

With each squish, squish that accompanied her every step, Maggie couldn't help but chuckle. The chicken broth that had spilled all over her feet and soaked her shoes never fully dried. Each step felt as if she was walking in wet mud. If it were anywhere other than New York City, she would have attempted to walk free-spirited and barefoot into the highlighted night.

"I can't believe what just happened. I'm so sorry. This is not how I wanted our first date night to turn out," Dom apologized profusely.

"It's alright, at least the steak was good and so was the soup since my feet are taking some home in a doggy bag," Maggie joked, trying to make Dom feel less responsible for the disastrous evening.

Dom hadn't stopped apologizing ever since they left the restaurant. She could tell he was experiencing a range of emotions, but pure disappointment mixed with regret was the most noticeable. He had even offered to replace Maggie's outfit, down to her unmentionables. She giggled to herself, thinking she had no intention of remaining fully clothed for the rest of the night.

Besides, there was no way she was getting stained red wine out of her ensemble. It was times like these that she wished her friend Charlie wasn't robbed of her sight. She desperately wanted to snap pictures of their outfits and send them to her for a good chuckle. Instead, she snapped a pic of her dress and sent it to her mother with an apologetic message.

Maggie: So *sorry mom, I know how much this dress means to you. I promise to make it up to you.*

Her message was followed by three crying emojis. Angel never responded.

Lucifer and Camila sauntered arm and arm several feet behind Dom and Maggie. His anticipation was growing thicker with each tap of his loafers.

"When they turn the corner, time will stop around them. The demons I've summoned are waiting in the darkness. They will grab Maggie, and we will disappear from there. She'll take us to Jesse for sure," Lucifer reassured coolly.

"What about the boyfriend?" Camila questioned, sounding as if Dom would be a liability.

"Ah, darling, you worry too much. The bloke will just be tossed to the side. I don't have time for him. Hell, I hate his stupid face and grabby little hands."

"Sire, am I sensing a bit of overprotectiveness?" Camila patted his muscular bicep using every opportunity for tactile contact.

"Only you would pick up on that. I can't help what you're sensing. The little monster is still my niece. Angels always have this pull toward their kin. Her gravitational pull is tugging harder on me than her mother once did."

"Good, then the sooner we get her, the sooner I get Jesse." Camila smiled triumphantly at the information she received.

The sky turned midnight black as if the moon had slipped unobtrusively into a black hole in space. Lucifer and Camila picked up their pace as Dom and Maggie turned the dimly-lit corner, oblivious to the trap they had just walked into.

"Showtime!" grinned Lucifer as his plan finally fell into place.

The night appeared peaceful and calm as Maggie and Dom engaged in deep conversation during their stroll to his place. She was learning so many interesting facts about him, things she would have known during a pillow talk session if she hadn't bolted as if she stole something after their rendezvous. They had more in common than she had expected, from their passion for music to an enduring love of books. Maggie was finding her date more intriguing by the minute. Although every now and then, a slight feeling of guilt would wash over her as reality kept reminding her that their relationship could not possibly be a real thing.

All these thoughts were flowing through her as Dom chatted about his summers in Korea and growing up as a Korean-American. He spoke highly of his family, especially his mother who was an exceedingly respected neurosurgeon at Clark University Hospital, the largest and most prestigious hospital in the metropolitan area. He had a younger sister in college, and his father had passed away a few years earlier from cancer. There had been a slight tremor in his voice at the mention of his death. Maggie wanted to know more about his dad, but she didn't want to press the issue as it appeared too touchy a subject. He explained how his mother wanted him to become a doctor, but he purposely failed out of medical school to pursue music instead. His mother wasn't happy. But as his disc jockey career took off, she learned to come to terms with his passion and later became proud of him.

"My mother figured that as long as I'm happy, and I'm not living off of her, then that's success in her book." Dom grinned from ear to ear, happily sharing his personal life with Maggie.

"That's amazing!"

Maggie was genuinely impressed. As they walked hand in hand, she snuggled closer and grinned, wanting to know more. They continued to walk in sync, completely oblivious to the light mist that was slowly descending along their path.

"I made my mom a mix playlist to help calm her nerves before surgery. Now, all her doctor friends want me to make one for them. That's what I've actually been working on," continued Dom, not skipping a beat in their conversation.

"Must be some playlist."

"It's not my best, but they like it. I'll play it for you when we get to my place. You can tell me what you think. You'll get a taste of nice sounding Korean music."

"That would be nice. I love all types of music." Maggie pulled Dom's arm over her shoulder and nestled closer to him, inhaling the masculine scent of his Burberry cologne.

Dom crinkled his nose from the stench of the red wine, soup, and perfume emitting from Maggie's dress.

"Yeah, so, before we do that, we need to get out of these smelly clothes."

"Getting naked is always a better idea." Maggie stated, her voice seductively low.

Dom chuckled at Maggie's comment and kissed her gently on the check. She felt her insides turning to molten gold and her heart fluttering from his touch. *The date wasn't turning out so bad after all,* she thought.

As they turned the corner leading toward Dom's apartment, the tiny hairs behind Maggie's neck tickled and rose like static.

"So, tell me about your family. What does your mom do for a living? What are your parents like?" The spurt of questions slipped out of Dom's mouth but fell on deaf ears.

Sensing that magic was around, Maggie stopped short and steadied her breath; there was a heaviness in the air that felt pregnant with doom. The magic didn't feel angelic—it felt dark, powerful, and dangerous. She frantically scanned the area, realizing that all sounds had ceased.

"Is something wrong, babe?" Dom asked, not understanding Maggie's sudden vigilant stance. He looked around, trying to discern what she saw.

She quickly lifted Dom's wrist and stared at his watch, listening for the ticking and waiting for the hour hands to move.

"Damn, time has stopped." her voice quivered with a mixture of anxiety.

"What? No way, this is a new watch. My battery can't be dead already." Dom lifted the watch to his ear and tapped the face, trying to kick it back to life.

The ground underneath their feet slightly trembled as Maggie watched two lines of smoky, dark shadows pass below their feet. She followed the shadows with her eyes, shoving Dom behind her, as the smoke manifested from the cement swirling in dark swooshing circles.

Dom froze, his eyes wide. He held Maggie's hand tightly; it appeared as if his brain had commanded him to run but his feet were still nailed to the ground. Within seconds two tall, male, human-like figures stood before them. Their eyes were as black as coal as they fixated on Maggie. One of them grinned widely, cutting his thin, purplish lips with his razor-sharp teeth. The other waved "hello," his nails long and as sharp as knives.

"Demons!" Maggie muttered as she frantically turned to Dom and urged him to make a break for it.

Before they could act, one of the demons had manifested in front of them blocking their path. He instantly grabbed Maggie by the neck.

"Mag.da.le.na," the demon whispered and snarled through his razor teeth.

The words snapped Dom into fight mode. On impulse, he used all his might and kicked the demon in the back. As it was hunched over, Dom punched it in the back of the head several times until the demon finally let go of Maggie.

Maggie fell on her bottom and quickly got up. She tried to use her kinetic powers to fling the demons out of their way but nothing happened. She noticed a garbage bin close by and tried to summon it. It didn't budge.

"Fuck, fuck, fuck, what's happening?" Maggie stated in a panic. She soon realized the injection she had been given a few days ago must have fully suppressed all of her abilities.

"Maggie, RUN!!" Dom called out as he wrestled on the ground with the same demon that rang her by the neck.

Before she could move, the other demon reached for her with his knives for fingernails. She quickly moved out of his way but not before the straps of her dress snagged on his nails and broke off. Maggie kicked off her shoes and used the heels as a weapon. She stood in a fighting stance and kicked and punched the demon with every one of her combatant skills. He windmilled his hands as she dipped and dodged each dangerous attack.

Again, she tried to summon her powers, and again, nothing happened.

When she saw an opportunity, she lunged for the demon's eye and plunged the heel deep into his left eye socket. The demon bellowed in pain and fell to the ground writhing in agony.

She quickly ran over to Dom who was badly losing his battle. The razor-teeth demon was kneeling over him, his monster-like hands squeezing the oxygen from his body. Maggie instantly jumped on his back. She tied her slender legs tightly around the demon's waist like a pretzel and held his head in a sleeper hold. Using every bit of her energy, she squeezed her arms and legs hoping to break the demon down, but she wasn't strong enough. She could feel her adrenaline fading as her body began to weaken like a human.

"GET OFF OF HIM!" Maggie screamed as she tried to tighten her grip, mentally pushing herself not to give up. As long as the demon didn't let go, neither would she.

The demon sank his teeth into Maggie's arm and bit down, chomping off a piece of her flesh. The initial slicing of the razor teeth into her skin didn't deter her from holding on to her opponent. But as the blood spewed in every direction and the demon began feasting on her flesh as if she was a Thanksgiving turkey leg, she had no choice but to let go.

She screamed in pain, her voice unrecognizable even to her ears. The burning sensation of her arm streamed through her body as she rolled helplessly onto her back in excruciating pain.

She tilted her head to the side only to witness the last of Dom's life choked from his fragile body right before her eyes. Tears streamed down her cheeks in disbelief and frustration as she heard him gasping and fighting for the final bit of his soul. She tried to move but was consumed by the coldness of the concrete. It sucked her energy and sapped her will.

"Let him go, please." was all she could mutter through her river of tears.

The demon grinned at Maggie as he tightened his grip around Dom's neck and squeezed tighter and tighter until his eyes rolled to the back of his head. She mentally tried to stop it, but her powers continued to fail her miserably. She stared at Dom, sobbing helplessly and uncontrollably until she heard the snap and crackle from his neck bones and arteries.

Something inside Maggie ignited as she blacked out. During the commotion, she never saw the two dark figures watching her from the shadows afar.

"Sire, the demons just killed an innocent human. This plan isn't turning out as you anticipated. Let's just grab Maggie and go."

Before Camila could insert herself in the equation, Lucifer

grabbed her by the arm in an act of deterrence. "No, I have a feeling this isn't the end. Look!"

Maggie bellowed, shattering the windows around her as glass rained down on everyone like a hail storm. They all held their ears, shielding themselves from the noise, except for Lucifer. He continued to watch in amazement at this unforeseen result.

Maggie turned onto her side and grabbed her head, protecting herself from the pounding inside. When that didn't help, she got on all fours and began to pant like a dog and moan in agony. She could feel her temples throbbing fiercely as her skull seemed to expand and contract, releasing the lumps that had been suppressed. These lumps transformed into two huge black horns that sat pertly on the top of her head.

Purple veins spiraled down Maggie's forehead and neck. Huge, silky, black wings emerged so suddenly from between her shoulder blades that she involuntarily flapped herself upward. She stared, bewildered, at her wounds as they stitched themselves up instantly without a bite or scratch mark in sight. Her dark, curly hair fell to her shoulders as her energy was rejuvenated and every ounce of her supernatural strength returned.

Dom's lifeless body struck Maggie like a lightning bolt to her soul. Her heart disintegrated inside her chest and replaced itself with an appetite for death and destruction. Her mouth felt as if it was filled with the ashes left over from burnt offerings. Vengeance would be hers.

The two demons extended to their full height ready for a fight. One demon plucked the stiletto heel from his eye and grew a new one. He was the ablest for combat.

Maggie gave the demons a hard glare that was filled with the promise of a prolonged and agonizing death. Her pupils burned red and dilated with fire and power. She rolled her neck back until it cracked and grounded her bare feet to the concrete. The battle between good and evil that had fought inside her head for years was finally set free. Evil completely dominated her mind and body as the angelic voice was lost to rage.

The two demons hissed and snarled, waiting for Maggie's next move.

"Bring me to those who sent you, and I may make it quick," her words boomed around them like a massive echo as she confronted the two beings like a boss—hands on her hips and wings outstretched.

Before they could answer, the demons were blinded by an all-encompassing green illuminating force. Angel, Keiko, and the two black panthers appeared through a magical portal that materialized behind her.

Angel and Keiko's eyes widened as they took in the crackling power of an angel-demon standing before them. Maggie looked over her shoulder, too angry to address her family face to face.

"Magdalena," gasped Angel in disbelief.

The two demons turned their attention to Angel and Keiko, ready to pull off their disappearing and reappearing act.

A simple nod from Keiko gave the panthers permission to attack. As they charged at full speed, Maggie swiftly snapped her fingers and instantly exploded the demons in a matter of seconds.

Blood and guts spilled everywhere as the panthers were hit in the mouth and eyes. They slid and tripped over blood and gore, trying to prevent themselves from getting caught in the mix, but everything happened so fast they didn't even have time to react appropriately. They whined in protest at their undignified positions and the fact that they were robbed of their fun.

The panthers shifted back to their human forms cussing out loud in annoyance.

"What the fuck was that about?" spat Coco, removing guts and blood from her long, glossy, black hair.

"Yeah, that was not cool at all, Maggie. We're all on the same side here," chimed Pearl, wiping the blood from her face.

The two women were in their birthday suits, appearing unbothered by it all. Coco stood taller and thinner than her sister, Pearl. It was not that Pearl was heavy, she was built like a powerhouse—thick and fit. A quarter could solidly bounce off her glutes. That's how tight it was.

Maggie ignored them as if they were invisible. She kneeled over Dom's lifeless body and shed tears of blood that fell pitifully onto his bowtie. The bowtie she found to be cute at the beginning of their date was now ruined.

"If everyone is done gawking at me, now would be a good time to try and bring my boyfriend back to life." Maggie's words hurt more saying them out loud.

"Coco and Pearl, go back home. We got it from here," ordered Keiko.

"But..." Before Coco could protest, Keiko shot her a look as if she were going to disintegrate her as Maggie had done with the demons. It was in their best interest not to challenge.

"Yes, Madam Keiko," the girls said in unison as they shifted back to their panther state and darted back through the portal.

Angel kneeled beside Dom and placed her delicate hands on his neck, checking for a pulse.

"Maggie, I'm sorry. Your friend is gone. He doesn't have an ounce of life left in him for me to try to revive him."

"No. NO. NO! You're the guardian of life. Give him LIFE!" Maggie's tone demanded more than a miracle.

Angel remained silent. She gently shook her head no, confirming there was nothing else she could do to change the situation.

"MOM, please." Maggie pleaded as the tears of blood continued to stream from her fiery orbs.

Angel attempted to hug her daughter, but Maggie gently shoved herself away,

"Please don't, that's not going to help," she stated as she stood up, wiping her bloody tears, feeling angry and helpless.

Keiko looked around, noticing that time had not yet resumed. They were still being watched. "Angel, we need to go. Something powerful is watching us."

Angel stood next to Keiko and scanned the area, as well, seeming to sense the same thing.

"I'm not leaving until I find more demons. I'm no longer hiding. *I'm* coming for them," Maggie declared with conviction.

"Maggie, you alone are no match for Lucifer and the Underworld." Angel reminded her.

"Lucifer? Lucifer as in the actual Devil?" Maggie asked incredulously.

Angel appeared disappointed at her ignorance. It was clear that Maggie wasn't up to speed on her history because she had never bothered to study Eden as much as Jesse did.

"Lucifer is your uncle," chimed Keiko.

"We don't have time to teach a lesson, Magdalena. We need to go," Angel urged.

Maggie shook her head in denial, unwilling to leave Dom. "I can't leave him like this, mom. He doesn't deserve to die in the street like a dog. He doesn't deserve to be alone."

"We'll alert the human authorities and make sure they take care of him. But we can't stick around," suggested Keiko.

"Even then I still can't go home. The portal is designed to keep out demons. That's me, right now, in this form. I'm sure once I'm normal again I'll be fine. But I can't go back now, and I refuse to go back."

Angel took a deep breath. "Then I'll stay with you."

"No, mom, please. I need time. Go back to Master Anu. I'll find a way back home in a few days. I promise." Maggie pleaded.

"Let her go, Angel. If Maggie says she'll find a way, then we'll wait for her." Keiko tried to sound convincing, but Maggie knew it took all her willpower to believe her own words.

"Fine." Angel finally conceded. She placed a gentle hand on her daughter's shoulder and lightly caressed her purple, veined cheeks, "I love you no matter what you are," she whispered.

Keiko and Angel disappeared through the portal, leaving Maggie alone with Dom's body. She kneeled next to him one last time and gently kissed his cold lips.

"Thank you for making me feel normal. I love you," she whispered in his dead ears.

Maggie grabbed her leather jacket and took to the skies, landing on the roof of a nearby building. Before she could wave her hand to unfreeze time, the sounds of ambulances rushing down the streets and cars honking were already in motion. It was as if someone was waiting for her to leave. She pulled out her cell phone from the jacket and began to call the human authorities, but when she glanced below, someone had already sent them. Maggie watched as the scene was closed off and Dom's body was wrapped in white sheets and later hauled away. The pain was too much to deal with head-on, and the longer she stayed, the more she blamed herself for his death. The guilt felt like a millstone weighing her down.

Maggie stepped on the ledge of the roof. She closed her eyes tightly, letting the night's breeze ripple over her body. As she spread her arms out wide, thoughts of the past few hours flashed in and out of her mind like a strobe light. Maggie leaned forward and free-fell about a hundred feet from the sky before she flapped her wings and disappeared into the night.

Camila paced back and forth inside Lucifer's lair, pissed by the events that had transpired during the night.

"It was reckless and a waste of time. I didn't get what I wanted and neither did you. Excuse me, Sire, but I cannot contain my anger. Forgive me in advance for speaking out of turn, but WHAT THE

FUCK WAS THAT ALL ABOUT?!" Camila's Spanish accent thickened with each high-pitched word.

"Darling, sit down. All your bloody pacing is making me dizzy." Lucifer reclined lazily on his red velvet sofa feeling sated by his accomplishments. The top four buttons of his shirt were open wide, exposing a chiseled, smooth chest.

Camila kneeled in front of Lucifer and laid her head on his upper thigh. "Sire. I didn't mean to be abrupt and question your every intention. But we killed an innocent human. The demons you sent weren't fit for the job. Why didn't you summon No Nose Tommy?"

"Camila, stop worrying. The bloke landed himself a trip into Eden; he's just fine. If Maggie is ever given the privilege of stepping foot there, she'll get her happily ever after."

Lucifer rose from the sofa, trying not to give into Camila's enticing touches. A good fight and death always excited him. He was inches away from tearing her out of her evening gown and showing her the power of the Prince of Darkness. It was taking all his willpower to decline her, and he wasn't known for having much of it.

Camila moved herself to the sofa and crossed her legs, the slit of her dress displaying more thigh than before. She stared straight ahead in a daze.

"Then what have we done?" she asked again.

"What *we* have done is unleash the Destroyer of Worlds. That child is so powerful that the Underworld could surely use her." answered Lucifer, feeling as if he had hit the jackpot with his prize on backorder.

CHAPTER 9
SOMETIMES LIFE IS A ROM-COM

As Maggie flew above the clumps of dark clouds with dazzling stars high above her, she savored the cool feeling of the wind whipping against her face. Although it had cooled her tears, it left a horrible streak of blood that was stuck to her cheeks like gorilla glue.

I need to fully investigate this "Uncle Lucifer," she thought as she soared through the skies.

Lucifer, a name that she hardly remembered learning about, was now haunting her mind. She thought about the people in her life, other than her family, who could help her understand Eden and the Underworld. All those times her mother tried to teach her, despite her stubborn lack of interest, about their family lineage and Jesse's constant rambling about Eden, had finally bitten her in the ass.

I should have paid more attention. she scolded herself.

Well, we didn't. But it doesn't mean it's too late to learn, chimed the Left voice that now seemed to be the dominant advisor of her inner conscience.

Maggie ran down the list of heathens and saints she knew until an idea slapped her in the back of the head. She was missing the big picture. Charlie, How could she have forgotten Charlie? Her best friend was pursuing her Master's degree in Religious Studies. She was her best bet.

Maggie hovered over the rusty, black steel of the fire escape before gingerly planting her cold, bare feet against it. Her dark wings slid silently between her shoulder blades as she carefully scanned her surroundings looking for any magical creature that could have followed her. The night was young, and the Upper West Side of the city gleamed with street and building lights and buzzed with a parade of colorful people seemingly ready to get into mischief.

A part of Maggie wanted to walk the city and destroy every demon that walked among the humans until their ruler appeared; however, her heart had experienced enough agitation for one night. She needed to decompress.

The burning red flares from Maggie's orbs reflected through the clear window as she soundlessly observed Charlie in her apartment. She was innocently sitting on her brown, comfy couch, munching on a huge red bowl of popcorn, and listening to her favorite rom-com movie, *Trainwreck*. Maggie instantly recognized the film the moment Amy Schumer popped into the scene.

Goodness, how many times is she going to play that movie? stated the Left voice as if it could eye roll.

"Quiet! She loves that movie. She's a big Schumer fan. Now shut up and let me concentrate," Maggie spoke out loud as if chastising someone near her.

With eyes closed tight and a slight bow of her head, Maggie didn't even break a sweat as she summoned a powerful protective shield around Charlie's apartment. The invisible shield could not be heard or seen by a typical human, but its magic would disintegrate any non-human at the slightest touch. It was a weak gift she inherited as an angel and one she rarely used. The problem was simply that the shield only held for a couple of hours, twelve tops to be exact. After that, she would be a sitting duck waiting to be plucked.

The thought of Charlie possibly succumbing to the same fate as Dom raced across Maggie's mind more times than she could count. However, she kept reassuring herself that she wouldn't let the same thing happen twice. She mentally stomped the thought down to the pit of her stomach and vowed that she would die a death by a million cuts before she lost another loved one. Now that she was in her full demon form, nothing was going to get past her defenses.

As the shield strongly vibrated with magical energy, Maggie made a mental note to contact her mother in the morning and have Charlie protected indefinitely. It was time she had her own guardian angel.

The dark silhouette of a shadowy figure lurking by the window caught Pete's attention. The black lab popped his head up from his resting spot near the couch and listened intently. He stared in the direction of the large window and slowly growled under his breath until the rumbling grew louder and then turned into vicious barks. Charlie leaned over the couch trying to shush her dog.

"Pete, be quiet. I'm trying to listen to my movie in peace."

He barked louder until Maggie could hear the dog trotting toward the window and barking in her direction.

"PETE!! SHUSH! My goodness, what has gotten into you tonight?"

Charlie shot up from the couch and followed the sounds of the barking dog to the window.

"Did I leave the window open again by accident?" she asked him.

Pete began jumping and scraping the window, trying desperately to claw his way to a scary intruder. Maggie gently pressed her index finger to her fuchsia-stained lips and gently shushed the black lab. Pete abruptly stopped his barking and stood pressed at the window obeying the commands.

"Sit," said Maggie quietly.

Pete sat watching the window as the obedient dog he was.

"PETE! What's happening, boy? I can hear you breathing, but why did you stop barking?"

Charlie stood completely still as she listened intently for any sudden movements. She yelped as light tapping broke her concentration, followed by the sound of her name. She automatically recognized the voice.

"MAGGIE?! What the fuck? You scared the SHIT out of me," she exclaimed as she felt around the window frame for the latch.

Maggie climbed inside, scraping the top of her black horns on the window seal.

"What are you doing out there? I live fifteen flights up. Why didn't you come through the front door like a normal person?"

"Normal," ha! Chuckled the Left voice. Maggie instantly ignored the comment.

"I didn't want to be seen."

"Why?" The sounds of Maggie's irregular breathing tipped Charlie off that things were not right with her friend.

"Maggie, what's wrong?"

Fresh tears of blood streamed down Maggie's cheeks again as she stared into Charlie's smokey, crystal ball-like eyes. Regurgitating the news of Dom's death wasn't going to be an easy task. The memory, and worse yet, the knowledge that his beautiful soul was no more sat in her heart like Sisyphus' Boulder. She couldn't say his name without the guilt eating away at her black heart.

"What happened to your date? Did Dom stand you up? Is that why you climbed up fifteen flights?"

Maggie's sobs became bone-wracking and fierce; she could no longer hide her sniffles under her breath.

Charlie leaned in and embraced her best friend. She held her tightly as her pajamas became stained with the crimson red droplets that flowed freely from Maggie's eyes. Her nose crinkled at the unpleasant scent of Maggie's leather jacket and hair. She reeked of rotten trash and sulfur.

"Hey, it's okay, I'm here for you." Charlie gently caressed her friend's back and slowly began to smooth her hair reassuringly, but Maggie instantly pulled away.

"I think I need a hot bath. Is it okay if I use your shower?" Maggie quickly asked.

Charlie placed her hand on Maggie's cheek, seeming unmoved by the feel of her rough dry skin under her silky fingertips. She was unknowingly caressing blood-red tears over purple streaked veins.

"Sure. Whatever you need. I'll get you a change of clothes and make some hot tea. We can talk when you're ready."

"I would like that. Thank you." For the first time, Maggie was grateful that her best friend was unable to see the miserable creature she had become. Her metamorphosis was even hard for her to grasp.

Maggie made her way through the narrow corridor that led to the pristine black and white checkerboard bathroom. Before disappearing behind the doors, she glanced at Pete and threw him an apologetic look.

"Sleep," she whispered.

The sound of Pete's paws skittering across the hardwood floor alerted Charlie of Pete's whereabouts.

"Pete, are you going to bed? That's so strange of you. You never sleep in your doggy bed. You're so weird tonight." She shook her head as she brought her tea kettle over to the stove to boil.

Charlie shut off her rom-com and tuned into regular television. She was obsessed with the news and constantly listened to *New York 1*. As she was making her way toward the bathroom with towel and pajamas in hand, she overheard the breaking news signal coming across the television screen as an anchorwoman spoke of the night's unforeseen events.

"*Tonight, cops are investigating the death of Kim Dae-Seong, known to his fans as Dominique Kim, a well-known Korean American DJ from right here in Manhattan. Kim was very popular among the DJ circuit with* having ties to play at several celebrity gatherings and high profile night clubs. Tonight that all came to an end. Kim was found brutally murdered mere inches from his home on 86th Street. The surrounding streets are blocked off as authorities are surveilling the neighborhood. The Kim family is seeking answers and asking for justice. If anyone has any information regarding the murder of Mr. Kim please contact the NYPD's local tip number at 555..."

Dominique Kim, the name seemed to reverberate inside Charlie's head as though she was standing inside a cavernous space with the bells of Notre Dame clanging vigorously with a horrible echo. *DOM!* The clothing in her hands fell to the floor as she rushed through the corridor and stormed into the bathroom.

Steam from the hot shower enveloped her as if walking into a blazing sauna. She could barely breathe as the boiling steam assailed her nostrils. Maggie's sobs were loud and clear through the mist. The sounds of ferocious hyperventilating combined with wailing weren't the cries of a murderer but that of someone who was stricken with unbearable grief, pain, and guilt. She knew that sob all too well. Those exact sounds had been ripped from her diaphragm when she lost her parents. If a shattered heart could speak, its words would be replaced with those horrific wails that no one would understand unless they, too, had suffered a similar loss.

Charlie felt for the shower curtain and slowly opened it. Maggie was sitting inside the tub, hugging her knees to her chest with her head buried between her legs, letting the hot water wash away her anguish. Her stomach twisted into a knot, and she instantly felt a sharp pain in her heart as it pounded against her chest cavity. She was releasing every bit of sadness left inside her heart.

Without hesitation, Charlie followed the whimpering sounds, knelt beside her, and caressed the wet skin on her best friend's back.

"I couldn't save him. I couldn't do anything to stop what happened," whispered Maggie between deep, steamy breaths knowing that Charlie had heard the news. Her demon ears had heard it crystal clear as well, as if she were standing in the same room.

Devastation washed over Charlie's face. It pained her to hear her friend so lost, tears streamed down her very own cheeks. After everything they both went through, Maggie couldn't catch a break. Fully clothed, she climbed her slender body into the bathtub letting all of her garments soak in the soiled bathwater. She wrapped her long arms around Maggie's shaken, naked body, and gently pressed her firm breasts against her back as she leaned her head on her shoulder. She slowly rocked her comfortably like a mother soothing a baby's cries. The hot rushing shower cascaded over the two young women like a calming waterfall. Charlie hugged Maggie tighter from behind, oblivious to the strange sound, like that of a scratching chalkboard, that was emanating from her best friend as they both sobbed out loud together.

Like two lost sisters finding comfort in their own misfortunes, Charlie's hug gave Maggie reassurance that everything would eventually be okay. The heartwarming feeling of Charlie's raw human emotions coated Maggie with undying sisterly love, a love she didn't feel from anyone or wouldn't allow anyone to share with her. It was at that moment that she felt her horns slither their way back inside her scalp. The scraping sound was so deafening to her own ears that she feared Charlie would question it. She cried a bit louder to camouflage the unsettling scraping noises. Crimson tears turned clear as joy settled in, knowing she wouldn't be stuck in her demon form. She held on tighter to Charlie's arms, allowing the warmth of her body against her wet skin to smother her with love.

CHAPTER 10
ALL I WANT IS LUCIFER

Lucifer stood comfortably in the middle of an immense cave that could have been the home to an early ancestor of humanity. A series of petroglyphs were carved into the rocks. One told a story of a revolt led by local villagers against their heartless king. In the end, many of the villagers were slaughtered while some were left nailed alive on wooden stakes in the open fields, for the animals to feast. The king had won his battle. Although he was deemed heartless and ruthless, he spared the women and children of those who defiantly fought against him by exiling them to other lands. It was a story Lucifer related to as it reminded him of his own misfortune. Usually, he would take a few moments to continue deciphering the carvings as they were sketched on every inch of the enormous space. However, the million thoughts and ideas that crossed his frustrated mind distracted him from concentrating on anything other than his research.

Through fire-breathing orbs, Lucifer remained focused on the ancient book hovering in front of him. It was written a millennia ago by a warlock that possessed the gift of a seer. His eyes couldn't settle on any particular page; they flipped over and over as though being sorted by a never-ending money counter.

"STOP!" Lucifer's exclamation was received like a lightning bolt that induced fear during a ferocious storm. The pages reluctantly settled and letters painstakingly began to appear on the pages as if an angry pen was scratching the words in the author's own blood.

> *It is crucial that the gates of the Unknown realms remain barred for all time—NEVER TO BE OPENED. For these worlds are not kind and will cause death and destruction to all creatures who encounter it. Not even the coexisting worlds will be able to stop the chaos. All and every supernatural being will be powerless against the ferocious monsters waiting eagerly to be unleashed. But alas, not all is lost and hope is at a distance. The Unknown has a weakness and its name is the Destroyer of Worlds. The half-demon, half-angel child will possess the power to lock the realms for all eternity and cleanse it from existence. The Destroyer is an abomination from the realm of Eden and Valhalla, whose only birth right is to eliminate the Unknown realms. Without the Destroyer, life as one knows it will be demolished. So it is written. You have been warned...*

Lucifer read the last few lines three more times as he did in the past, finally connecting the dots to Maggie, his half-angel, half-demon, trainwreck of a niece. She was planted by the seed of a fallen angel from Valhalla, Jack, and born from the womb of an angel from Eden, Angel. Her history made sense, more than her brother Jesse who is half-angel and half-human. Before the words shimmered out of existence, he pondered whether she was even capable of such a task. Saving worlds was more her mother's speed. Maggie was more of a headache than a heroine.

"We're fucking doomed," he lamented as the ancient, dusty tome slammed its pages shut with a determined bang.

"The Seer must have not been seeing correctly," he ridiculed as he flicked the book away with a dismissive thought and turned his back as it floated away to be absorbed with the rest of the collection of tomes in his library. He gazed around the jagged shelves, mentally summoning every ancient scroll and book, searching vigorously for information pertaining to the Destroyer of Worlds and the Unknown realms. Most of his library was filled with research he confiscated from witches and warlocks and other magical creatures over time, books he most certainly felt were in the wrong hands.

Cluttered books accumulated on every available surface in the room and were scattered haphazardly on his writing desk. Lucifer removed his grey suit jacket and discarded it on top of the many dusty manuscripts piled on his leather throne. He rolled up the sleeves to his off-white dress shirt and stretched his fingers, cracking his knuckles in the process. The floating torches slowly danced around the high ceiling illuminating hundreds of black, leather-bound tomes on the tall shelves. The caved library was the only room in the Underworld, other than some of the simulated torture rooms, that wasn't scorching hot. The temperature was purposely kept cool to prevent the books and ancient scrolls from withering and cracking.

The usual scent of leather and sulfur was overpowered by a sweet lavender aroma emanating from hidden alcoves around the room. It was as if the lavender candles magically appeared. He'd been so occupied in his research that he missed the minor details.

Under normal circumstances, no one was allowed into Lucifer's library. It was his personal sanctuary and his escape from the drivel of the Underworld. However, it dawned on him that he recently granted Camila access to his little retreat, a perk she received for being his most loyal and obedient servant.

Before Lucifer resumed rummaging through the endless piles of knowledge, he summoned the candle from across the room and examined it.

"Smells nice," he mused, admiring the candle as it hovered and sparked a flicker in his sea-green eyes. He watched with pride as the library door creaked open and a small, golden, nine-inch-heel sandal stepped lightly across the devil's threshold.

Startled to see her master standing before her, Camila's satisfied smile died on her full sensual lips.

"Apologies, Sire. I didn't mean to interrupt. I thought you were at the torture chambers."

Lucifer floated the candle back into the alcove and folded his arms tightly across his chest. He lightly rubbed his beard and stared at her provocative ensemble. The top of her black lace gown hugged every inch of her assets. Its long v-neck dipped slightly below her cleavage, displaying a pushed-up bosom that commanded submission if only to bury one's face between her ample breasts. The rest of her gown flowed openly past her hips like open blinds on a windowpane. It tapered to direct the eyes down to the ultimate source of her power that was encased in a diamond-encrusted, leather thong. Her neck twinkled with the diamond choker Lucifer had gifted her. It matched her leather thong perfectly.

For a half-second, his eyes landed on her pink nipples that desperately tried to hide behind the black lace material. The sight of it caused an instantaneous reaction in his nether regions. His monster was the hardest it had been in centuries.

"Sire?" Camila found it hard to meet his gaze. She was distracted by the definite bulge that was still, um, rising.

Her dark, straight hair hung past her shoulders as she slightly bit down on the bottom of her glossy lips, seeming to wait for him to make the next move. It was as if she knew, without a doubt, that her pussy was in charge. But it was a thirst trap that Lucifer was internally fighting not to fall into.

"Why are you dressed in that manner?" His voice was rough with repressed desire.

"I was behind Door #1 in the simulation chamber. A damned soul wanted his 'Eternal Happiness' to be with a sex goddess. Poor bastard didn't know how brutal goddesses could be."

Lucifer had to admit, the Doors of Hell were always good times, especially Door #1—Eternal Happiness. The simulation suffocated a person with their deepest desires, eventually leading them to commit suicide repeatedly in order to escape their depraved pleasures. He wondered if he would have picked a goddess as his deepest desire had he been locked away in one of the never-ending chambers. He would, if it were Camila delivering the naughty pleasures. The thought of another wanting her lit a wave of anger inside of him and deflated the bulge in his pants.

Lucifer furrowed his brows. His lips pressed tightly as his flared nostrils exhaled his irritation. Out of all the demon women that could have role played, why did Camila volunteer? The task was beneath her. After all, he told her on numerous occasions that she was retired from role-playing inside the simulation chamber. Her duty was to consult and oversee the other demons. He couldn't help but feel possessive over her.

Lucifer squinted his eyes. His jaw clenched as he tried not to overreact. "Is that so?" was all he could mutter.

"Lucky me, I got to dress the part." Camila gave a delighted twirl, knowing that her perky ass showed to perfection with the line of diamonds twinkling from between her cheeks. She brought her hands together as if holding an imaginary baseball bat. She swung her invisible bat over her shoulders as if she was striking out in the middle of a ball game.

"Then I got to beat him over and over again until he begged me to kill him. I thought my arms were going to fall off from the amount of whipping he could take. He's finally committing suicide in a loop. My job is done. It's time for me to relax."

Lucifer turned his back on Camila and leaned against his writing desk, pressing his fingertips firmly on the oak wood. He lowered his head as thoughts of anger and uncertainty ran through his mind. He wasn't sure if it was her attire, her nonchalant attitude, or the stress of his research that was ticking him off. He only knew he wasn't feeling right, and he was ready to explode.

"I thought I gave you specific orders that I no longer wanted you working in the simulation chamber," Lucifer scolded.

"Sire, I...eh..didn't think..."

"Didn't think WHAT?!"

Lucifer swiftly turned to face Camila, furiously knocking over some of the leather books that cluttered his desk.

"You didn't think it would be a big deal? When I give an order, I want you pesky demons to OBEY. How hard is it for any of YOU TO UNDERSTAND AN ORDER? How many more of you little arseholes do I need to burn into the void before I'M BEING TAKEN SERIOUSLY?"

With Lucifer's last words, he morphed into his red devilish demon face and was upon Camila in nanoseconds, pinning her against the door. Black smoke spewed from his wide nostrils in anger, spotting her neck with dark ashes.

Camila stiffened and hardened her back against the cold wooden door as if desperately begging the wood to swallow her to safety. Tears trailed down her cheeks as she quickly turned her head and tightly closed her eyes; anticipating her punishment. The heat of Lucifer's sulfur breath was turning her neck a purplish red as if it were lava melting her skin. The shimmering, diamond choker she wore around her neck halfway disintegrated and slipped off. Her legs quivered beneath her. One could almost hear her teeth clattering with fear.

In all of her years in the Underworld, Lucifer had never gotten this angry with her. Even when she was kidnapped and returned, she suffered no real consequences. However, she disobeyed one order and was two seconds away from joining her fellow demons inside the void. Lucifer was making it known that no one was safe.

Camila held her breath, trying to hide her whimpers. She clenched her teeth, balled her fists, and begged for mercy through harsh whispers.

"Please, please, stop Sire..it..burns."

Lucifer continued breathing heat down her neck, not realizing he was torturing his most prized servant. He mentally summoned her arms above her head and pressed them tightly against the wall as he continued to sniff away like a dog in heat. Her whispered pleas of agony sent enticing shivers down his spine. She brought out the sadist in him.

Camila's perfume was the embodiment of the scent of the lavender candle. Her skin was shimmering with gold specks, and the scent of her hair seemed to be infused with a heady, hypnotic aroma of flowers. Anger raged in his veins and fueled his massive desire—the proof was pressing painfully against the zipper of his pants.

His roar shook the Underworld.

Loud shrills escaped Camila's lips until her throat was hoarse and cracked. Out of instinct, she spiked her heel onto her master's foot with all her might, freeing her arms from its restraint. She sent her right hand crashing to the side of his demon face. The harsh, painless slap sent Lucifer's face turning in the opposite direction and morphing back to normal. He took several steps back, hand to face, trying to assess the situation.

"WHAT THE FUCK HAS COME OVER YOU?!"

Camila wiped her tears and nursed her neck, pressing her hand tightly on her wound. It was a fight or flight moment, and he wasn't the least bit surprised she chose to fight. He was, however, stunned at his own jealous and sadistic behavior toward her. The slap to the face snapped him back to reality. He knew very well he deserved every bit of anger thrown at him.

"How. Dare. You. After everything I do for you, you treat me as less than shit. You tell me I'm your most valuable, and yet you burn me and threaten to throw me inside the void."

Lucifer took his scolding silently. He knew that if it were any other demon, he would have taken pleasure at pulverizing their very essence before banishing them to oblivion. When in the world had Camila come to mean so much more to him? How is it possible for his chest cavity to contract with such agonizing pain at realizing that he had been a massive prick? *So, this is what jealousy feels like,* he thought.

"If you feel I disobeyed you, then throw me inside the void," she challenged as she settled into a strong defiant stance, her hands balanced assertively on her hips.

"NO." Lucifer commanded as he gilded toward Camila with his hands outstretched, willing to help mend her wound.

"Get away from me." she demanded, shoving him at arm's length.

"You have to let me help."

"No, you've done...enough."

Unexpectedly, Camila hunched over, biting down on her lip and breathing heavily as she sucked in her agony. It was clear by her actions that the burn on her neck was intensifying. Unable to withstand the Mount Everest of feelings that threatened to engulf him at the sight of her anguish, Lucifer ignored her demands and placed his heavy hand on her open wound. She flinched at his touch against her skin. Within seconds the burn healed without a scar as though it had never existed.

It seemed to take forever for Camila to finally make eye contact with her sire. He stared into her bright blue eyes feeling as if he might fall down a very dangerous rabbit hole. He didn't know how to begin to apologize; he had never found the need. At this moment, he felt he would give it an "honest" shot. He gently slid his hands down her arms.

"I don't know what came over me. I don't know why I said all those horrible things or why I felt it was the appropriate moment to swing my cock around. Quite frankly, I'm embarrassed."

"You're embarrassed?" Camila's eyes widened in surprise.

"I was a complete twat for what I did." Lucifer took two steps back, running his hands through his dark short hair. "The truth is, you're doing something to me, Camila. And I don't know what to do about it."

Camila folded her arms across her chest tightly and leaned against the door.

"And what exactly am I doing, Sire?"

"You're doing all this." Lucifer waved his hands at her seductive clothing.

"I'm doing my job," she responded, unmoved.

"No, you're turning me on." He took a few steps closer to get a better read from her. The King of the Underworld never let a woman become a distraction, but Camila was becoming just that, a distraction. He needed to air everything out before his jealous rages accidentally harmed her again. He needed her more than she knew. In his mind, he couldn't rule the Underworld without her by his side.

"You have my back during every decision I make. You genuinely praise and adore me. When I need situations taken care of, you handle them with zero mistakes and no questions asked. You're ready to put up a fight even with the strongest creatures, knowing it's a battle you'll lose. I've never witnessed such loyalty. Every step you take with every swish of your hips spins my head and puts me in an awkward place."

Camila released her hands from across her chest and drew closer to Lucifer. She gently clasped his hands in hers.

"It doesn't have to be awkward, Sire. You are my master; I am here for you. If you want me to stop..."

"That's the problem," he quickly interjected. "I don't want you to stop. I. Need. To stop. I need to stop doubting you and the feelings I have for you."

Camila gasped. "Sire..."

The long uncomfortable pause between them felt as though it lasted centuries.

Lucifer, feeling as if he had said too much, slowly walked over to the door and reached for the knob. He figured it would be best to have her leave before he did something he may regret but also enjoy.

"You're free to return to the torture chambers as you please."

Unable to move, Camila nodded her head in understanding.

"But before you go, I hope you forgive me for hurting you. You're too good for me, Camila, and I don't deserve you. My cursed soul does not deserve the sort of devotion you have for me. I am incapable of love. That is my punishment. It's what I have to live with." It pained him to admit that he was incapable of love when deep down in the pit of his stomach he felt it was far from the truth.

Camila turned on her golden-heeled sandals and stopped in front of her master. They stood nose to nose, staring into each other's eyes. The silent passion that burned between them began to grow stronger. Lucifer could hear Camila's heart racing inside her chest as if it were running circles in a marathon. She gently placed her delicate fingers on his cheek and smoothed her thumb down over his mouth while tracing the outline of his lips.

"Even the most horrific monsters are capable of love," whispered Camila, her words sounding erotic in her enticing Spanish accent.

Lucifer held her hand in place and gently planted a kiss on the back of it. Her expression remained as sincere as her words.

"I believe you have punished yourself long enough, Sire."

"Perhaps. Or maybe it is you that is punishing me." Lucifer's flirtatious glare was enough to make any woman melt with burning desire.

"I would never. I adore you too much."

Without any further thought, Camila crashed her soft lips against his luscious mouth. The encounter was unexpected, thrilling, and intense. He pulled her in closer as his tongue explored all the corners of the inside of her mouth. She relaxed in his arms as he rubbed the center of her back and ran his fingers through her long, dark, straight hair.

He could have easily lost himself if it weren't for the heat that crept up inside of him. He pulled away, fighting the desire to tear Camila's clothes off and bend her over on his desk as he pounded into her without a care in the world. He wanted nothing more than to fill her up until he was legless. The heat of his selfish desire was intoxicating. He tightly closed his eyes for less than a second and went against it. For the first time in a long time, he wanted to give someone his all. After all, she was right, *Even the most horrific monsters are capable of love.*

Lucifer turned the tables and pressed Camila's back against the door and passionately devoured her mouth as if it were the last kiss in their lifetime. She wrapped her arms around him tightly, inviting him in for more while pressing her firm breasts against his chest. She raised her leg onto his hip to level herself. Lucifer got the hint and caressed her thighs and picked her up, cradling her on his waist and squeezing her butt cheeks.

With one turn, Lucifer transported them from his library to his private bedroom. It was in the comfort of his own space where he knew he would not be disturbed. No one was ever allowed into his personal quarters, not even the many women he previously bedded. He had several places in the Underworld where he engaged in his sexual liaisons; however, his bedroom was not one of them. He was breaking all his own rules by bringing Camila to his personal space. But he didn't care; he wanted to please her in every way imaginable and prove to her that he was more than just her sire.

The room gleamed of pure whiteness combined with a dreamy aesthetic feel. It was as if Lucifer was holding onto a piece of Eden with the angelic decor of his room. Even the air smelled of Eden's well-kept flowers.

Lucifer held onto Camila as he made his way to the large, plush bed in the center of the room. He gently placed her back on his pure white, silk sheets ready to explore every line, crevice, and curve of her body. Her emerald lipstick was smeared all over his lips and collar. She couldn't help but chuckle as she gently rubbed the lipstick off his full beautiful lips and rough beard. He took a moment to slowly caress her body with his hands, first gently stroking her rock-hard nipples through her lace gown, then sliding his hand down to her warmth. He felt her shiver under his touch, not sure if it was out of fear or pleasure.

"I will stop if you want me to. This will only go as far as you allow."

"Sire, don't stop," she squirmed between breaths.

"Please, call me Lucifer."

Camila wrapped her legs tighter around his hips and gyrated for a few seconds until the bulge in his pants hardened and pressed against her as if it were looking for an escape.

"All I want is Lucifer," she moaned seductively in his ear.

Lucifer was lost in the trance of her dancing blue orbs. He knew this moment wasn't going to be a casual romp. It was going to be meaningful, joyous, and magical. This was going to be an incredible experience with the woman he was falling for, and he wasn't going to hold back.

With one hard tug from Camila's hands, the buttons on Lucifer's white dress shirt went flying around them. She kissed his muscular chest and eased her way down to unbutton his pants. She bit down on the button, ready to tear it apart with her teeth. She tried to release what she desperately wanted to taste, but she was stopped by the gentle tug on her hair.

Lucifer winked at her devilishly and gently lowered her gown from her shoulders exposing her bare tits. He slowly guided her shoulders to lay back and relax.

"Let me handle this," he smiled erotically.

He let her hands wander as she caressed his shoulders and ran the tips of her finger down his smooth chest.

Lucifer undressed and stood before his lover in all his naked glory. He pulled off Camila's thong and slid off the remainder of her gown. He admired her body, running his strong hands down her hips and gently slipping his pointer and middle finger inside of her vagina. Camila moaned in pleasure as he slowly eased his fingers in and out as his thumb tickled her clit while he smothered her neck with luscious kisses. He could feel her juices wetting his fingers as she gyrated, fucking them as if she were dancing to a slow and sensual Sade song. Before she could climax, Lucifer quickly removed his fingers and brought them to his lips. He licked them seductively, tasting every bit of her juices.

"Not yet," he whispered as he kissed and sucked his way down between her quivering legs. He gracefully wrapped Camila's silky, long legs around his neck. His rough masculine hands felt as though they were touching satin for the first time as he caressed her thighs and slightly propped her hips to his nose. The pure scent of her internal essence drove him wild with passion. He could no longer hold himself back from devouring her pussy like a forbidden fruit. He licked and sucked his way inside of her as she grabbed the back of his head, begging him for more. Her shrills of cosmic pleasure turned him on, and he swallowed every bit of her orgasm as she spilled herself into his hungry mouth.

The sounds of her panting had his cock rock hard. He was just getting started. Lucifer made his way to her now discolored emerald lips and kissed her passionately. He had never felt so connected with his past lovers, not even Gia. He took a moment to catch his breath that was being stolen by the vixen before him and stared at her beauty. Camila smiled lovingly. He could feel behind the darkness in his heart that he wanted her more than life itself.

"Are you ready for Round 2?" he whispered, knowing that this was going to be the act that locked them together.

"Always."

Camila caressed his chest and down to his cock and guided him inside her. She was warm, tight, and wet, just as he liked it. They moved together in sync, finding a rhythm that pleasured them both. Lucifer bit down on his lip as he pumped and thrust inside her, feeling her get wetter and wetter. With one easy flip over, Camila changed positions and rode her lover until his eyes rolled to the back of his head. What started as something sweet and lovely turned into Camila gaining the upper hand and fucking his brains to mush.

The bouncing of her breasts and her rhythm was sending him to his peek.

"Bloody HELL..." was all Lucifer could choke out before Camila stuck her two fingers in his mouth to silence him.

She closed her eyes and cocked her head back as she squeezed the walls of her vagina tighter to make him cum. Within seconds Lucifer had filled her up with everything he had left as they climaxed together.

Camila collapsed in her sire's arms as he held her tight and kissed the top of her head lovingly.

"You owe me a new diamond choker," she said while slapping his chest playfully.

"Darling, I will buy you a diamond house if it pleases you."

They both chuckled with amusement. *This is just the beginning of us*, thought Lucifer.

CHAPTER 11
IT SHOULD HAVE BEEN ME

Maggie spent the past few days at Charlie's place researching and learning everything she could about Eden and the Underworld. After reviewing Charlie's research papers, audiobooks, and going over the first couple of pages of her thesis paper, it appeared that the humans knew more about Eden than she did. Although most of the research was based on mythology, with more than a few writings from non-credible sources and lunatics with zero evidence, the humans strongly believed that most of the events were factual.

With every piece of information Maggie gathered, she made it her business to cross-reference it with Jesse's research. To her dismay, most of it proved to be true. Every day that passed she wanted to spill the beans about herself to her best friend. The secret of hiding her true identity, along with the details of Dom's death, was burning a hole in her insides. Even when she was on the brink of confessing, Angel sternly advised her against it. *"Ignorance is bliss"* was her mother's sound reasoning.

The smell of coffee lingered in the air as Charlie exited the bathroom and followed the clinking sound of rattling dishes into her kitchenette. Maggie sat comfortably with one knee pulled to her chest at the small table as she absentmindedly swirled the creamer mix into her coffee mug. Her gaze wandered and focused rather hazily on the cupboard and mentally summoned it open. The doors obeyed with a somewhat tired groan of creaking hinges. A purple ceramic mug floated toward her just as Charlie entered the room. Using her magic around her blind friend was one of the small advantages that she relished. It was something she could not do with other humans who had complete use of their eyes.

"Morning! I was just pouring you some coffee," she stated as the coffee pot began pouring itself into the mug.

"Smells delicious. Thank you."

Charlie felt around for the seat directly across from Maggie as the coffee pot floated smoothly past her and landed soundlessly on the top of the stove. Pete sat obediently beside his handler staring back and forth at the floating objects, his tongue out, mesmerized by the flying items within his surroundings.

Charlie inhaled the fragrant aroma of her coffee and began surveying the table with her expert fingers as if searching for items to complement her drink. She placed her hands on a few scattered papers before Maggie intercepted the hunt with a kind inquiry.

"What do you need, creamer?" Maggie gently placed the creamer into Charlie's palm.

"No, a spoon, but thank you. Is there someone else here?"

"No, Just us. Why?" The question was tossed nonchalantly, and Maggie was a bit taken aback.

Charlie set the creamer aside and brought the coffee mug tentatively to her lips. With a few smooth, slow breaths to cool her steaming "pick me up," she sipped casually before answering.

"Either you move really fast or the coffee pot just grew legs and ran to the stove."

Maggie awkwardly giggled. "What do you mean?"

"I sensed you sitting here, but I could have sworn I heard the pot ding against the stove."

"You must still be half asleep. The pot is still on the table," Maggie fibbed as she materialized the pot into her hands.

"More coffee?" she offered, pouring herself another cup before Charlie could answer.

"No, I'm good, thanks." Charlie waved the pot away as Maggie casually popped up from her chair to place the coffee pot on the stove the old-fashioned way. She made sure to shuffle her feet on her way back to the table.

"What are you reading?" Charlie curiously asked as she felt around the scattered papers.

"Just some notes I've been taking from your and Jesse's studies of Eden."

"Oh, I didn't know Jesse had an interest in religious studies."

Maggie gathered the papers together, saving them from possible coffee spills.

"Well, you know my brother. He's always been the nerdy one. Always studying about someone or something." The casual shrug of her shoulders was for her own benefit since Charlie would not have been able to see it.

"I'm curious to hear his views on Eden. Do you mind sharing your notes?" Charlie inquired.

"You want to read them?" Maggie's surprise was genuine.

"I was banking on *you* reading them *to* me. I have this legit blind thing going on and unless it comes in braille..."

Maggie playfully slapped Charlie on the arm with the papers, giggling at her usual forthright sarcasm. She wasn't making fun by asking if she wanted to read it; she was surprised more than anything. She wasn't prepared to share her information with Charlie.

Maggie shuffled through the pages, making split decisions as to which pages would be appropriate to share as Charlie continued to innocently sip her coffee. The voices inside Maggie's head began whispering loudly and felt more like annoying buzzing that seemed to fill the cavity of her skull. Shoving the papers to her face, she inhaled and began whispering out loud to herself.

"Just shut up you two. Shut-up, shut-up, shut-up." There was a thin thread of panic in her tone.

The troubled thump of Charlie's coffee cup against the table brought her back to reality.

"Is something wrong, Maggie?"

"I'm just trying to pick the right page. My handwriting is chicken scratch. I can hardly read it myself," she replied nervously.

"Oh, well, don't worry about it. Just give me your verbal synopsis."

Maggie paused and gently inhaled, willing her slightly shaking hands to be still.

"You know what, Charlie? Why don't we skip this conversation for another time? Today is Dom's funeral, and I want to make sure I say my last goodbye."

"Oh, shoot, what time is it? Let me start getting ready so I can go with you."

"NO!" The force of her denial surprised them both. The word was an unusual occurrence between them.

Maggie's hands unconsciously slammed the papers on the table. The rattling nearly tipped over the coffee mugs. Charlie's head swiveled sharply in her direction as if she had just insulted her. Her piercing grey eyes stared intently, if unseeing, at her friend. It wasn't like Maggie to snap, especially since her best friend had been nothing but accommodating.

"I'm sorry, but I need to do this alone. I hope you're not offended and can understand."

"I'm not offended, but I think my table is. Did you have to slam down so hard? This thing is on its last legs."

"I'm sorry. I really am," Maggie continued, apologizing as she gathered her papers to make herself scarce.

"Hey, Mags, before you go, I have one question."

Maggie stopped short and stood behind Charlie who remained at the table drinking her coffee.

"Do you believe Dom made it to Eden?"

"Excuse me?" The thought sent a shiver of fear through her.

"Do. You. Believe. Dom. Made it. To Eden?" Charlie repeated staccato. She repeated her statement loudly and slowly as if her friend had suddenly become hard of hearing. It wasn't that Maggie's ears had miraculously decided to go on vacation; the question had thrown her off guard. She decided to answer it as honestly as possible.

"I would surely like to believe it, but Dom wasn't much into religion. So who knows."

Charlie crossed her legs and straightened her back, setting herself up to kick some serious knowledge.

"The creator of Eden doesn't choose his army based on their religious belief but by the notion that the human had the purest of hearts and soul. In my studies, it was said to believe that there were defective humans unknowingly sent to Earth. The defectives were just plain evil and caused chaos in everything they encountered. They don't possess a pure heart even if they try to be kind. I'm not the creator of Eden, but in my opinion, Dom had a pure heart. He was one of the most genuine and kindest people I have ever met. If I were you, I would find peace in knowing that he is resting safely in his afterlife." Charlie looked in the direction of Maggie's shallow breathing as soon as the last words were out of her mouth. Though she could not see it, she could tell that her friend was trying to find peace.

Guilt quickly washed over Maggie's very essence. The Right side suddenly became very chatty and drowned her out.

She's right, Dom had the purest of hearts. He was the kindest human that deserved to live a longer, happy life. And we took that away from him. Our selfishness got him killed.

Don't blame me for that shit. I was trying to fight while you were weeping in the corner, chimed the Left.

As she wiped the tears that slowly streaked down her cheeks, she silently shushed the voices in an attempt to get them under control.

"Do you believe that what you study is truly real?" inquired Maggie, deeply curious.

"I would be lying if I said I didn't. Learning about Eden is what kept me going after my accident. It gave me closure knowing that what happened to my parents wasn't my fault and that one day I'll see them again. Isn't that why you began reading about Eden? To get closure, to free yourself from the guilt?" Charlie uncrossed her legs and relaxed her shoulders, seeming to patiently wait for Maggie to respond.

Maggie had almost forgotten that Charlie blamed herself for her parents' death. She knew that Charlie often felt that if she hadn't begged her parents to go to Vermont, they would be alive today. What if she would have quit skiing, as planned, and pursued swimming instead? What if they would have flown instead of driven? What if she had gotten sick that day and couldn't travel? And what if she wasn't so damned spoiled, the thought of a road trip would never have crossed her mind? The "what ifs" ate her up like a rotting disease. It was a savage case of survivor's guilt. Maggie now understood her friend's pain on so many levels.

Charlie maneuvered around the kitchen flawlessly, finding things instantly without needing to feel out objects. Keeping things at a particular spot helped her immensely. Aside from the clattering of Pete's breakfast being served, the air grew thin and silent.

Maggie couldn't help to ponder the question, *Was she looking for closure?*

"I'm not looking for closure," she admitted as if it were the only thing tying her to her never-ending feeling of guilt.

"I'm looking for revenge."

"Unless you know who killed Dom, then revenge will be hard to come by," stated Charlie nonchalantly, not taking her best friend seriously. It wasn't uncommon for Maggie to talk crazy every once in a while. She was not only reckless with her actions but also her words.

Charlie placed Pete's doggie bowl on the kitchen floor and patted him on the head as he devoured his breakfast.

"It was Lucifer. And I'm going to kill him."

The name echoed through Charlie's head. She spun around as if she had heard a ghost.

The crowd of mourners flocked around Dom's casket as if he was having his own personal party at the cemetery. People from all walks of life paraded around to pay their respect to their fellow DJ brother, friend, and family member. It was easy to point out Dom's mother. She sat front and center of the casket with bloodshot eyes, seeming almost catatonic.

Maggie stood hidden in the shadows, several feet away from the crowd standing beneath a leafy, shady tree. Although mother nature was putting on perfect funeral weather: greyish sky, dark clouds, with a huge sign of rain, it didn't stop Maggie from sporting the aviators she took from Dom a few weeks earlier. She reached into the pocket of her dark leather jacket and pulled out a slender cigarette and skeleton lighter. She rarely ever smoked, but today she felt that smoking would help her feel more human and ease the tension coursing through her nerves.

She watched intently as people spoke kind words, sung songs, and threw flowers into his grave as they lowered his casket. Her heart shattered into a million pieces as she watched his mother drop to her knees and wail to the skies, begging and pleading to the angels above to take her instead of her son.

"Pssh, you can forget about that happening," huffed Maggie as she dropped the cigarette and stomped on it as if it were an annoying ant.

As the crowd finally dispersed, leaving no one behind but the gravediggers, Maggie reluctantly dragged her carcass to Dom's plot.

Each footstep she took sunk her heels into the half-muddy grass, making it feel as if she was walking with weights on her ankles.

Pulling a white rose hidden in her jacket and another cigarette, she gazed over at the two gravediggers.

"Excuse me, can I have one minute here alone, please?" Grief was written all over her and it looked to the gravediggers as if she was just holding on by a very thin thread.

"Sure, no problem. We'll give you five," answered the gravedigger, pulling his co-worker away.

"Thanks." It was a grateful grunt, but it was all the gratitude she had left.

Maggie inhaled the aroma of the white rose, reminiscing on the times that Dom would show up to her sets surprising her with a single white rose. It was his way of letting her know he was her number one fan. Now she felt as if she was surprising him with one. On the verge of tears, she kissed the white rose and threw it inside the open grave, watching it fall heavily to the bottom as if it weighed a ton. She lit another cigarette, blowing out thick clouds of smoke as she ranted.

"I'm so stupid, Dom. This is all my fault. I swear to you. I'm going to make this right. If I would have never fallen for you, this would have never happened. I should be in there. Not you. It should have been me. It should have been me, I swear, it should have been me. You were just an innocent human. And I… Well… I was being a huge selfish…"

"Asshole."

Maggie quickly spun her head around toward the voice nearly giving herself whiplash. Jesse was standing behind her. He was clean-shaven with his hair groomed and was holding six black roses that matched his fitted turtleneck and slacks.

"Yep, we all know that feeling," he stated as he chucked the roses into the grave.

"How did you find me?"

"It's not as if you were hiding." His sarcasm slightly annoyed her.

He took the slim cigarette from between Maggie's delicate fingers and inhaled an everlasting hard pull. The sound of him exhaling seemed as if he was releasing ten years of stress from his shoulders.

"When did you start smoking?" Maggie asked grudgingly.

"When did you start wearing those ridiculous sunglasses? It was typical of Jesse to respond to a question with a question. His clear-cut way of letting one know he didn't want to be interrogated about his actions.

"Is mom or Keiko with you? And my aviators are not ridiculous, they belonged to Dom."

Maggie scanned the area, making sure no one else was hidden in plain sight as she was. She felt as if their friendly sibling banter was about to go down. Instead, Jesse glanced over at her and dismissed her last statement.

"Nope, Just me." White puffs of smoke blew out between his words.

"Charlie called me. She told me where you were."

"Charlie? Ugh, I told her I didn't want company."

The sky turned darker as thunder rumbled in the clouds above. Small droplets of rain began to make their presence known on their skin.

"She's worried about you. Especially since you spooked her with all that talk about killing the devil." Jesse stated, smoking the cigarette nearly down to the filter.

"Before you go on scolding me, I know I was out of line. I fucked up. I nearly told her everything about us. But I didn't. I just need Charlie to give me everything she has researched on the Underworld. She has more books and papers than you do, and I need every scrap of it," Maggie replied, trying to convince her brother.

Jesse listened carefully as if he was hearing his little sister speak for the first time.

"Master Anu has research, as well. Have you ever thought about just coming home and reading his work? Or talking to mom? I'm sure together we can work something out," Jesse calmly advised.

"No, I don't want help from Master Anu or mom. They are in this mess because of me. Everything that is happening or has happened is ALL my fault. I've been nothing but a black cloud since the day I was born."

"Stop, Everything that is happening is Jack's fault, not yours," he corrected.

Hearing their father's name mentioned by Jesse as Jack and not dad, in the manner he used to call him as a child, hurt her soul. They were once a happy family until tragedy tore them apart. The situation boiled over when Maggie was kidnapped by her own father. Even then, she never once blamed him for the hardship she was going through. She only wanted it to end.

The touch of Jesse's hands resting on her shoulders weighed heavily. She immediately pulled away, ready to give him a piece of her mind.

"Keep my father's name out of your mouth. My father is a good man. He did nothing but keep me safe." Maggie's eyes glowed a bloody, angry red.

Jesse raised his right eyebrow, seeming not even the least bit impressed. He threw out the cigarette butt and put it out with the tip of his loafers as he took the hint of the glowing eyes and walked away.

"Call me when you're done being so high and mighty."

Stunned by her brother's reaction, her bloody angry eyes slowly transformed to their original state. Maggie raced after Jesse feeling like a complete jerk and hoping to smooth things over.

"Jesse, wait, wait. I'm sorry. I... I just don't know what's coming over me. I know everyone wants to help, but I don't want anyone else to get hurt. I won't be able to live with myself if I lose any more people that I love. I can barely hold it together now."

The hurt in Maggie's eyes was enough to change the temperament of the most coldhearted person. With a deep sigh, Jesse kissed Maggie on her forehead as he brought her in for a comforting embrace.

"It's going to be alright. We all have to go at some point, and if we all go out protecting each other, then we have truly died a glorious death."

A glorious death? repeated the Right. *Dom, for sure, died a glorious death.*

As Maggie and Jesse stood outside the gates of the cemetery, she couldn't help but feel lucky to have her brother by her side. When she needed a good kick in the ass to get herself out of a rut, he was first in line to give it to her. After many tears and coming to Jesus moments, Jesse finally convinced his little sister to seek help from their mother, Angel. Picking a fight with the Prince of Darkness alone would not end well for anyone. It was time to pull out the guns and call in the cavalry.

Now that Maggie's demon side had grown supremely powerful, she could no longer transport herself through the portal to go home. It was "open season" on her while she remained stuck in New York City, but oddly enough, not one demon dared approach her. Even when she roamed the troubled streets late at night, screaming into the crowds as if she were insane, antagonizing Lucifer to show himself, nothing happened. It was as if they were afraid of her.

As the droplets of water turned into sprinkles of rain, Jesse stared at his sister with reassuring eyes.

"So, I'll see you later tonight?"

"I guess so," sighed Maggie deeply at the thought of seeing the look of despair on her mother's face.

"You have to trust in us, Mags. No running away this time."

"I promise I won't run. I'm just thinking about Charlie now. I really freaked her out." Maggie finally came to terms as her anxiety cleared.

"Yeah, you did. But no worries. Master Anu will wipe away that little minor detail. She won't remember a thing."

"Ugh, Vs are so fucking cool. It's sickening."

It took a lot for Maggie to admit that about them, for some Vs possessed incomprehensible powers. Hypnosis, erasing memories, flight, speed as if they were the new and improved Flash, and having the strength of a thousand horses were just a few of their abilities. The older a V became, the more its powers increased. Or if they were someone like Master Anu that feasted on angel blood, their abilities heightened to the hundredth power. Although she felt that many of them were nothing more than worthless, bloodthirsty, sex-crazed animals, the ones Maggie knew personally she held near and dear to her heart.

They walked a few blocks away from the cemetery before they stopped in front of a large, tinted-out, black truck. Two females quickly hopped out. One opened the door while the other humbly greeted Jesse. Maggie stared at them through curious eyes, wondering where she had seen them before. Their matching dark, fitted suits adorned with a golden-red letter "A" pinned neatly to the lapels screamed "property of Master Anu." However, they were not Vs or humans. Their scent was different and their bronze skin flawlessly gleamed, even under the gloomy skies.

"Do you need a ride anywhere?" Jesse interrupted as her mind pondered the sighting of the two women.

"Naw, I'm good. When did you start walking around with bodyguards?" questioned Maggie, feeling as if she had put everyone in danger.

"Since I was given two bad-ass shifters as escorts."

The word 'shifter' hit Maggie like a full-speed boomerang. It was Pearl and Coco as fully-clothed humans.

"I knew they looked familiar. The panthers! Hey, how's it going, ya'll?"

Without hesitation, Maggie stretched out her hand to greet them. They both turned away in unison, reacting as if she had sneezed in her palm and then decided to extend it to them. She never felt so foolish.

"You sure know how to make friends," teased Jesse.

"Yeah, you know me, little miss outgoing. They must still be sour about the demon fight. I got demon guts all over them. But I get the feeling they never really liked me to begin with," Maggie sarcastically confessed.

"I wouldn't take it personally. They barely talked to me the entire ride here, strictly business. And for some odd reason, they only seem to be loyal to Keiko."

Maggie turned her focus to her brother after picking up her face from the ground and dismissing the awkward encounter.

"So, where are you off to?"

"A bar, I have some investigating to do," responded Jesse.

"More research? Need some company?"

"No, not this time. I want you to contact mom, and I'll meet up with you later. Just be careful," he stated, his words sounding shaky.

"I'm always careful. I move around the city in the best mode of transportation."

Maggie removed her aviators and secured them in her leather jacket. Her heels levitated inches from the ground. She winked at Jesse as her silky wings stretched out and shot her up into the sky without a trace. The wind nearly knocked him over as a single black, silk, feather floated into his hair. He plucked it off and examined its beauty before stuffing it into his pocket.

With no sign of Maggie, Jesse hopped into the backseat of the truck. He pulled out the little black book and read an address scribbled on the bottom of one of the pages.

"Hey, Coco, take me to O'Riley's Pub."

CHAPTER 12
THERE ARE NO MORALS IN HELL

There was no denying that the Underworld seemed to have, for the first time, a queen among them. Although Lucifer didn't publicly announce it, everyone knew that the relationship between him and Camila had become more than just a servant and her sire. For instance, she no longer consulted on the punishments in the torture chambers. That job was now left to No-Nose Tommy. She also spent less time appearing at the demon parties and more time inside her master's lair.

In the beginning, their relationship was just loose-lip gossip.

Either they are already fucking or Camila is trying very hard to get laid, whispered one bold demon when no senior demon was within earshot.

I heard she's purposely trying to land herself in the void to be with Castus, mused another who took joy in spreading every piece of gossip overheard, whether factual or not.

Helen of Troy told me that she and Lucifer are still having sex. He even promised her a seat by his throne. The shocked gasps from that little tidbit had raced all the way down to the seventh circle of hell as fast as an ice skater trying to outrun breaking thin ice.

These were just a few of the rumors that were spreading like wildfire among the forces of the Underworld, especially the one about Helen of Troy. She had started that lie herself out of pure jealousy and her salty emotions toward Lucifer. He had brushed off their sexual romps eons ago as he couldn't understand how someone with so much beauty could be so boringly bland. He couldn't grasp how someone like she could be the cause of the Trojan War. In his opinion, it was better that empty-headed beauties be seen and not heard.

The demons gossiped more when they would see Camila often entering passageways and doors that were forbidden to them. No-Nose Tommy warned her on several occasions that her disobedience would land her in the void. But all she ever did was shrug her shoulders and dare him to rat her out. Which he never did.

It became clear that Camila would be held to a higher standard the day "Lucifer's Eyes," or the "Eyes" as they were known in the Underworld, arrived for their weekly report. Demons that hid in the shadows—watching, observing, lurking, reporting, and never engaging—were Lucifer's most valuable soldiers. It was how he kept up with Angel and her band of Vs on Earth for years. Lucifer's Eyes saw and heard it all.

Two Eyes entered Lucifer's lair in human form. One sported platinum blonde hair that was nearly white and stood tall and slender. The other had short dark hair, was extremely heavy set for his height, and sported a long caveman beard on his wide face. Both men kneeled in respect then quickly rose as they noticed Camila standing sternly behind their king, arms folded as if she were ready to scold them.

"Ahhh, brilliant! My Eyes have arrived. Let's have a seat, gentlemen." At the snap of his finger, the environment changed and all four of them were sitting outside of a brightly-lit cafe. The sun's rays warmed their tanned skin, and the scent of freshly-baked bread and brewed coffee lingered in the air. The trendy crowd of people who elegantly strolled by with their expensive dogs and high-end shopping bags elicited a feeling of somehow being trapped inside the pages of *Vogue* magazine. In a blink of an eye, their surroundings had been transformed from a darkened room with floating torches, blazing fire pits, and golden mirrors to a sunny day on Rodeo Drive.

With each head turn and stare, it was obvious that the Eyes were two fish out of water. Lucifer and Camila sat casually blending in with the patrons and appearing nonchalant as they sipped on their coffees.

"You look stunning, darling," Lucifer whispered to Camila, admiring her all-white pantsuit and matching big, floppy-brimmed hat. She smiled seductively at his comment.

"Sire, with all due respect, where are we?" inquired the blonde nervously.

"It's Beverly Hills. You don't like Beverly Hills?"

The simulation room replicated Beverly Hills down to every last detail. The modern cars parked on the streets, the vibrant boutiques, the feel of summer, and the shady trees made them forget that their surroundings weren't real.

"I...uhh..." The blonde had lost his tongue.

The bearded man nudged his demon partner and finished his sentence. "We love Beverly Hills. It's very trendy."

"Yes...uh...trendy. And hot!" emphasized the blonde, loosening the collar of his sky blue dress shirt.

"Don't worry your head, mate. It's only a simulation," Lucifer reassured.

"Sire, maybe he'll feel better after he's had some food. Croissants?" Camila offered the freshly-baked goods as if she were hosting a tea party. The whites of her satin gloves glimmered under the warm sun.

"I'll pass," replied the blonde, turning up his nose.

"Wait, is this edible?" asked the bearded man excitedly.

Camila nodded a cool and casual yes as she pouted her velvet rose lips.

"SWEET!" The bearded man helped himself, stuffing his overweight face as if he hadn't eaten in days.

"I believe in change, gentlemen. Must we always be in the dark when having a meeting? All the screaming and whining is so distracting. From now on, we conduct business in the simulation chambers," exclaimed Lucifer.

Camila smiled brightly. After all, it was *her* idea to change the scenery.

The blonde scanned the streets, nervously whispering his last sentence. "But Sire, aren't all the faces here demons? They will hear us."

Lucifer sipped on his coffee, almost forgetting one last detail.

"Oh, yes."

He waved his hand in dismissal, and every human form silently exited through a storefront as though they were mindless zombies about to fetch breakfast.

"Umm, Sire, aren't you forgetting one more?" The blonde pointed toward Camila.

"No, she stays." Lightning cracked through the sunny skies at Lucifer's command.

The warbling of birds chirping nearby broke the awkward silence as Lucifer changed the subject.

"Now, what do you have for me?" he prompted in a gentler tone.

The blonde cleared his throat and tried to speak effortlessly under pressure, but Lucifer could sense his unease.

"The half-breed demon child was calling you out for a fight. She's apparently still pissy about her boyfriend being killed. She's staying with a human who can't see two shits in front of her face, in the middle of Manhattan, supposedly a 'best friend.' Angel or the Vs haven't been seen since the day the half-breed went ballistic. Not sure if they're planning a retaliation, but the half-breed is stopping at nothing to find you."

Lucifer crossed his legs, listening with a surprising level of amusement.

With a mouth filled with croissants, the bearded man picked up the remainder of the report.

"Jesse is on his way to O'Riley's Pub. And Maggie is supposedly going to see Angel. The three of them will eventually meet up. We just don't know where yet."

Lucifer and Camila's attention perked up at the sound of O'Riley's Pub. Intrigued, Lucifer leaned forward and caressed the hair on his chin trying to make sense of the situation.

"My stars, Jesse's going where it all began." There was an admiration that seeped out in Lucifer's voice.

"What do you think this all means, Sire?" Camila questioned. The Eyes noticed that she was bold enough to join in their conversation. It was rare for Lucifer to bring lovers around when conducting business; it was even rarer when they spoke.

"I'm not sure." Without turning to her, he placed his hand on hers that was resting lightly on his shoulder. There was a level of intimacy that could not be hidden in that small gesture between them. The Eyes exchanged knowing looks with each other.

"O'Riley's was the location of Angel's and Castus' first mission. They were sent to retrieve a rogue angel but failed. That's where Castus experienced his true death and ended up here. And if it hadn't been for Mendulous and me, Angel would have ended up here alongside him. It's also where Mendulous decided to temporarily erase her memory. I wonder what Jesse is up to?"

Lucifer rubbed his beard, then leaned back and sipped on his coffee, pondering Jesse's intentions. The blonde appeared to get antsy and spoke hurriedly as if he had somewhere special to be.

"Jesse is carrying the little black book. We need that book. I could easily kill him and take it. We'll make his death seem like a suicide, quick and messy."

"YOU WILL NOT TOUCH HIM!"

Without hesitation, Camila reached over and grabbed the blonde by his lapels faster than Lucifer could answer. The crashing of dishes and the thumping of the table landing on its top were enough to draw stares from a crowd, had there been one. With swift speed, but rather shaky feet, the blonde stood up and forcefully shoved her back down to her seat. He snatched the coffee mug out of his partner's hands and splashed it all over her face and white pantsuit.

Camila shrieked as the heat of the coffee scalded her forehead and trickled inside of her top, burning her chest.

In uncontrollable fury, the blonde morphed into his blood-red demon face, his black pitch eyes focusing on her.

"WOMAN, know your place. Have you lost your FUCKING mind?! I will..."

The scent of burning flesh, dark smoke, and fluttering ashes suddenly filled their space. It was as though a fire pit had been waiting patiently between the cracks of the ground to destroy the lives of those who dared overstep the Prince of Darkness. Tortured shrieks did not fill their ears with agony; there was simply no time. The blonde never suffered during his final seconds; the memory of him was quickly obliterated.

Startled, the bearded man shot up from his seat and frantically patted himself, believing he was also on fire. He shook ashes from his clothes and heavy beard as he exhaled in relief that he was unharmed.

"What a twat," Lucifer stated, annoyed. "Are you alright, darling?"

He extended his hand to Camila, pulling her to stand by his side as if she were his damsel in distress. He needed her to understand that he would diminish a hundred more of his demons if they spoke out of turn again. Camila wasn't just any demon woman in the Underworld anymore where he would normally let them fight their own battles. She belonged to him, and now her battles were his to permanently end.

Within seconds the simulation room faded and they were back to standing near burning fire pits, golden mirrors, and floating torches. He held her tightly and caressed her now clean, dry face. He traced his fingertips along the lace collar trimming of her now dark blue, satin gown. Stealing a few seconds to admire her beauty in her seductive new attire, Lucifer gave a silent wolf whistle of appreciation.

His next words were thick with an unmistakable and dangerous tone that made sure his meaning would be understood and obeyed without delay or discussion.

"Listen up, Fatso. Let it be known that the next time any of you put your hands on Camila, I will burn you to your final death without a second thought."

The bearded man dropped to his large knees, fearing his lord more than ever before. "Yes, My Lord," he quavered.

"Now, get up. I don't have all day to watch you struggle to your feet. I have to find you another Eye and quick."

Lucifer examined the mirrors that monitored his demons, wondering who he could trust.

"Ugh, what arsehole isn't going to mess this up?" he muttered.

Burning the blonde wasn't the best decision. He was his most reliable and a damn good Eye. However, he was willing to eliminate even the best demons in his path if they dared test the waters.

After giving it some thought, Lucifer knew exactly who he could promote for the job. It was time for this trusty demon to step up and step out of his comfort zone.

"Camila, darling, summon No-Nose Tommy."

Lucifer carefully observed Camila as she slipped on her robe over the curves of her sultry, naked body. From his eagle's perch, the view would never get old. He settled lazily onto his side with his head propped up against his hand and watched her graceful and sensual movements that were on full display for him. Even the silence between them was arousing. Their lovemaking had become more frequent, thrilling, and intoxicating. She became the aphrodisiac to dominate his erotic addiction. A drug by any other name would be

Camila. He felt his manhood swell and thicken just at the thought of her name.

Most of the time, he couldn't keep his wandering, eager hands to himself or his dick in his pants. The fire she ignited inside of him, just by the sound of her voice alone, was hard to put out. He fell in love hard and fast, even if he didn't want to admit it in public. However, his whispers or passionate cries during their love sessions often included a seductive, yet passionate "I love you" behind closed doors.

The innocent woman who had ended up in the Underworld because she would rather end her human life than be taken into slavery by a mob of raving savages was now becoming the death of him. The same woman with whom his nephew Castus had fallen in love with during his time in Hell and with whom he had a child was now bringing him to his knees. Hell, by this standard, was definitely the true definition of lacking morals.

Camila gently brushed her long, dark hair in the mirror, meticulously dismantling every knot and tangle acquired during their romp. Lucifer watched every stroke of her hand and smiled. He loved everything about her, even her quite obvious ploy of refusing to meet his gaze. He knew that it was not out of shyness but to heighten their desire for each other.

He casually walked behind her and gently kissed her neck, giving his penis what it wanted from the moment it woke from its short slumber. He removed the hairbrush from her hand and brought it before them. They both looked at each other through the mirror. Camila's deep blue ocean eyes remained locked on Lucifer, anticipating his next move.

"You are beautiful," he seductively whispered in her ear. His British accent sounded even thicker and more intriguing than normal.

She smiled brightly and tormented him even more by remaining quiet. She was stealing his breath away.

"I would give you the moon if you asked me to," he said, the words surprising himself.

"Sire, the moon isn't what I want."

Lucifer kissed her again on her smooth neck, sensing the shivers he was sending down her spin. His penis throbbed and begged to get deeper as he whispered.

"Watch."

Camila turned her attention to the mirror. The brush that Lucifer was holding transformed into a diamond and emerald-studded choker. It was just as extravagant as the original one he gifted her, then later destroyed. Her eyes brightened in surprise.

"Sire, it's beautiful," she glowed as he placed it around her neck.

"So is the person wearing it."

She smoothed her fingers across the diamonds and emeralds, feeling its rough edges and admiring the twinkles between the stones. Demons that have been lucky enough to work alongside Lucifer knew the significance of the emeralds. Camila was nearly in tears.

"You will now be able to enter in and out of Earth as you please, without me."

Stunned, Camila quickly turned her body and hugged Lucifer tightly. Before he could utter another word, she jumped up and wrapped her sleek legs around his waist in excitement as she crashed her lips against his. He wobbled backward, losing his balance, and landing on his king-sized bed. The fall never caused her to come up for air; she was like a mermaid in water breathing happily in her habitat.

Lucifer finally broke the kiss and stared into her wide eyes, nearly losing himself in her fiery desire. His next words were spoken with sincerity as he ran his rough hands through her hair.

"I don't do this for anyone, but I trust you will do the right thing. Go and get your son, the black book, and let us live out the rest of our days ruling the Underworld, together."

"Sire, I'm not sure what you mean?" A look of confusion pressed against her face.

"It's time for the Underworld to have a queen, and I choose you."

"I'm no queen."

"Yes. You are. You are my queen and now the ruler of the Underworld."

Camila stood up and fixed her robe as if she was turned off by the proposition Lucifer had dropped on her. He could tell by her actions that she was not the least bit interested. Her hands shook as she scurried around the room looking for her undergarments.

"Is everything alright, darling?" he asked, concerned that he might have fucked everything up between them.

"I...I need to go, my apologies."

"What? Why? Did I say something wrong?"

Camila continued gathering her clothing and dressing. Guilt and fear washed over Lucifer as the thought of losing her entertained his thoughts.

"Stop, you need to tell me what is wrong," he demanded.

"I CAN'T BE YOUR QUEEN."

Lucifer remained unmoved at her sudden outburst, wondering where her doubts were deriving from.

"And why not?"

"Hell isn't made for two rulers, just one, and that's you," stated Camila as she pointed her finger at his chest.

Lucifer clutched her hand and brought it to his lips, but she snatched it away.

"It's just the way the Underworld was created. This place is solely under your command. Only you obtain the power to control it. My title as Queen will be a complete joke. These demons won't listen to me; you saw what happened earlier with the Eyes. I'm only a human branded as a demon. I have nothing to bring to the table as a ruler."

Camila bowed her head in disappointment as if it were the first time she was acknowledging her powerless human existence.

"Then forget the Underworld. Be more to me than whatever this is we are doing," he compromised, lifting her chin toward him. It was difficult for anyone to resist Lucifer; his charm alone was a hands-down, panty dropper.

Camila hesitated, "Are you asking me to be your girlfriend?"

"Ugh, that sounds so human and temporary. I want commitment."

"Then, are you asking me to marry you?" she pressed.

"Goodness, this is complicated?" Lucifer stated, nearly giving up.

Camila chuckled, quickly moving past the fear she displayed earlier. She wrapped her arms around his neck and snuggled against his body.

"You have my heart as much as I have yours. I'm not going anywhere. I belong to you. And I don't need to be the queen of this shit hole to prove that I'm yours."

"Finally, progress." he joked as he pulled her in and smothered her neck with wet kisses.

Knowing where his playfulness would often lead, Camila gently pulled away and began gathering her belongings.

"I'm not going to Earth alone. We are getting Jesse and your little black book together. We better get going," she urged, as she playfully tossed his clothes at him.

CHAPTER 13
MENDULOUS

The Hand of Father sat motionless, with closed eyes, in the orchard of cherry blossom trees. This orchard was his favorite place to frequent when he needed solace to clear his mind and decompress. The ground was covered in cotton candy-colored petals as a few young souls of Eden galloped around playing a never-ending game of hide-and-go-seek. Their joy could be heard yards away as it radiated throughout the long rows of trees, adding an incredible warmth and tranquility to the atmosphere. It didn't occur to him that during his state of meditation he was being watched. A place where he went to be alone was no longer a place of sanctuary.

"So, this is how the mighty Hand of Father spends his days?"

The sarcasm was enough to make anyone else cringe.

"This is how I spend my days when I seek solitude." Mendulous remained unmoved, never budging or fluttering his eyes open at the sound of the interloper's voice. He knew that frequency all too well. Helena, the daughter of Father and mother to Castus and Angel, stood behind him, arms folded as if she were annoyed by his every breath. She was an intimidating woman, even at five-foot-four inches tall, but held her ground as though she were six-foot-three who could shake the gravel beneath every step. Out of all of Father's children, she was the most fearless, clever, and verbal. When she spoke, people listened; and where she led, people followed.

At times, her mouth held no filter and neither did her actions. Even Lucifer had his limits with her. Mendulous often felt that Helena would have been better suited to rule the Underworld. Not because she was evil, she didn't have a monstrous bone in her tiny body, but because she had a knack for order, structure, and putting people in their respective places.

All the meditation in the world couldn't mentally prepare Mendulous for the wrath of Helena. She tiptoed into his sanctuary like a cunning lioness ready to sink her teeth into what was left of his pride.

"And what is it that you're pondering?" Helena asked as she walked in front of Mendulous, her arms still hugged to her chest.

"Nothing that should concern you." His voice was calm with suppressed resignation.

Mendulous could hear the steam fizzing from her pores.

"How dare you?! Everything in Eden concerns me, especially when it involves my children."

His dark eyelids shot open as if cocking a gun for battle, staring at Helena argumentatively. Usually, their banter was friendly like two old pals sparring over a game of chess. But ever since the day he took matters into his own hands and erased Angel's memory, he had been on her long-winded shit list.

Within seconds Mendulous was on his feet towering over Helena as if physically willing her to scurry away like a frightened little house mouse. Instead, she straightened her stance, glaring at him through incandescent, dark brown eyes. She never shied away from intimidating quarrels or a good fight. Being the eldest of ten children taught her to be tough and resilient. Growing up, slapping her brothers around became her favorite pastime, and many of them were taller than Mendulous' six-foot-three-inch Olympian frame.

Mendulous clenched his jaw, trying to prevent his patience from escaping from his core.

"Helena, now is not the right time. I am busy trying to…"

"To WHAT! THINK?!"

The air grew deadly silent as Helena's outburst caused an awkwardness he couldn't shake. She had never raised her voice at him, but he believed he had it coming.

"All of your thinking is not bringing my boy back from that wretched place. You left him behind as if he deserved to be there."

"I had to leave him. I had NO CHOICE!"

The baritone of Mendulous' voice shook the petals off a few nearby cherry blossom trees.

"CHOICE?! Is that what my son was to you? A choice?"

Helena's orbs glowed as brightly as the golden sun in her indignation. Her eyebrows narrowed as she took a few steps forward to close the small gap between them. Her body levitated to his full height so she could look him in his eyes. The softness of her breasts bumped him a few inches back as she huffed herself against him in frustration.

"When you walked through the gates of Hell, bringing Castus home wasn't a choice, it was an ORDER!"

"Father is the one who gives the orders, not you. And my orders were to free every angel I could without starting a war with Lucifer," Mendulous answered without hesitation.

"Father should have sent me instead. This is more of a family matter than a business transaction."

Helena slowly levitated away, closing her eyes and bringing them back to normalcy.

Mendulous remained unmoved, his face hard as stone. It was often difficult to read him because he constantly wore a mean poker face. Expressing emotions was not part of his character, even when things pained him. He despised withholding information from Helena, but he was advised by Father that it was for her own protection. The less she knew, the better. However, he wasn't sure how it was protecting her. Every day she appeared as if she were taken down from a painful crucifixion. He knew one thing for sure, it was time she heard the truth.

"Helena." Mendulous called out before she glided further away.

She crossed her arms and stared past him, seemingly disinterested in what he had to say.

"Castus is more valuable to Eden if he remains in the Underworld a bit longer. We need him," stated Mendulous.

"WE need him? What do you mean?" An expression of deep confusion flitted across Helena's face.

"The little black book was smuggled out of Eden."

Helena's hands flew to her mouth as she gasped, "No. That can't be true."

"It is true. Lucifer gave it to Angel before her first journey to help her assimilate with the humans. He didn't think she would take it with her, but she did. She lost it during her travels. But, somehow, the book made its way back to her again," confessed Mendulous.

A sigh of relief as low as a warm breeze escaped Helena's mouth.

"Thank Eden, the book is back with Angel. We can just retrieve it from her."

"It's not that simple. The book is actually with Jesse."

"Jesse? Angel's adopted human son?" Helena repeated for clarity.

"Yes!" answered Medulous, realizing this was his opportunity to unlock the flood gates.

Helena had been so fixated on getting Castus out of the Underworld that she hardly troubled herself with Angel's life. She boldly mentioned on several different occasions that, *The angel chosen by the Divine Right shouldn't have their mother butting into their affairs. They are chosen warriors, not fumbling cry babies.*

It was her nice way of saying, "Angel needs to figure out her own shit." Which is the reason why she never bothered to stay in the "know" when it came to her daughter. Although everyone knew she loved her daughter with every inch of her angelic soul, the chosen warrior was not her greatest concern, Castus was. But things had shifted and it appeared that Angel and Castus' worlds were colliding.

The thin curves of Helena's eyebrows straightened, and her eyelids lowered as she looked on in deep thought. She was known for tackling one issue at a time. But now that the little black book had entered the situation like a rowdy, uninvited party guest, things just got even more complicated.

Helena fidgeted with the seams of her sleeves, appearing overwhelmed. It internally hurt Mendulous to watch the suffering in her eyes. It was as if he were watching her drown and didn't have the means to save her.

She rubbed her temples before asking, "The little black book is the key to unlocking the Unknown worlds. Does Angel know that?"

"I don't think so. Lucifer believes they are oblivious to the power the book contains, but I don't trust his words. This is Lucifer we're talking about." He shrugged his shoulders in resignation.

Mendulous took a deep breath, reflecting on the waist-deep level of shit they were in.

"Mend, I'm not going to ask why this is the first I am hearing of this. I need to know *how* we will fix it. If my brother gets possession of that book, he will have leverage against us. He will threaten to unlock the worlds even if it means destroying his own pathetic kingdom."

"I had a similar thought, but I don't think that is his plan," Mendulous carefully disagreed. "He seems rather protective of his world. His demons are extremely loyal to him. I don't see him destroying it. Let's walk for a moment. I will explain it all."

Mendulous led the way as he and Helena walked through the cherry blossom orchard. The sweet scent of fresh petals and newly-trimmed grass relaxed the angry lines on his hardened forehead as their bare feet left behind a trail of deep, pink footprints. He enjoyed the softness of the petals between his toes and how they stuck like glue to the bottom of his heels, although no one would have ever guessed because he seldom smiled or expressed happiness toward anything.

The small, joyful souls that had been running through the orchard giggling had dispersed. The summer's warm breeze lightly blew the brown curls away from Helena's stiff shoulders.

Mendulous discussed how he walked through the gates of Hell and tussled with Lucifer. He talked about all of the angels he saved, in and out of the void. He then smoothly transitioned the conversation to discuss the deal he struck with Lucifer.

"I left Castus behind because we both agreed it would be best to have Castus retrieve the little black book from Jesse."

"Why? Why don't we get it ourselves?" Helena's rapid response proved that her mind was running a mile a minute.

"Because Jesse is..." Mendulous lowered his head, breaking the news to Helena as he remembered it being told to him by Lucifer. Even Angel's story was complex to explain. But he was going to go there. This was about Castus.

"Jesse is...Castus' biological son," he finally spat out, feeling fifty pounds of weight lifted off his shoulders.

"What? Lies!!!" Helena gasped, trying to make sense of things. She leaned against a cherry blossom tree, her face as white as a porcelain doll.

"Are you ill?" He placed his strong hand on Helena's shaky shoulder.

"The human child is my grandson?" It appeared as if nothing would be able to wipe the look of surprise from her face as she ventured into her next question.

"How?"

Mendulous cleared the frog lingering in his throat as he explained Castus' relationship with Camila. Since so much time had passed, it wasn't easy for Helena to acknowledge that her son, who had left Eden as a young and helpless sixteen-year-old teenager, was now a man well in his thirties.

The most difficult part was confessing to Helena that Castus had been sentenced to an afterlife in the void after he smuggled a pregnant Camila out of the Underworld against her will. Agreeing to have Castus retrieve the little black book would be his redemption and bring less conflict to an already damaged situation.

Running her fingers through her curls, Helena locked her golden-brown, boiling eyes on Mendulous. Hearing the news of her son's cruel punishment propelled her emotions into overdrive.

Mendulous took a few steps back as Helena's hard fist landed straight through the bark of the cherry blossom tree. The tree rained down pink petals as she shook it nearly bald. She drew back an unscathed hand as the fury that ignited inside her body sent deep shrills in the air.

"Helena," Mendulous thought quickly as he grabbed her hand and pressed down firmly, filling her angelic soul with tranquility.

His power rushed through her nerves sending messages of calmness to her brain. The slow rise of her chest and her serene voice confirmed his magic had been effective.

"My brother hurts my family all because of his hatred for us," she stated softly.

"Possibly, but just like we have rules in our world, so does he. Smuggling a demon out of the Underworld is a violation of his law, and Castus was not immune to the consequences," Mendulous replied calmly.

Helena closed her eyes tightly and leaned against the broken cherry blossom tree. The last of the pink petals cascaded over her hair and shoulders as she took long yoga breaths, inhaling the sweet aroma of the whispering warm breeze. She rubbed her hands against her cream-colored chiffon dress as if she were drying the sweat off of her palms.

"This is such a huge mess. What a huge, huge, mess!" She repeated, as though Mendulous didn't understand her the first time.

"Did Father agree with using Castus as bait?" She couldn't help but question her father's involvement. She was committed to knowing everything.

Mendulous raised his dark eyebrows but didn't respond.

"Is this *his* plan?" she pressed.

"Father is refusing to meddle in this ordeal. He informed me that everything is as it should be," explained Mendulous.

"Which means he will sit around and do nothing." retorted Helena, raising her hands in defeat.

"For now, yes."

The pain in Helena's eyes widened as she looked up to the sky as if seeking guidance.

"Mendulous," she whispered for his ears only, "we need a plan."

"We have a plan," he confessed. "Lucifer agreed to release Castus as long as he's able to retrieve the little black book from Jesse. The exchange is Castus' way out. According to Lucifer, Jesse has been searching for the identity of his biological father for some time. Lucifer is convinced that this family reunion will save both of our worlds."

Out of the deep pockets of his tan cloak, Mendulous dug out the brightest emerald Helena had ever seen in all of her existence. The glare of the emerald sparkled as she took a closer look at it in admiration.

"Mend, it's breathtaking," she marveled as she scooped it into her petite hands.

"The Underworld is filled with them. Lucifer uses them to transport demons in and out of Hell and for communicating. He will be contacting me through this once he has released Castus."

Helena continued admiring the stone as if mentally questioning its power.

"Once Castus has the little black book, I will return with him and the book. It's a fair exchange for the sake of our worlds," Medulous announced as if his good deed would not go unnoticed.

Helena angrily squeezed the emerald into her small hands and crushed it until it shattered into tiny fragments of class. She shoved it against Mendulous' broad chest.

"You must be one large fool if you think my brother will keep his word. Lucifer doesn't do anything unless it's for Lucifer. So what's in it for him?"

Mendulous slightly hesitated before he responded, "Jesse!"

"Jesse? NO!"

"Yes." Mendulous retorted. "Turns out, Camila wants her son back and Lucifer agreed to help her. I'm sure you can understand her struggles all too well. A devoted mother cheated out of having time with her son. One will do anything to get their child back. Even make a deal with the devil himself."

Mendulous could hear Helena's heart racing in her chest as if it were exhausting its last fuel of energy to cross the finish line. Her face hardened as she rubbed her forehead in dismay.

"This is going to be a never-ending cycle. Castus will be heartbroken, and his torment will shatter me to pieces. He sacrificed himself for that boy; his fight would have been in vain," responded a grief-stricken Helena.

"Agreed, which is why I have been pondering an alternative. Even though Lucifer sounded sincere, I don't trust him as far as I can throw him."

Helena shot Mendulous a stern look. He knew that look all too well. It was the look of a determined warrior preparing herself for battle.

"Whatever your alternative is, include me in it. I refuse to stand idle and watch this exchange unfold. I couldn't care less what this Camila wants. Half-breed or not, Jesse is one of us. The Underworld is no home for him. We need to protect him."

Mendulous nodded his head in agreement.

"Mend, we leave for Earth at nightfall."

"Are you certain?" he asked, needing reassurance.

"I've never been more certain in my life."

"Then nightfall it is." he casually agreed as he watched Helena turn on her heels and vanish into the cherry blossom orchard.

CHAPTER 14
SWEET CHILD OF MINE

The misty rain finally let up as the clouds remained grey and somber. Maggie walked the wet streets up to Charlie's apartment without doing her usual surveillance of the crowd. Again, she was inviting a demon to sneak up on her. She eagerly welcomed it. She stopped at the entrance to Charlie's building and casually pulled out another cigarette. This time she didn't light it, she only stared at it as if she was examining it for poison.

The creak of the metal front door and the tiny taps of Pete's paws against the cement floor pulled Maggie out of her trance. Pete rubbed his shiny, dark coat against her knees and sniffed her shoes with his pink wet nose as he wagged his tail in excitement.

"Look who's happy to finally be outside," Maggie teased in a childlike voice as she smoothly ran her fingers over Pete's head. Relief washed over her knowing that Charlie was safe. She hadn't been sure what she was going to walk into.

"Mags, you're back already?" Charlie questioned as she lightly pulled on Pete's harness, trying to calm him down. Her honey-blond hair blew in several directions as her violet skirt flared in a wind that suddenly whirled around them, echoing Marilyn Monroe's iconic photo as it began swirling above her knees. With a plop of her arm, she frantically tried to deflate it back to normal. But the gusts only became stronger, louder, and more domineering.

The few pedestrians leisurely strolling down the block held onto their hats and handbags, trying to walk against the wind as if it was just another day in the city. It wasn't until one man lost his footing on the pavement, became one with the wind, and began rolling down the street that the people became panic-stricken. Nearby storefronts and apartment buildings welcomed the herd of strangers desperately fleeing the windstorm. Intense shrills and shrieks could be heard for blocks on end as tree branches hit the pavement, bodies rolled and collided into each other, and emergency sirens rushed into the distant, consuming fog.

Cars swerved and skidded in the street, trying to avoid head-on collisions and property damage. Many drivers abandoned their vehicles and took cover, grabbing their distraught passengers with them.

"Mag's, WHAT'S HAPPENING?!" Charlie screamed, holding on tighter to Pete's harness as he barked loudly in fear.

Pete quickly scrambled, then used his hind legs to jump on the closed entrance door to their building. He frantically scratched his front paws on the black door knob using all of his doggy skills to turn it open and pull his master to safety. He could only do so much before the wind began lifting his little hind legs off of the ground. Within seconds Pete became airborne, gasping and whimpering for help as the harness tightened around his neck as though he were being hung.

Pete's yelping and never-before-heard doggy cries caused Charlie to drastically pull his harness closer to her until she was able to hold him under her arm.

"I got you, boy, I got you." She cried as she kissed his forehead in relief, the wind swirling her hair and skirt in a thousand directions and clumsily knocking her backward.

Maggie quickly reached for the doorknob, but the wind beat her to it. With one huge gust, the metal door flung from its hinges with violent velocity and magnetized toward her forehead

Dazed and blurred, Maggie could hear the despair of the people around her as she glided in the wind as though floating in a calm, soothing sea. She wanted nothing more than to surrender to her inner anguish and the consuming windstorm.

Maggie...Maggie...wake up...WAKE UP! called a male voice inside her head that was neither hers nor the Left or Right.

Fiery crimson eyes shot open as she dodged the silver lamp post that nearly collided with her cranium. With one hand, she grasped the lamp post and clung on to it as she surveyed the immediate area. Nothing could be seen in the dense fog except for a flying object that she could barely make out. However, she knew the screams all too well.

Charlie's shrieks could be heard through the swirl of fog as she swooshed through the air holding on to Pete as if her life depended on it.

A current of terror electrified Maggie's body as she helplessly watched her dear friend being swallowed by the raging fog. Black wings clawed their way out of her shoulder blades as she stretched her hands out and channeled her energy toward Charlie's swirling body. Going against the mini-tornado proved to be much more challenging than she anticipated. Through clenched teeth, tireless flapping, and fatigued hands, she summoned all of her energy to mentally force Charlie and Pete to crash inside the lobby of their apartment building. Their bodies rolled across the black and white checkered floor as if someone had used them as bowling balls. The thud of their heads hitting the wooden walls temporarily knocked them unconscious.

Maggie fought against the windstorm trying to scan for any more flying human bodies. The clouds grew thicker and slowly embraced her in a tight bear hug as it passed over Charlie's neighborhood, leaving things in disarray.

This is it. The moment we've been waiting for. It's Lucifer!, claimed the Left voice.

"GRRRRR," growled Maggie as she feverishly fought to escape the grip of the tornado. Large, black horns manifested themselves from the tip of her head as purple veins covered the cheeks of her caramel skin. Burning anger coursed through her veins as she bellowed in frustration. Unable to control the direction of the windstorm or the amount of air that was smothering her lungs, breathing became burdensome.

"SHITTT," was the only comprehensible word that broke free from Maggie's lips as she slammed chest-first into a swirling tree trunk.

"Ooof," she howled as a sharp pain encased her insides. The sweet luxury of breathing clean air was knocked out of her lungs as she felt her collarbone rattling and her sternum on the verge of collapsing. The world around her went dark and deadly as her body fell limp and her thoughts went silent. She flipped and dived through the fierce cyclone until she was finally released in an open, secluded green field.

Maggie came crashing down like a falling meteorite, fast, bright, and loud. She face-planted in front of Angel, Master Anu, and Keiko. The mini-tornado relaxed into a calm breeze, and the sun beamed with warmth and radiance. Not even the slightest wind blew to provide Master Anu the dramatic effect of his silky hair blowing in the wind like a dashing supermodel.

To the ordinary eye, it seemed as if Keiko and Angel were guarding Master Anu as they stood to the right and left of him. The three of them positioned themselves in a defensive stance, waiting for any surprises that Maggie might throw at them.

A sign of life twitched from her fingertips as she confirmed to herself that she was, indeed, still alive. Excruciating pain stabbed her chest; the smallest task of taking a breath became a battle to the death. A deafening smoker's cough reverberated in everyone's ears as Maggie gained the strength to roll onto her back and gasp for warm, clean air. She flashed her bloody eyes at the three figures in front of her as she tried to make sense of her surroundings.

Using the sleeve of her leather jacket, she rubbed it over her face trying to remove the dirt and debris from her rough skin. Instead, it smeared everywhere.

Cough, cough. "Am I...in Hell?" Maggie struggled to say as sharp pains crept throughout her chest cavity. Falling chest-first to the ground with broken bones hurt more than anything she'd ever experienced.

"Hardly," answered Keiko, taking the opportunity to speak up.

Master Anu raised his right eyebrow, taking in Maggie's appearance for the first time. She wasn't the sweet innocent angel he was used to seeing. She was different, unrecognizable, and deadly. Her devil horns were something one would see in a mythological book; and her wings, although still fluffed with silky, shiny feathers, were the darkest shade of black coal one could imagine.

"Magdalena, are you alright?" asked Angel, not moving from Master Anu's side to help her up. She remained stuck like a statue nailed to the ground.

With the ounce of energy that Maggie had left, she sat up on the plush grass, realizing they were huddled in the middle of an open field.

"Yeah, I think so," she lied as she held her hand on her collarbone, feeling it wiggle and sway about.

Yep, it's broken, confirmed the Left voice.

"No shit," muttered Maggie out loud as she squinted in agony, mentally fighting back tears.

"It's obvious she's hurt," Keiko announced to the group. "I doubt she will be a threat." She bent in front of Maggie and placed her hand on the same spot she was nursing. The feel of her smooth hands triggered a burning sensation on her aching bone. She instantly flinched and huffed a soft growl under her breath.

Ignoring her growl, Keiko stood up, unfazed, and addressed Angel. "The collarbone is broken along with some other damage."

"Do you think she will be able to heal herself?" Angel asked Master Anu.

Master Anu didn't reply as quickly as he normally would. Instead, he loudly sighed before acknowledging the question. There was an awkward pause before Master Anu finally broke the silence.

"Oh, you're asking me? Shit, beats me." he shrugged uncaringly.

The three of them studied Maggie closely as she allowed her body to surrender back against the ground as if she were slowly dying inside.

After a few drawn-out seconds, Angel kneeled in front of Maggie and placed her hands on her chest. The glow of her hands penetrated her aching, broken bones with divine healing energy. The collarbone repositioned itself as fragments of bones could be heard aligning and mending. As gruesome as it sounded, no one looked away.

Maggie stared at her mother quizzically as though seeing her for the first time. Full-length, white, silk wings shimmered and sparkled under the sun's rays, nearly blinding her vision. It had been a while since she had seen her mother in her true angelic form. She'd almost forgotten how elegant and beautiful she appeared. If one dreamed of angels, it would be her mother they would visualize. Her smooth bronze skin, long, dark hair, full lips, and her essence of angelic calmness and innocence radiated a celestial glow. It would make anyone drop to their knees in prayer while shedding a few tears in rejoicing. She gave off the feeling of hope and inner peace. Hope is what Maggie clung to at this very moment.

The essence of Angel's magic enveloped Maggie's body like a warm blanket. She could feel the power flowing through her blood like a roaring river. Inner peace danced in her soul as her horns retreated inside the fortress of her skull, the purplish veins that circled her forehead and cheeks diminished, and her wings slowly crawled back between her shoulder blades.

Master Anu and Keiko watched in astonishment.

"Incredible!" stated Master Anu. "How were you able to calm her inner demon?"

"It's a mother's touch," answered Angel confidently.

"This is all so fascinating. Your species are self-healers, yet Maggie struggled with that ability. She appears more fragile as a demon," responded Master Anu, taking a closer look at an unconscious Maggie.

"She's a weak demon," Keiko spat, tightly crossing her arms over her chest.

"Ugggg," moaned Maggie as her soft brown eyes fluttered open.

She slowly sat up and firmly closed her eyes, preventing her head from spinning any further.

"Mom, what did you do?"

Taken aback, Angel answered as honestly as she could, "I healed you. You were hurt."

"But I feel different."

"How different?" interjected Master Anu, needing to feed his curious mind.

Maggie glanced around the open field; the smell of freshly cut grass stung her nostrils. Birds could be heard chirping and squeaking in the trees above and beyond the open plain. Her senses felt heightened to the tenth power. She moved her head around at every noise like a bobbing chicken's head.

"I feel as if everything is magnified," she rose from the ground and steadied her hands in front of her face.

"My hands are glowing," her voice slightly quivered.

"No, they're not," Keiko responded, sounding annoyed and popping her bubble.

"What do you think is happening, Anu?" Angel questioned.

"I think she absorbed some of your energy."

"Is that even possible?" she challenged, pulling on Maggie's hands as she examined them.

"Anything is possible at this point. It's the only explanation that makes sense right now," he responded, moving closer to Maggie and deeply surveying her pupils. It was almost as if he was trying to hypnotize her.

Maggie backed away from Master Anu's creepy V stare. She yanked her hands away from Angel as her recollection of the windstorm interrupted her thoughts. She pulled her hair back and straightened her stance, trying to appear as tough as possible. The thought of Charlie and Pete being seriously hurt sent tiny tremors of fear down her spine.

"Mom, did you guys create that cyclone?" she asked, fearing the truth.

"We had a witch conjure it," admitted Keiko.

Maggie gasped, "Why? Humans were seriously hurt. Charlie and her dog were nearly killed. Shit, I was nearly killed. That was so irresponsible of you three," she scolded as if speaking to a bunch of five-year-olds.

"I'm sure your friends are fine, but we had to make sure," answered Angel.

"Make sure of what?" spat Maggie.

"That your uncontrollable demon side wouldn't kill us," chimed Keiko.

Maggie's eyes rolled in annoyance. "Kill you? But you guys nearly killed me." Her hands waved in front of her as she was making her point.

"Do you seriously think I can't control my inner demon? That I will slaughter the people I love? I would never!" Maggie's emotions were getting the better of her as a tear slid down her right cheek.

"I think we need to be more honest with Maggie," stated Master Anu, walking in between Angel and Maggie. "I believe she can handle it." He patted her on the top of her head as if she were an obedient lap dog.

Maggie backed away and sized up Master Anu. He was acting extremely peculiar, almost out of character. Patting her on the head and not being quick on his toes were traits he never exhibited. Even his speech was a bit off.

"Maggie, the storm was created to test your strength. You want to fight with your Uncle Lucifer so bad, yet you could barely handle a small cyclone. You reacted too slowly, you almost let your friends die, you got dinged on the forehead by a metal door, and got the shit knocked out of you by a flying tree trunk. Overall, this proves that you are inadequate to fight and can't take a few hard hits." Master Anu paused to glance at Maggie's expression. It was as if he was watching a fighter hear for the first time that he wasn't good enough to make it to the pros.

"If it wasn't for me intervening inside your head and telling you to wake up, you would have become one with the lamp post." He confessed with irritation.

"That was you?" Maggie was stunned to hear Master Anu was able to get inside her head.

"The point is, your uncle is going to rain down ten times stronger than a baby cyclone. And you're not the least bit prepared. I wanted to see for myself what you were capable of, and quite frankly, I'm unimpressed. Be happy that he didn't show himself when you tried to force him out of the shadows. I believe he was doing you a favor."

Master Anu turned his back and began slowly walking away as if he had just mic dropped and exited a stage as the crowd went apeshit. It was clear he was no longer entertaining the conversation. Keiko took one last glance and followed in Anu's footsteps. She had never turned her back on Maggie, but today was an exception.

To hear Master Anu bluntly disrespect her and watch Keiko turn on her heels and walk away as if she didn't matter, turned her stomach upside down. He had never spoken to her with such brutal honesty. She felt her heart explode inside her chest with hurt and crumble to a million pieces, only to be reconstructed and filled with rage and anger. The Left and Right voices were speaking at once; she couldn't find her own tongue to formulate words.

Just who does this stupid Vamp think he is? I was born ready. I'm always ready, said the Left.

Yep! He's right, we let our guard down. We didn't scan the perimeter as we were taught. We didn't look for signs of danger and we didn't expect the unexpected. We're not ready, retorted the Right.

Oh, hush, you damn people-pleaser, commanded the Left.

Angel looked into Maggie's hurt-filled eyes and stretched her arms out to embrace her daughter. Maggie dove into her mother's comforting arms like an injured child who needed soothing as pent-up tears streamed down her polished cinnamon cheeks.

"I wish this would all go away. I wish this would just stop. I don't know what to do. Please, mom, tell me what to do." Maggie buried her face into Angel's neck, feeling her skin warmer than usual. For the first time in years, she cried like a baby.

She wailed over Dom's death, her father's absence, Ruby Jane's disappearance, the way she treated her mother, and most importantly, her erratic behavior. Since she needed a hard lesson, this was it. She came to terms that she was a complete screw-up and wasn't as tough or as badass as she portrayed herself to be. The realization that she was not winning kicked her in the ass harder than Dom's death.

As Maggie's weeping began to calm, she squinted into the distance only to notice Keiko watching her from a few yards away, stone-faced and unreadable. It wasn't her normal reaction, but it was enough to convince Maggie that her worst fears had come true. The people she loved most had turned their backs on her.

"Shhhh, it's alright. I got you," Angel reassured as she continued to comfort and console her distraught daughter. She kissed her forehead and wiped the remaining tears from her cheeks.

"So, what now?" asked Maggie in a shaky voice, not sure if she wanted to go on. Part of her wanted to call it a day and hide inside her room for the next ten years.

"Now? We will go home," replied Angel, trying to sound convincing as she fixed the collar on Maggie's leather jacket.

"Wait, what about Master Anu? He seems angry with me."

Angel glanced in Master Anu's direction. He and Keiko were standing patiently under a shady tree, idly watching without any conversation exchanged between them.

"He isn't angry with you. He's just giving you a bit of tough love." Angel smiled, lightening the mood.

"Tough love?" Maggie whispered to herself, thinking of how human the term was. She stopped short in her tracks and gave in to the nagging feeling that lingered in the back of her head. Something wasn't quite right. She stared over at Keiko again, who seemed to be biting her nails and huffing and puffing under her breath out of boredom. Her eyes then shifted to Master Anu who stood in the same spot, motionless and expressionless, vigilantly watching her every move. There was also the fact that she couldn't go home because her demon side wouldn't allow her to pass through the portal. Angel knew that. Her gut twisted inside her stomach as she began to feel suspicious about her surroundings.

"Where is everyone?" whispered Maggie to herself as she scanned around for another sign of life throughout the open green fields.

She quickly faced Angel with a serious expression pasted across her face.

"Mom?"

"Yes? Sweet child of mine," using a phrase she had never used before.

Angel placed her hand on Maggie's cheek, accidentally scraping her chin with the tips of her fingernails. The palm of her hand felt like sandpaper against her silky skin.

"Ouch!"

Maggie grabbed Angel's hand and noticed its skin had changed to a reddish-purple and the fingernails were long and sharp as knives. Small droplets of blood trailed down her chin as she realized the scrape was a large slit. She looked over Angel's shoulder and noticed Master Anu and Keiko had vanished with the wind. Only the breeze and the leaves circling in a twirling motion were left in their place.

Panic rose inside her throat and remained there like an elevator jammed between floors.

"Yes? Sweet child of mine," repeated Angel once again, sounding like a broken record, the cadence in her voice never changing.

Maggie dropped Angel's hand and gazed up into the sky as the sun bled a fiery orange followed by the sounds of thunder. The air transformed from its sweet, clean scent of grassy fragrances to the pungent smell of sulfur. The green grass melted and withered away, leaving bits of tar and gravel.

Sweat trickled from Maggie's forehead as the temperature felt as if someone raised the thermostat to one-hundred-and-ten trillion degrees. She turned to Angel who, before her very eyes, morphed into a razor-tooth, six-foot demon with a large head, black spiral horns, and hollow eyes. Looking into its eyes was the equivalent of staring into a soul-sucking abyss.

"AHHAAHHAAAHHH," the demon laughed diabolically. It closed the gap two inches from her face as it hissed and ridiculed while spitting out black lava.

"Yessss? Ssssweet child of mineeee?"

Maggie's heartbeat accelerated and must have stopped pounding midway because she couldn't feel it trying to escape anymore. Her scream sounded unrecognizable to her own ears as she took off running blindly into the nothingness. She spread her wings as she gained momentum and shot up into the fiery sky.

Lucifer and Camila observed Maggie's simulated torture chamber intently through the golden, floating mirrors of his lair. He sighed as he watched his niece retreat in fear and take flight. It wasn't what he was expecting.

Camila rubbed his shoulders as he waved his hand and blackened the mirror in front of him, shutting it off as if it were an irritating television program.

"I told you, my love. She is just a child. So much power yet still afraid."

Listening to Camila's Spanish accent always enticed Lucifer, even when he was trying to remain focused.

He gently removed her hands and kissed them as if worshiping a goddess.

"I know, darling. I'm just a little disappointed. I expected more from this "Destroyer of Worlds," He mocked. "Look at her. Scurrying away like a scared little mouse. What a bloody waste!" Lucifer walked over to his desk where two drinks filled with aged whisky patiently waited for them. He handed one to his lover and took a relaxing sip as he savored the heat of the alcohol on the tip of his tongue. He leaned against his desk in deep thought.

"We did make her face her worst fears. Abandonment and heartbreak seem to defeat even the most ferocious people. I believe it's her brokenness that prevented her from putting on the show that you expected, my love," stated Camila, breaking his train of thought. She sat close to him and sipped her drink, then nestled her head on his shoulder.

"I know. But broken or not, that behavior would have never flown in Eden," Lucifer stated, pointing his whisky to the mirror.

"Eden is made up of warriors. Angels never shy from a battle. That girl right there is more like her father, pathetic. Her mother should have taught her better. And she dared challenge me? Claiming to end me which, for the record, is damned near impossible." Lucifer paused to sip, trying his best to calm his anger. "I went easy on her, too. I sent my weakest demons to that torture chamber. Those bastards wouldn't hurt a fly. They are all glitz and glamor, just like she is. Either way, I had to see for myself what sort of power she was going to unleash."

"It's clear that it's nothing you can't handle," flattered Camila.

"I never doubted that, darling. But one can never be too sure. Getting the little black book from her brother is going to be easier than taking candy from an infant," Lucifer grinned.

"It definitely will be." agreed Camila, clinking her glass to his.

Lucifer downed his drink and slammed it on the table before popping himself off his sturdy desk. "Finish up, darling. Before I send her off into the real world, I need to have a chat with my niece. It's time we meet face to face," he grinned from ear to ear.

CHAPTER 15
FROM WIND STORM TO HELL

Lucifer and No-Nose Tommy stood directly across the street watching Maggie as she stood in front of Charlie's apartment building twirling a cigarette between her fingers. The usual press of New Yorkers walked around them as if they were just another set of tourists pausing in their leisurely walk to admire the building's structure.

No-Nose Tommy continued rubbing his neck and hands, scratching and picking at his skin.

"You'll get used to it, Tommy. Give it a couple of more days, and you'll hardly notice it," Lucifer assured without taking his eyes off of Maggie.

"Sire, I don't want to be one to complain, but I hate this skin. Why is it so itchy?" He rubbed his hands again then quickly inserted them into his pants pocket trying to refrain from scratching himself raw.

"Because you're not an actual human. You never were. If I'd sent you to Earth more often, you would have adjusted to your skin." He faced his trusty demon and patted his shoulder, giving him a half-smile. "Now, I need you here. As one of my 'Eyes.' So far, you're doing a hell of a great job. You've managed to tail her, unnoticed."

No-Nose Tommy grinned brightly showing off his human, pearly-white teeth. He tightened his tie and stood tall and proud as he smoothed the wrinkles from his striped navy blue suit. His attire was made of the finest material. He appeared as if he worked for an Italian mob boss. All of Lucifer's 'Eyes' generally did.

"Thank you, Sire, I'm grateful that..."

"Hush now! As much as I would like to hear your praise, just know I wouldn't have chosen you if I didn't find you worthy. Besides, Camila thinks highly of you, and her opinion is most valued."

No-Nose Tommy's eyes widened at the sound of Camila's name. She was always one to look out for him. But reality was they looked out for each other like a close knit family.

Lucifer continued giving commands, ignoring Tommy's reaction. "Continue finding leads on Angel and her entourage. I will take things from here. Go. Now."

"Yes, Sire," he obeyed. He took one last glance at Maggie as if it would be his last chance to see her alive. Aside from his compulsive need to constantly scratch and rub his hands and neck, he blended in with society perfectly well. He made his way around the street corner then vanished within the rushing throng of humans.

Without batting an eye, Lucifer raised his palms waist-high, summoning fumes of white smoke buried deep from the trenches of the Underworld. The grey, thick clouds, combined with the mounting breeze, blew with ease as it readied itself for the ultimate chaos of a cyclone.

With only the sounds of his heels crushing the gravel beneath them, Lucifer walked through the mazed corridor of the Underworld wondering if throwing Maggie behind a simulation chamber was the appropriate thing to do. After all, she was still family, a bit of a pest, but still family. The sulfur-flavored hallway flamed to life, each floating torch igniting as he strolled by comfortably like a king in his kingdom.

Lucifer straightened the jacket of his navy suit and gazed upon the six silver doors of his torture chambers, reading the signs on the metal doors as if taking them in for the first time. *Damn, they are glorious*, he mentally reveled in his own magnificence.

The doors were created by his nephew Castus and had become the way of order in the Underworld. Every door led to a damned soul's never-ending, agonizing hell loop.

He entered through torture chamber number three and quickly scanned the fiery sky searching for signs of Maggie. He chuckled under his breath as he realized he was standing in a simulation of the old version of Hell. Sulfur-filled air, temperature hotter than molten lava, screams of terror, and the sky bleeding a fiery orange was enough to make even the non-believers fall to their knees and beg for mercy. He surveyed the pits of fire and smoke and continued drawing his sea-green eyes to the skies. Still, there was no sign of her.

Crunching noises and snickering could be heard within earshot as Lucifer swiftly turned on his heels to face the unknown forces behind him. Three demons stood baffled by the unexpected presence of their sire. One of them quickly knelt as the rest of them, a bit delayed, followed suit.

"Sire, apologies, we weren't expecting you," spoke a long-headed demon in a raspy voice.

"Surprise!" Lucifer joked, his voice dripping with sour sarcasm. "Where is the gal, and what the bloody hell happened to your voice, William?"

The demon, William, lowered his head and cleared his throat, trying to make it better with no success.

"Apologies again, Sire, the screaming and sinister laughing strained my throat."

"Well then, why didn't you two pick up the slack for William?"

he questioned the other two demons who seemed as if they wanted to become one and vanish into the pits.

One demon with long horns spoke up, "He lost the coin toss. It was his turn to do the screaming. It's how we handle things here in the torture chambers. The screaming and screeching laughter are even too tortuous for us to continue, so we coin toss. The loser screams until the next soul arrives."

"Is that so?" Lucifer rubbed his beard, finding the situation fascinating. Never in a million years had he considered that screaming would tire out his demons. He thought they were biologically built for it.

"Sire, is it possible we can install more simulated sounds in the chambers? It would really help us out. We love our job, but screaming until our vocal cords burst is taking a toll on us. We're starting to sound less intimidating," stated the third demon with razor-sharp teeth, appearing as if he was making his first complaint to the Human Resources department.

Not wanting to waste any more time, Lucifer clapped his hands together signaling the demons to rise.

"Come now, you three blokes bring your complaints to Camila and she'll fix it. By the way, who is in charge of the simulation chambers now?"

"It was No-Nose Tommy, but he has a new job. No one has been appointed yet," rasped William.

Lucifer stared at the demon with razor-sharp teeth and landed his palm on his broad, ripply shoulder. He gave it a light squeeze as if they had been pals for millennia.

"What's your name, mate?"

"I'm, uh, Steven, Master," he said in response, his voice quivering, fearing the worst.

"Well, uh, Steven, since you have such great ideas, YOU are currently in charge here. Congratulations on your promotion!" Lucifer playfully cuffed Steven's square chin. "Make sure you do right by your fellow demons."

Steven grinned his razor-sharp teeth happily and shook Lucifer's hand proudly as his fellow demon friends patted him on the back for a job well done.

"Wow! Thank you, Sire. My wife will be thrilled to hear about this. She always said I should be in charge. I have such…"

"Yes, Yes, Yes," interjected Lucifer. "Tell it to Camila; she will set you up. Now you three scatter. I need to find the gal," Lucifer rushed.

"Oh, the girl," shot William, remembering why his sire was originally there. "She's hiding behind the big rock that looks like a cock."

Lucifer looked beyond the pits and noticed a long, pointed, grey, cement block similar to an erection. He turned to the demons and back at the rock, then slowly turned to the demons again in search of answers.

Without hesitation William quickly and raspily snitched.

"That was No-Nose Tommy's idea."

"Now that I'm in charge I will take it down, Sire," intervened Steven, trying to smooth the situation and save his fellow friends from the unexpected.

"No, It's pleasantly fine." Lucifer fought a chuckle under his breath, thinking of No-Nose Tommy's childish humor. As goofy and silly as Tommy was, he admitted to himself that he missed having him around, although he would never confess that out loud. "The knob stays. Just turn off the theatrics on your way out. I don't want to relive the old version of hell again. It's beyond dreadful."

"Yes, Sire." Steven responded as he bowed his demon head in acknowledgment.

The three demons walked over to a blazing fire pit and casually reached their skeletal hand into the rising heat. The heat parted as a dark hole opened to the size of a door, revealing the mazed corridor on the other side. Their chatter and praise could be heard as they exited away.

Within seconds the simulation began to fade, screams turned into soft chirping, and fire pits evolved into calm streams. The cold, black gravel under his loafers transformed into fresh, shimmering, emerald grass covered in patches of yellow and orange. The sun became a normal stone of fire yellow as the temperature dropped to a refreshing breezy fall. Ranch-style houses and livestock could be seen a few yards away. Lucifer relaxed his shoulders and brought his hands together, content with the choice of scenery. In his opinion, anything was better than standing in the old version of the Underworld.

The pointed cock rock stood a few feet away from him. As Lucifer leaned to the side to get a better glimpse, he could see black feathers peeking from the edges of the cement.

"You can come out now," he called out reassuringly. "I'm not going to hurt you."

Before he could react, a gust of wind blew behind him as a strong arm wrapped tightly around his neck, drawing him backward. The hard pull nearly caused him to fall, but he managed to secure his balance.

Maggie tightened her sleeper hold grip as the heat of her angry whisper nipped Lucifer's ear. "But I'm going to hurt you."

Amused, Lucifer dematerialized from her arms and stood facing her a few feet away. Confused, she charged at him head first, ready to use her long, black horns as a battering ram. Lucifer poofed himself from her vision and stood behind her.

"Maggie, I think we need to stop this," Lucifer suggested coolly, unbuttoning his suit jacket.

Maggie spun herself around, nearly giving herself whiplash. She balled her fist, cranked her right arm back like a slingshot, and let it rip forward. Waves of orange and red flames shot in her uncle's direction.

Lucifer rolled his eyes in annoyance. *Oh, bloody hell*, he said to himself as he counteracted by mentally disintegrating the fireballs to ash. The wave of ashes fluttered with the cooling breeze as Maggie looked on in astonishment.

"Stop, you'll tire yourself, gal," he stated.

"Shut up and fight me!" Maggie took another chance and

charged at Lucifer again. This time she leaped in the air but never dropped back down to finish her power move.

Lucifer grew restless and gave a "talk to the hand" gesture, pausing her actions in mid-air. Maggie was paralyzed in a split position, unable to move the slightest muscle as if she was a human statue. Lucifer moved her limbs and positioned her like a wooden soldier, making sure she wouldn't be able to break free. He slowly drew her closer and stared into her bloodshot eyes.

"Behave yourself," he commanded.

"Uggh, grrrr," she grunted as she desperately tried to break away from his magic. It was no use, she was trapped inside her own body.

"I believe it is time for you to listen for a change," he stated as he held a floating Maggie frozen like ice.

"First and foremost, welcome to the Underworld." Lucifer slowly turned three-hundred-and-sixty degrees, his hands spread out as if introducing his guest to his grand luxury lifestyle.

"I'm your uncle, Lucifer Morning Star. It is a pleasure to make your acquaintance." His British accent sounded sly yet charming.

Maggie breathed heavily, darting her eyes from side to side as if taking in her environment for the first time. It seemed as if she hadn't noticed the shift in scenery since encountering Lucifer.

"You may speak," Lucifer granted, removing his magic from her neck up. Maggie moved her head around, but her body remained paralyzed. The veins on her cheeks pulsed as if they were going to explode.

"Am I dead?" she rapidly questioned.

"No, Do you want to be?"

"Then how did I get here? I thought one had to die to cross here," she frantically asked, trying to move her limbs with no success.

"Humans must die to get here; you're not human. You're one of us. You can come and go as you please," Lucifer schooled.

Maggie stared in confusion, "Did I manifest myself here?"

"No. I brought you here using my powerful windstorm," he couldn't help the slight chuckle that escaped his lips.

"That was real? I thought I dreamt it."

"No, that was very real," he confirmed.

"My friends, are they okay?"

"Yes, you personally saved them. Bravo to you!" Lucifer gave a sarcastic applause.

Maggie lowered her head and sighed in relief.

"Maggie?" He raised her chin and spoke sincerely, keeping his attention on her demon eyes.

"I'm going to set you free. But before I do, you have to promise me that you're not going to attack. It will be a fight you cannot win. You're in my world; I can dispose of you with one touch of my pinky. But, I won't."

"Then WHY won't you?" Maggie pressed. "You already tried to kill me once, but instead you killed Dom. He was innocent; he didn't deserve to die." Her voice cracked at the mention of her lover's name. It was clear to Lucifer that her feelings for him were much stronger than he anticipated.

"Because you're family. And I didn't intentionally kill Dom. That was a misunderstanding. It's what happens when I send bloodthirsty demons to play in the sandbox—they don't behave. Besides, if it accounts for anything, Dom is safe in Eden, probably growing baby wings by now."

"What?" Maggie couldn't believe what she was hearing. "How do you know that for sure?"

"Because he isn't here. And humans can only go two places." Lucifer could see a relaxed expression wash over her face.

"Anyway, you killed two of my best and vicious demons. That was tough for me to process."

"It should have been you," she mumbled.

"Well, good news! It wasn't. So let's call it an eye for an eye then." Lucifer raised his hand to his chest and withdrew the magic holding Maggie. Magnetic swirls swiveled and found refuge in the cracks of his palm.

Maggie dropped to her knees and retracted her wings. She swiftly stood up, brushed her knees, and took a few deep breaths.

"Well, you got what you came for, now what?" she folded her arms tightly across her chest.

"I got what I came for? Do you mean you?" puzzled Lucifer.

"Yes, Isn't that why you brought me down here? You've been following my mother and father for years because you wanted your hands on me, the half-breed child with unpredictable powers. My mother did everything to protect me, and yet…I failed her." Maggie paused, appearing as if the last sentence hit her like a ton of bricks to the ribcage.

Lucifer bit down on the bottom of his lip until he could no longer suppress the laughter inside. He laughed so hard he bent over holding his belly, nearly in tears.

"YOU!" He tried speaking between his chuckles, but it was damned near impossible.

"What's so funny?" Maggie stared at him as if he were losing his mind.

"Hahaha…, we were never after you. HAHAHAHAHA." Lucifer stood tall and began walking toward the cock rock.

"Oh, gosh, this is classic." He leaned against the rock, regaining his composure.

"What do you mean? My father hid me for years because the Underworld was after us."

"Darling, excuse my language when I say this, but your father is a shithead. He should have known better about who we were chasing."

A puzzled expression crossed Maggie's face as she stood silent.

"It is true, we were following Jack for a while. But did he tell you he assisted in smuggling a pregnant demon out of the Underworld?"

Maggie shook her head no, appearing more confused than before.

"A pregnant demon?" she questioned, seeming not to understand how a demon could ever be pregnant.

"Oh, well then, come along. We have plenty to discuss." Lucifer gave the cock rock one hard stare. It gradually moved slightly to the left revealing the exit door of the simulation chamber.

They walked into the dim corridor and watched the silver door shut behind them. Maggie glanced up at the red and black sign centered in the middle of the door

"Door 3 - Back to Earth to make things right."

"It tricks the damned into thinking they will make amends, but it mostly involves them facing their worst fears," Lucifer answered before she could spit out a question.

"I saw my mother and the people that I love there. How did you do it?" Maggie spoke in a whisper and stared into Lucifer's eyes in search of the truth.

"It's a simulated torture chamber. It's designed to manifest your deepest fears into reality.

"But it felt so real." Her voice shook as she planted her palm on the metal door as if wishing she could go back inside to see her mother one last time.

"That's the idea. I can stand here all day and talk about my torture rooms, as you can see I have six. But I think we should get some food and discuss your brother Jesse. Are you hungry?"

"Wait, Jesse?" Maggie repeated, ignoring Lucifer's invitation to food.

A sudden creak of an open door and the crunch of nine-inch heels against the dark gravel at the far end of the corridor had interrupted their conversation. Camila stepped out appearing as alluring as usual in a black, skin-tight corset with a chiffon train attached to the end. It opened in the middle revealing black leather pants. Maggie's jaw almost dropped at her beauty. It was as if her sparkling blue eyes illuminated the entire hallway.

"This way, Sire," Camila motioned for them to enter through the steel door she was holding.

"Who's that?" Maggie asked sternly.

"That is Jesse's *real* mum," he answered nonchalantly, turning on his heels and making his way toward Camila.

"Camila Del Rio," she whispered to herself stunned, remembering the name she read on Jesse's documents the day she was in his lab.

Maggie watched, shocked, as she witnessed Lucifer kissing Jesse's mother.

CHAPTER 16
PIZZA ANYONE!

As Maggie followed Camila and Lucifer through the impenetrable steel door, she was led into a world like no other. It was a mini-city similar to the streets of New York, just not as large and the buildings not as tall. It was nightfall and the streets glimmered and glared with lights everywhere, illuminating each restaurant, shopping center, entertainment bar, and apartment building.

Maggie's eyes were glued to each demon and human walking around as if they were enjoying their life in the Underworld. Cars zoomed by in the streets, demons were pushing strollers, and couples were leisurely jogging down concrete-paved blocks without a care in the world. Maggie shook her head and breathed in heavily, a hint of sulfur stung her nostrils as she inhaled. She almost toppled over but held onto the brick wall behind her in hopes of easing her anxiety.

"Is something wrong?" asked Lucifer, seeming concerned.

Maggie firmly pressed her hand against her chest trying to quell the throbbing of sharp pains within.

"I believe she is having a panic attack," Camila suggested as she soothingly rubbed Maggie's back in comfort.

"It's okay. Just breathe, breathe. Follow me. One. Two. Inhale. Hold your breath. One. Two. Exhale," Camila walked Maggie through her breathing techniques as if she were giving birth.

Maggie leaned her body against the wall and expelled strong breaths as she stared into the dark sky. Each time she inhaled, her entire body cringed as if she was smelling something foul. Every pore and cell tried to retreat from the pungent stench.

"The smell takes some time getting used to. Don't worry, it gets easier," Lucifer reassured. "I masked my kingdom to not seem so dramatically scary, but I could not mask the smell very much. Sulfur and death are embedded in this place."

Camila rubbed Maggie's arm, doing her best to console her; but she gently pulled away.

"I'm fine, I'm fine." Maggie straightened her stance and donned her best poker face, but inside she was dying.

She fanned her face dry and pulled her curly hair back; the sweat that trickled down her temples didn't seem to let up. She removed her leather jacket and wiped her forehead. If the smell wasn't going to kill her, the heat surely was.

"Let's find a table at this place. I love the pizza there," Lucifer pointed to a small restaurant that only had a few patrons inside. As they walked in, all eyes were on them. The hostess, who was human, quickly ran toward Lucifer alongside a demon that sported a chef hat. They smiled brightly and respectfully bowed, as though seeing their king for the first time.

"Master! I...I'm honored to serve you tonight. I mean..." the young waitress slapped herself on her forehead and quickly corrected her statement. "Gino's is happy to serve you tonight." She glanced over at the demon with the chef hat.

"Sire, I'm thrilled to serve you, always. I'm Gino the owner and head chef..." the demon was ready to give his best kiss ass speech until Lucifer cut him short.

"I know who you are, Gino. No need for pleasantries. You're doing a magnificent job with this place," Lucifer patted the demon on the shoulder that appeared to stand shorter than most of his kind in the Underworld.

"Thank you Master." The demon beamed a toothy smile. "Please let me get you my finest table. Whatever you and your party want I will make sure it is specially made only with the finest and freshest ingredients."

"We'll sit outside," smiled Lucifer.

"Yes, Master, wherever you desire."

"I'll run and grab some menus," chimed the waitress pleasantly.

"No need, Just bring me a bottle of your best red wine and three of your specials. My niece is visiting from out of town, and I want to make her feel at home," Lucifer grinned at Maggie as she slightly huffed under her breath.

"Yes, Master, I'll get on your specials right away. We will not disappoint." Gino excitedly bowed his head as he dashed to the kitchen.

The young waitress turned to Maggie, "Welcome to the Underworld. Cool eyes!" she smiled, admiring the dark, bloodshot eyes Maggie sported in her demon form. Maggie acknowledged her with a small smile but remained silent as the young waitress walked away to attend to her duties.

The three of them sat outside at a small, round table with an open red and white striped umbrella over it. Maggie thought it silly to have an umbrella table as there was no sun; however, once she sat down, she could feel the cool breeze drying her neck and rejuvenating her skin. It was as if she had temporarily escaped the summer's heat.

The young waitress brought out a tall bottle of red wine with a skeleton head corkscrew and three extravagantly bejeweled wine glasses that may have possibly dated back to medieval times. Warm garlic bread and fresh ice water followed. She chuckled at the ridiculousness of it all. In the back of her mind, she felt she must still be dreaming. The young waitress poured the wine and smiled brightly as she retreated inside the restaurant.

Lucifer held up the dazzling glass, appearing more rich and powerful than he already was.

"Let's have a toast," he suggested enthusiastically.

"Yes!" happily agreed Camila, raising her glass.

Maggie folded her arms tightly across her chest and leaned back, wanting no part of the festivities.

"Oh, come now, Maggie. You don't need to be such a bugger," Lucifer chided.

Maggie took a deep breath and snatched up her fancy wine glass, disregarding its delicate nature. "Fine!"

"That's the spirit," he grinned. "Cheers. To family!"

"Si, a la familia," joined Camila.

"This is complete bullshit." mumbled Maggie before she fully said, "To family," smiling sarcastically.

They all sipped their wine as Maggie watched the two of them carefully.

"This wine is delicious, my love. Is it from the new vineyard?" Camila savored each sip, then tapped her glass for a refill as Lucifer obeyed her command.

"Yes, can you believe the bloke that came last month was a real vintner? Finally, someone who knows what they're doing. Now we have really good-tasting wine and not the shite we've been having before. I love it when humans with real skills land here. It makes our communities so much better."

"Indeed," Camila continued sipping as she leaned back in her chair and crossed her legs. Her cherry-colored lipstick never smeared on the glass.

"Okay, Can we please stop this shit?" Fury trembled in the brutal steel of Maggie's voice. She quickly stood up as her fingers ached with the burning desire to flip over the table. It took an abundance of effort not to throw a kiddie tantrum.

"I need to know about my brother, my father, my mother, and this place. Why does this fucking place look like this?!"

She pointed to the joggers and cars passing by.

"Why does everyone look so happy to be here? What kind of FUCKING HELL is this?" Maggie lifted the bottle of wine and stared at the skeleton head corkscrew.

"The only thing scary about this shithole is the corkscrew. I don't understand, what's happening?"

She abruptly stopped raging and stared into Lucifer's sea-green eyes.

"Why does it feel as if you're..." She glanced at Camila who was clutching a diamond and emerald studded choker. It momentarily caught her attention as the most stunning piece of jewelry she'd ever seen.

"What the Fuck?! They have diamond mines in hell, too?" she questioned, distracted by each twinkle of Camila's glam.

Things continued hustling and bustling. Demons and humans walked alongside the brick buildings, seeming as if it was a regular day in the neighborhood. Everything that she read about the Underworld appeared untrue. Maggie sat down and placed her head in her hands.

"It's as if you're torturing me," she said in a soft voice, finishing her last comment.

"Three pizza specials!" the young waitress interrupted, placing the personal-sized pizzas on the center of the table. The aroma of garlic hit Maggie's nostrils as her stomach growled and begged for a taste. The young waitress beamed and departed as fast as she entered.

Camila rested her hand on Maggie's arm. "Sire is not trying to punish you. This place has a way of twisting things around. But I assure you, your uncle means well."

Maggie looked at Camila, not knowing what to make of her words. She stared at Lucifer who was just glaring back at her as if she had miraculously grown three heads.

"It is true. I'm not trying to torture you. It's just the way Hell is designed," he implied with a nonchalant shrug.

"Well, then start talking. Why does Hell look like a bad version of New York City? And why is she here?" Maggie pointed to the waitress who was taking an order from a long-faced demon and dark-haired human that appeared to be on a date.

"Don't believe everything you read. Humans can be such idiots," Lucifer stated. "The humans you see walking among us are here because I chose them. They were not evil people, just misunderstood."

"Misunderstood?" Maggie imitated Master Anu and raised her right eyebrow.

"Correct," responded Lucifer. "Do you think I should torture a soul that has committed suicide to escape their dreadful human life or people who have denounced a faith because of confusion, despair, and loss?"

Maggie remained silent.

"I could go on and on as to why I let humans roam the Underworld, but I will cut to the chase. Only the most scum of the earth land in my torture chambers for eternity. The few I cherry pick get to live out their afterlife contributing to my world. Whether it's by work or pleasure." Lucifer pointed to a huge neon purple and white sign that floated above a darkened creepy building. Maggie couldn't remember if the place had previously been there or if it appeared with the motion of his finger. The blinking sign read *"Hell's Dolls"* with small lettering underneath that stated, *"A demon's gentlemens club."* Maggie huffed and shook her head in disdain at the irony of it all, as Lucifer replenished everyone's glass.

"Now, I will tell you everything about your parents, but you have to remain open to the truth and take it for what it is," he said as he drew his extravagant wine glass to his smooth lips.

Their conversation consumed hours as Lucifer explained all he could. He told Maggie how Angel first lost her memory. How Jack, her father, screwed up his obligation to protect Angel, and deceived the Underworld. He told her about her Uncle Castus (her mother's little brother), his trip to Earth, his death, and his fate that landed him in the void. Lucifer then confessed that Castus and Camila were Jesse's biological parents but that their relationship was nothing more than one huge, tragic, love story. He explained in detail Camila's regretful decision to leave Jesse in Angel's care.

Maggie's brain was running on overload. The more information she received, the more she drank.

"Maggie, you were never my intended target. It was always Jesse," Lucifer stated as if knocking her off her high horse.

Maggie's jaw dropped as she tried to recap her life on the run. But the effects of the wine weren't helping her memory very much.

"You followed me my entire childhood. I was in danger."

"Was I really following *you*?" Lucifer was making her second-guess herself.

"You sent demons after me."

"I had demons follow you."

"Bullshit, the minute I let my guard down, your demons killed my boyfriend." Maggie couldn't help but continue throwing that major detail in her uncle's face.

Lucifer slightly smirked and refilled everyone's wine glass as if he were bartending at a dinner party.

"There is no debating that. But if demons were after, specifically you, your entire childhood, understand this, they were not *my* demons."

The air grew deadly as Maggie tried to make sense of Lucifer's last statement. Her voice came down to a near whisper.

"Then whose demons were they?"

"That's what we're here to sort out." Lucifer laid the ultimate bomb on her, one minor detail of which she was unaware. "Do you know about the little black book and the Unknown worlds?"

Maggie sipped on her sixth, maybe even seventh, glass of wine feeling her senses wobbling. She giggled like an annoyingly tipsy, first-time drinker as Lucifer told her everything she needed to know about the little black book's power, and the key it harbored to release the creatures inside the Underworld.

"Is he always this serious?" she asked Camila, not being able to hide her inebriated, immature antics.

"No, he's usually very entertaining. But when he is serious, it's best to listen," Camila explained.

Maggie shrugged and mocked Camila's Spanish accent in a very low voice, as she sipped the remains of her red wine. *"It's best to listen. Whatever!"* She rolled her eyes derisively.

"You have significant power, Maggie. You could use your skills to help us to secure the little black book instead of mocking and ridiculing others," Lucifer scolded. "Have you heard anything I've been saying to you?"

Maggie relaxed back in her chair. "Yep, Little black book is bad. Jesse has it. Need to get it before bad things happen. Yeah, I think I pretty much have it covered."

Lucifer inhaled deeply, seemingly losing his patience. "We need your help. I want to ensure that the Unknown worlds remain Unknown." He pulled a cigar from the inside of his suit jacket and held it to his nose, admiring the fresh scent of the tobacco.

Maggie, ignoring Lucifer, stared at Camila trying to stop her surroundings from spinning. She rested her elbow on the table and leaned her head in her hand, marveling over her beauty.

"You're sooo pretty. Ugh, I hate how damn pretty you are," she stated, pouring herself more red wine from the last bottle they received.

"Thank you," Camila casually responded as she lit Lucifer's cigar.

"So, since Castus is locked away in a black hole somewhere, are you two a serious thing now? I mean it's one thing banging his ex but turning it into a relationship. Is ehhh...kinda awkward." Maggie was not checking her tongue the least bit.

Lucifer slightly chuckled at the comment, "Awkwardness has no place here. Camila is, as the humans would say, *my* girlfriend." He placed his free arm around Camila's shoulder, pulling her into his chest.

Maggie raised her glass in acknowledgement, "Here's to Hell having zero morals." She sipped and left the glass floating in the air in front of her face.

"Are you just going to leave that there?" asked Lucifer, seeming a bit annoyed at this point.

Maggie gazed at him with lowered eyelids, then focused back on the glass.

"Sit," She commanded the wine glass.

The glass floated past the table and was making a freefall down to the ground before Lucifer mentally caught it and placed it back in its respective place, the wine still intact.

"Maybe you just had a tad too many," he stated.

Maggie looked past Lucifer as if he were invisible. She hiccupped then giggled like an intoxicated teenager and rambled to Camila.

"I hate what happened to my brother. His pain is my pain. He's been looking for you forever. But I guess if you had never left him behind, then I wouldn't have been so lucky to have him as an awesome brother. So I should be thanking you."

Camila remained silent as she squeezed Lucifer's hand under the table, signaling him to keep Maggie on track.

"Maggie, the little black book," he reminded, "will you help?"

"Yeah, sure! Whatever! Anything to help the world be a better place," she agreed. "But under one condition." She pointed a swaying index finger in the air.

Intrigued, Lucifer leaned in closer to get a better listen. "What do you have in mind?"

"You weave. My family. A. Lone. And zhat includes my wother. My wother? Hehe." Maggie found humor in her slurred words. "My Brother," she finally corrected herself. "You seem like a nice lady, Camila, but Hell is not his home."

Camila shot Lucifer a concerned look.

He leaned back in his chair and took a puff of his cigar.

"I think we will let Jesse decide where he wants to be. In the meantime, let's get the little black book from him first."

"Deal!" Maggie shook Lucifer's hand as she downed her last swallow of red wine. Steam rose from their handshake and she heard crackling and sizzling as if a plate of fajitas was cooking. She frantically pulled her hand away and stared at the number six that was bubbling and forming in the palm of her once-smooth hand. Her vision blurred then cleared again.

"It's just a brand to give you right of passage to the Underworld," stated Lucifer.

Maggie stared at the six on her palm feeling drunk and confused.

"I thought you said I can come whenever I want? I didn't know I needed a special key."

"That will bring you straight to me when you enter, no torture rooms, no gates, no games," he assured.

"Oh, okay, Thanks." Maggie leaned back on her chair watching the six on her palm fade in and out of her vision.

"Tell me what you need me to do," she replied, confirming her deal with the devil.

CHAPTER 17
THE MEET UP

The rushing sound of multiple ambulance sirens blasted Maggie's way back to consciousness. The annoying wailing of their warning signals felt like lightning bolts in the sensitive canals of her ears. She jerked her body abruptly into a seated position, feeling as if she were a zombie awakening from the dead. The sound of Pete's barking caused Charlie's fingertips to pause over the braille on her book.

"Maggie, are you alright?" asked Charlie with genuine concern as she walked over to the sound of heavy breathing. She gently placed her hands around Maggie's shoulder as if comforting her from a terrible nightmare.

Puzzled and suffering from a splitting headache, Maggie shot her hands to the top of her head searching for her horns. They were gone. Without answering, she stood up and checked her reflection in the spotless glass of the apartment window, the closest thing she could find to a mirror. A regular, frazzled, curly-haired Maggie was staring back at her. She pressed her cold hands to the window and scanned across the city streets looking for signs of destruction, but everything appeared as normal as the day before.

People were bustling in the streets, business as usual. She rubbed her eyes, thinking that her mind was playing tricks on her or that she was being tortured again. She was still wearing the same black jeans she had worn to the funeral except she was stripped down to her nude-colored cami. Her leather jacket was draped over the kitchen chair. The room remained consistent with the scent of Charlie's Hawaiian coconut plug-ins. Nothing reeked of sulfur.

Maggie became spooked at the sound of Charlie's voice as she interrupted her from her trance.

"I can hear you shuffling around, is everything alright? You're making me nervous."

"What day is it?" asked Maggie, unsure of what to think.

"It's Saturday. Are you sure you're alright? You're breathing mighty hard. Did something happen at Dom's funeral?"

"Dom's funeral?" Maggie paused, confusion washing over her face.

"Yes, Dom's funeral. That is where you went earlier, right? Oh, no. Maggie, did you ditch Dom's funeral for a booty call? I know you were in a dark place but..."

"NO!" Maggie interjected as if the comment pinched a nerve and sickened her stomach—it could have easily been true. "No, I didn't ditch his funeral. I was there. And so was... my brother," she stated as if trying to differentiate the facts from fiction.

"Good, he made it. I called him to go check on you. You had me concerned with all your devil talk."

"Sorry about that; I was having a moment." Maggie exhaled in relief, knowing that one part of her memory was firmly embedded in reality. She ran her hands through her curly dark hair until it finally hit her. *The devil. The number six.*

She raised her hands to her face and saw the number six fading in and out of her right palm as if it were pulsing itself into view. She moved her hand closer to the light and could see it trying to rear its ugly head from under her skin.

"Fuck me," she whispered to herself, silently freaking out. Hell was real.

"Say what, now?" asked Charlie, seeming to need answers.

"Nothing," It was more of a groan rather than a statement. Maggie sat next to Charlie on her comfy couch and laid her throbbing head in between her hands.

"Did you and Jesse go anywhere after the funeral?" asked Charlie.

"No. We parted ways after…" Her voice trailed off to hide her uncertainty.

"Pete and I went to visit my grandparents today. We had a big lunch, played games, then ended up back here. I tried calling you, but it went to voicemail. I wasn't sure if I gave you the spare keys to the apartment. I guess you grabbed them because when I got home you were sound asleep on the couch." Charlie stood up and dug into the pockets of her violet flared skirt and handed Maggie her smartphone. Maggie took notice of her attire and realized it was the same skirt she had sported during the windstorm.

He turned back time, said the Left voice.

It's the only logical explanation, sarcastically responded the Right.

Welcome to the party! You're finally here.

Hmm, I thought your genius self would have realized by now that when you're full demon, you shut me out. There isn't enough room for the both of us in there. The Right voice was peeved that it was being dominated.

"Shhh," Maggie didn't realize her shushing was loud enough for the room to hear.

"Why are you shushing me?" Charlie asked in curiosity.

"I'm not. I was actually shushing Pete. He's breathing kinda loud." Maggie thought quickly, trying to detour the subject. "Pete, shush, I can't hear mamma talking."

Pete slightly whimpered as if ashamed of her for using him as an excuse. Charlie appeared as if she could smell the bullshit from a mile away. She kindly geared back to her conversation, seemingly to avoid Maggie's foolishness.

"Anyway, here you go. You must have dropped this while you were sleeping. It was ringing from under the coffee table." Charlie handed Maggie her phone and began to head toward her bedroom.

"Now that I know you're alright, I'm going to get ready to step out."

Enthralled in her smartphone, Maggie missed Charlie's last statement as she tapped on her screen, revealing seven missed calls from her mother and five text messages from her brother.

Jesse: Hey, meet me at O'Riley's Pub tonight @ 9:00 p.m. Corner of 81st

and Lexington.

Jesse: Don't forget to call mom, she's looking for you.

Jesse: I know it's early but I'm at O'Riley's if you want to get here earlier.

Jesse: Where the hell are you? Why aren't you answering?

Jesse: I swear if I find out you're ditching me for a guy, Imma be pissed!

He emphasized with an angry, steamed-headed emoji at the end.

Maggie noted the time was fifteen minutes to nine. *Thanks a lot, Uncle Lucifer. You couldn't get me here sooner,* she thought.

Maggie: Hey, I didn't ditch. Why does everyone keep saying that? Be there in 10 min.

As she responded, she couldn't help to think why the name O'Riley sounded so familiar. *O'Riley, O'Riley, damn. Think, Maggie.*

"Mom's downfall!" Maggie said to no one, snapping her fingers at her eureka moment. At that minute, her phone lit up with a message.

Jesse: About time you answered. I got some info, hurry up!

Before she could respond, Angel rang on the line. Maggie picked up on the first ring.

"Mom?"

"Maggie, where have you been?"

"Mom, you're not going to believe this. I have so much to tell you..."

"Meet me tonight. We need to talk," interrupted Angel, her voice sounding concerned and anxiety-stricken.

"Tonight? I'm going to meet up with Jesse now. Can we meet up after?" Maggie wanted to avoid dragging her mother to O'Riley's.

"Perfect, then I'll meet you both. Name the place."

Maggie paused, not sure what to say. She swallowed hard, but the rock in her throat remained stuck in her esophagus.

"Maggie. Maggie. Are you there?" Angel pressed.

"O'Riley's," she finally blurted.

There was an eerie silence on the other end of the phone. She could practically hear a pin drop.

"I'll be there in ten." Angel hesitantly answered.

Maggie remained stuck to the couch as if Gorilla-glued to the seat. Charlie appeared seconds later with her hair fashioned in a neat updo. She fumbled through her closet and grabbed her big shoulder bag and began discreetly stuffing clothes inside. She paused and turned at the sound of Maggie's intense breathing, again.

"Mags, is everything alright? I overheard you talking to your mom."

"Yeah, I'm good. I'm just going to meet her for a late dinner," Maggie lied. She rose from the couch and took one look at her friend who had changed into a pair of denim skinny jeans with a skin-tight, black top that looked extremely familiar. She glanced at Charlie's open bag and could visibly see lace underwear, a condom box, and toiletries peeking out, proof that she was getting into naughty deeds tonight.

"Are you going out to shag wearing my black shirt?" she teased, changing the subject.

"Seriously, I'm wearing your top? I thought it was mine. That explains why it's a little snug on top." She pulled the breast area of her shirt, trying to loosen it from squeezing the life out of her. "I'll go change."

"No. No need. It looks great on you," Maggie assured with a

smile. She didn't know what the night would hold for her. Charlie could keep the damn shirt for all she cared.

"So, where are you off to?"

Charlie's hesitation caused Maggie to give the famous Master Anu raised right eyebrow look. It was an expression that had become contagious.

Charlie sensed her friend's silent reproof. "Don't judge me," Charlie half-pleaded. "I'm off to see my cello player," she couldn't help but giggle like a schoolgirl. "I know I said he was a terrible lay, but I'm willing to give him another chance to redeem himself. Besides, he's laying the charm on pretty hard. He even mailed me my old sunglasses without me asking for them." Charlie reached into her bag and put on the original dark shades she had left behind during her one-night stand.

Maggie smiled, thinking how refreshing it was to see her best friend genuinely gushing over someone.

Charlie continued, "I'm kinda breaking all my rules. But I figured, hey, I only live once and maybe it's time I find someone special. Like you did with Dom."

Maggie embraced her friend tightly. "Oh, Charlie, you deserve all the love and then some." She clasped Charlie's delicate face between her hands and touched their foreheads together.

"Break all your rules tonight but be safe."

"I'm always safe." The jingle of Charlie's text message broke their embrace.

"I better run, the car he sent for me is downstairs." Charlie pursed her pink-colored lips together and whistled to grab Pete's attention. He happily obeyed and brought his harness over, readily waiting to get strapped in as if he were going for his usual leisurely walk.

"It's a good thing this cello player is a dog lover. There is no way I was ever leaving Pete behind," Charlie mused.

"That's a good thing," Maggie turned away, not sure how to respond. Her thoughts raced with the contemplation of confessing that she wasn't sure if she would ever see her best friend again. Maggie may be reckless, but she wasn't an idiot. She knew that meeting her mother and brother at the same spot where her mother was nearly killed only meant a set-up. She felt as if she were walking blindfolded into a cave, not knowing what was waiting inside. She knew one thing—she had to retrieve the little black book from Jesse.

The pit of her stomach twisted and turned with the anxiety that was swimming in her gut. She began to feel nauseous as she swallowed the puke that was threatening to erupt. Before she could sit for a few seconds, Charlie interrupted her thoughts.

"Hey...you'll be here when I get back, right?" Charlie's voice sounded a bit concerned, almost as if she knew Maggie wasn't going to be there when she returned. Her words sliced open a wound in Maggie's heart.

"Even if I'm not, just know that I'll come back soon, I promise."

"I hope so. It was nice having you around."

Without exchanging further words, Charlie grinned and waved goodbye. She shut the door behind her, only to turn around and silently press her hand on the knob, second-guessing her exit. She rested her forehead on the wooden door as Pete whimpered, then heavily sighed as if her thoughts were weighing upon her like boulders.

"I'm sure she'll be okay, Pete."

CHAPTER 18
THE FAMOUS O'RILEY'S

O'Riley's Pub received an upgrade. Last Lucifer remembered the joint had been trashed to near extinction. Although it had been hanging on loose wooden boards and nails prior to Angel and Castus' semi-war, there was no denying that O'Riley's should have been condemned. However, it made a miraculous recovery and the place appeared modernized and cozy, no longer attracting the neighborhood drunks and off-duty cops but a different class of people.

Lucifer and Camila sat at the far corner of the bar watching humans as they strolled in for their evening gatherings. The bar extended nearly to the dining area but cut off before the restroom entrance. Flat-screen TVs surrounded the walls displaying old reruns of boxing matches and a variety of different sports. The aroma of fried chicken wings and fries caused Camila to stare at the man sitting three stools away from her. She nearly salivated at the presentation of his plate.

"Would you like me to order you some food?" whispered Lucifer in her ear as he put his arm around her shoulder.

"No, I refuse to get chicken between my teeth before I meet my son. A drink will do just fine."

"As you wish," he replied as he summoned the bartender.

A tall, dark-haired male with a gleaming smile approached them without hesitation.

"What can I get for you two?"

"A Manhattan for the lady and a bourbon on the rocks for me." Lucifer placed his clip of Benjamins on the bar.

"Sure thing!" The bartender beamed as he quickly made their drinks and sat them on the table, working faster than usual for an expected fat tip.

Camila sipped her drink and folded her hands delicately on the top of the bar, patiently waiting. Lucifer drowned out the chatter of the patrons with magic and focused on his woman. She wasn't wearing her usual extravagant gowns or skin-tight bustier tops. Tonight, she sported a black jumpsuit with an open V-neck and golden lace trimming on the sleeves and cleavage. Her dark eyeliner traced the edges of her deep blue eyes perfectly. She pressed her glossy, fire-engine-red lips together and caressed her shimmering diamond choker before she slowly turned her head to stare back at Lucifer.

"What?" she asked with just a touch of uncertainty laced within her voice.

"You seem nervous. Beautiful as ever, but nervous," was his dry comment.

"I am a little nervous. I haven't decided how I will approach Jesse yet. I can't just walk up to him and say, 'Hola, soy tu madre."

"Well, why not?" chuckled Lucifer, enchanted by yet another of her moods—*especially her Spanish accent.*

Camila shook her head helplessly and took another sip of her drink, seemingly to calm her nerves.

"Darling, whatever you decide to say, you best think quickly. Your boy just walked in."

At that moment, a tall, blonde with black-rimmed glasses

appeared at the other side of the bar. One would have guessed he was a sleek-looking professor in his black turtleneck and a camel-colored peacoat, or perhaps a blonde Clark Kent. He casually removed his coat and draped it over the stool next to him as if holding the spot for someone. He ordered a beer and pulled out his cell phone, texting away as if it were important.

"Do you think he's messaging Maggie?" asked Camila.

"I'm sure he is. I've probably sent Maggie too far back in time. I would say they haven't even spoken yet." Lucifer cautiously glared at Jesse.

"So, what does this mean, Sire?"

"This means we resume as planned. As my father always says, 'Everything is as it should be.'"

"I'm on it," Camila shot off her stool and clicked and clattered to the other end of the bar, turning heads in the process. She wedged herself in between Jesse and the empty stool as she forcefully shoved her arm against his, pretending to get the bartender's attention.

Jesse spun his head in annoyance; he was nearly knocked off his seat as though the bar was overcrowded. He looked around and realized she could have stood anywhere but, instead, decided to squeeze herself next to him. Camila gently smiled, but Jesse ignored her and brought his attention back to his Smartphone.

"Whatever you're reading, it must be very important," she stated over the loud conversations surrounding them. The pub was beginning to fill with a crowd.

"Kind of," he answered, sending his last message before he acknowledged the beautiful woman standing before him.

Camila waved her long, dark hair over her shoulder; she locked her blue eyes on Jesse. He stared back at her, appearing to wait for her to say something, but she stared blankly as if she were starstruck.

"You have my eyes," she finally blurted out.

"I guess so," shrugged Jesse, seeming puzzled as if the woman before him was very odd. "Blue eyes are very common these days; everyone has them."

"And you have his sense of humor," she marveled at the irony.

"I'm sorry, whose sense of humor? Do we know each other?" Jesse finally drew all of his attention to Camila who was now seated on his peacoat.

"We do know each other. Would you believe me if I told you I'm your mother?" she stated fearlessly.

It was as if everything around Jesse had stopped. His focus became solely on the strange woman conversing with him.

"My what?"

"Your mother."

Jesse shook his head in disbelief, "I don't know who sent you or what kind of sick game this is, but my real mother is dead."

"Dead?" Camila placed her hands on her choker, seeming confused.

"Yes, dead. She disappeared several years ago. Besides, I'm sure my real mom would look a hell of a lot older than you."

"So, you believe she's dead, yet, you never stopped searching for her or your father?" Camila was willing to push every line to get Jesse to believe her.

"Who sent you?" He drew closer to her with a threatening glare.

Before she could answer, Lucifer manifested next to them, interrupting their conversation before things became heated.

"Hey, mate, I take it from your displeased stare that she broke the news to you?"

"Who are you?" Jesse vexed.

"I'm your Uncle Lucifer."

"FUCK!" Jesse breathed heavily as he tried to make a beeline for the exit door. He was making no attempt to stick around for this family reunion. Lucifer bolted him back down on the stool with one hard force of magic.

"Are you alright, Jesse? You're turning extremely pale." Camila asked with truly concerned eyes.

"Is this the part when you kill me?" His voice quivered as his fingers twitched nervously.

"Kill you? No. Never," replied Camila, she rested a gentle hand on his shoulder.

"This is the part when I take you home."

"Take me home? Where?"

"Back to the Underworld," chimed Lucifer, letting him know his time on Earth was up!

Jessie appeared to nearly faint in his chair. There was a slight pause before he could form actual words.

"Hell? Absolutely not! Not even over my dead body."

"We can take you that way, too, if you prefer," Lucifer chuckled. "But I may have to fight Eden for your soul, and I don't have the bandwidth for that right now. We would rather have you come willingly."

Jesse's bones could be heard rattling with fear. "I.. I... I can't," was all he could mutter.

"I believe you can. And I know just the person to help convince you that the Underworld is where you belong. There is someone I would like you to meet," Lucifer stated, a stern expression crossing his face.

The dim lights inside O'Riley's blinked off and on like a strobe light. Within the flashes, the loud cafeteria conversations went deadly silent. It was like watching a scene transition from one storyline to the next.

All the patrons had disappeared, leaving them as the only occupants inside the pub. Jesse was finally able to stand up from his stool, he looked around the dancing lights, trying to avoid any surprise attack. He pressed his back against the wall, a look of sheer panic danced across his features.

Glass rained down upon them like a cascading waterfall as the flat-screen TVs shattered into confetti. Jesse cowered on the floor, holding his hands above his head to protect himself from harm's way. Most of the liquor bottles on the shelves exploded, and the floorboards underneath their feet shook as if a high-magnitude earthquake was passing beneath them. After a few trembling moments, things began to steady and the lights were turned up to a fluorescent state.

Before them stood a blue-eyed, slender male, nearly identical to Jesse. His dark, blonde hair sat straight on his shoulders. His nose was narrow, and his upper lip was thinner than the lower.

The scent of sulfur filled the room as Jesse choked and coughed from the strength of the fumes. Once he regained his composure, he stared at the male in confusion as if he were staring at himself twenty years into the future.

Camila gasped at the sight of the man. Lucifer was stopping at nothing to take Jesse back to the Underworld, which was all she ever wanted. She stared at her man with renewed admiration.

The male figure never moved from his position, as if he was waiting for his next command. His hands remained pinned to his sides, and his eyes shifted aimlessly around in a zombie-like manner. His skin was as pale as snow, and his dark grey suit appeared two sizes too large.

Lucifer walked up to the male and placed a comforting hand on his shoulder, signaling the end of his hard feelings.

"Good to see you, nephew. Jesse, I want to introduce you to your father, Castus!"

Jesse stared at the man who seemed dead inside. His eyes nearly watered.

"What's wrong with him?" Jesse's voice quavered with gloomy concern.

"Everything. Let's have a chat." Lucifer summoned a bottle of bourbon and three glasses over to where they were originally sitting. The bottle magically traversed the space as if it were taking a dog for a casual walk in the park.

Camila grabbed the floating bottle and began pouring their drinks while Jesse walked over to a lifeless Castus. He stared into his eyes and waved his hands in front of his face, looking for a sign of existence. He didn't even receive a blink in return.

"He won't move. He has no soul," Lucifer said as he sipped on his whisky.

"What happened to his soul?"

"I took it. As punishment for smuggling your mother out of the Underworld," Lucifer gestured toward Camila.

A stunned expression crossed Jesse's face. "There is no way *he* could have kidnapped my mother out of Hell. My mother was a human already living on Earth." Jesse furiously pointed to a mindless Castus as he tried debating his facts with Lucifer.

Camila threw back her bourbon, not bothering to recap her details of the events that had transpired. It was as if she grew tired of repeating herself. She was leaving the convincing up to her sire.

Lucifer mentally pushed Jesse's bottom onto a stool again and nailed him there.

"Alright, let me get you up to speed. It's obvious that you're lost. Your mother, Angel, is really your aunt. That arse standing there foolishly," Lucifer pointed to Castus, "is your stubborn father. Those two siblings were brought here to this 'famous pub' to collect a rogue angel..."

"Things went sideways and he died," interjected Jesse, speeding up the conversation. "Yeah, yeah, I already know that. Mom told me the story about her brother's final death."

Camila, who had seemed extremely disinterested as she yawned during their friendly banter, finally chimed in. "But he didn't die. He landed in the Underworld with us. That's where we met, and during a moment of weakness, we made you."

She stared at Castus as if reminiscing on their time together. "He wanted nothing more than the best for you. So with Jack's help, he smuggled me out. But Lucifer came for me. To protect you, I left you behind so that I could endure the suffering for the both of us. Fortunately, Sire welcomed me back with open arms. My biggest regret was leaving you."

Jesse gazed into Camila's ice-blue eyes as if they were validating every detail of her story. She raised her hand and softly caressed his cheek.

"I am your mother, and I never stopped thinking about you," Camila's words were smooth and sincere like a lost mother finally able to release her deepest fears.

Jesse's breathing accelerated upon hearing the sudden truth about his parents. His blank face suddenly flushed red with fury as he cussed Jack's name.

"JACK! That fucking bastard. He knew about you this entire time and never breathed a word. I've been searching for my parents for years, and he stood there and watched me suffer from the never-ending questions that tormented me." Jesse grew more furious by the minute.

"Maggie knew, too. Why didn't she tell you?" Lucifer couldn't help but add fuel to the fire.

"She did?" Jesse asked, puzzled.

"But of course. She visited the Underworld. We talked over drinks and pizza. I'm surprised she didn't share this with you. Aren't you two close?"

"She visited Hell? What the fuck!" Jesse couldn't hide his poker face any longer. The information he received struck a nerve. Lucifer enjoyed watching Jesse's burst of outrage under his calm and collected facade. It gave him a natural high.

"That explains everything. Her walking around like an open target when we were supposed to be hiding, her irresponsible behavior. She was always more demon than angel. She must have known you would never touch her." Jesse shook his head in disappointment, unknowingly feeding into Lucifer's web of manipulation.

"I would have never touched any of you. After all, we're family." Lucifer reassured.

Jesse glanced over at Castus with a bleeding heart.

"How can I help my dad?" He drew his attention to the man he'd been searching for nearly his entire life.

"That all depends on what you're willing to do, Jesse," Lucifer responded.

"Come back with us to the Underworld." Camila held her hands out in the hope that Jesse would accept her invitation. He hesitated then firmly locked his hands with hers. The gesture brought tears to her deep blue eyes as she squeezed Jesse's hands, making it known that this time around she was not letting go.

"My only condition is that you give my father back his soul," Jesse commanded.

Lucifer grinned at the unexpected twist in the deal. He had planned to propose it the other way around and also ask for the little black book. But Jesse's idea was even better.

"That would work!" responded Lucifer, picking up Jesse's camel-colored peacoat from the stool not before sneakily shaking it and making all the contents fall out of its pockets. The little black book, along with cigarettes and a lighter, clattered to the floor.

"Oh, my apologies, how clumsy of me," Lucifer smirked.

"It's fine." Jesse responded as he and Camila picked up his belongings.

Camila grabbed the little black book and handed it to Lucifer. He quickly flipped through the pages, excited to finally have it in his possession.

"Hey, that's mine." Jesse tried to reach for the book, but Lucifer shooed him away.

"Actually, I believe it is mine. My name is written inside. Or have you not noticed that?"

"Whatever. You can have it. Just give me my dad's soul."

"Very well," Lucifer placed the book inside his suit jacket and rubbed his hands together. It was almost as if he were rolling an invisible ball in his hands until a tiny, white twinkle appeared. He expanded the orb to the size of a single grape and delicately held it between his thumb and index finger as it pulsed like a baby's beating heart. The soul illuminated the entire room as if the sun suddenly appeared indoors.

Jesse's eyes widened at the sight of the most beautiful angelic light he'd ever seen. His deep blue eyes remained mesmerized by its power, not even realizing that Lucifer was handing the soul over to him.

Camila slightly nudged Jesse back into reality. "I believe Sire would like you to do the honors."

"What am I supposed to do?" Jesse hesitantly reached for the pulsing twinkle. His initial reaction was to pluck it from Lucifer's fingers, but he opted to open his hand instead and have him gently place it in the center of his warm palm.

"Place this in the center of his chest. It will find its own way back home," Lucifer directed.

Jesse took a deep breath and slowly walked over to the zombie-like Castus, making sure he covered his left hand over the right so as not to drop the soul. Camila stood silently next to Lucifer and intertwined her fingers with his. He gripped her hand tightly as she leaned her head on his shoulder.

Crunching glass and creaking floorboards were all that could be heard with each slow and steady step that Jesse took to approach Castus. His eyes focused on Castus' blank expression and slouched posture. He scanned him from head to toe with a look of guilt and pity all at once. He stood toe to toe with his father, desperately holding back tears that wanted to escape like a broken dam. He paused for what seemed like an eternity as he stared at the man he longed to meet. With shaky hands, Jesse slowly raised his right palm to Castus' boney chest and watched as the pulsing twinkle floated without direction and inserted itself into its home.

Rays of blinding light shot out from the center of Castus' chest. The brightness was so intense that Jesse, Camila, and Lucifer raised their arms to shield themselves from near blindness.

Gasping, followed by deep breaths and simultaneous screams, echoed throughout the bar. The sensation of his soul finding its place back inside the body caused Castus to drop to the floor like a ragdoll.

Jesse quickly rushed to his side as Camila remained glued to Lucifer's hip.

"Dad? Dad? Are you alright?" Jesse checked his pulse and breathing, but everything appeared normal. "WHAT'S HAPPENING?" he frantically asked Lucifer over his shoulder, never taking his eyes from Castus.

"You have to give him a moment. The soul needs to work its angelic magic," replied Lucifer, feeling bored. He had what he wanted and was ready to split.

Castus' body shimmered and gleamed with a magical essence that quickly disappeared. His eyelids fluttered as they struggled to open. When he finally came to, he glared at the face that was nearly identical to his. He locked eyes with Jesse as a look of bewilderment crossed over his face.

"Dad?" Jesse whispered.

Castus remained silent but blinked rapidly as if trying to wake up from a terrible dream.

"It's me, Dad. Your son, Jesse," he implored, unsure of exactly how much time he had left on this plane. He should have negotiated a better deal with the Devil.

Again, Castus remained silent, trying to process his surroundings. He slowly brought himself to a sitting position and looked around. Ignoring Jesse's presence, he let his hands feel the floorboards and looked up at the ceiling and back at the bar. He noticed the bright, orange and black cursive sign illuminated above the liquor shelf and nearly went faint.

"O'Riley's," were the first words that crossed his chapped, cracked lips.

On wobbly legs, Castus stood up with Jesse's help. He quickly adjusted his grey suit jacket and turned to Jesse.

"We have to save my sister. Do you know where I can find her?"

"Castus, Angel doesn't need your saving," Lucifer interjected, approaching a nearly insane Castus.

"Uncle!" He turned to see a beautiful Camila standing observant by the bar.

"Camila!" He walked past Lucifer and went to welcome Camila with open arms, but she extended her arm and stopped him short as if he were contagious.

"Camila, it's me. Castus," he pleaded.

"What's wrong with him?" Jesse asked Lucifer.

"He's not fully there yet. It may take a few minutes before his brain finishes rewiring. When the soul is outside of the body for too long, the brain tends to take a vacation."

"What does that even mean? That his brain may permanently turn to mush?" inquired Jesse.

"I didn't have his soul long enough for that to happen. Do you really think I'm that evil?" The family's addiction to sarcasm fairly dripped from Lucifer's sensual, full lips.

Jesse shrugged and looked at his father who was now on the floor, arms wrapped around Camila's stilettos as he begged her to talk to him.

"Sire, get him before I start kicking sense into his empty skull," Camila threatened. She was like a goddess carved from a block of solid ice.

"Castus, Bloody Hell, what has gotten into you. Don't embarrass yourself." Lucifer stood him up using his magic and straightened his suit.

"Now, there is someone you need to meet, so be on your best behavior. This young, fine-looking bloke is your son. Remember, your son?" Lucifer brought Jesse closer to Castus as he glared at him for a few seconds and turned away.

"Never met him."

Jesse rolled his eyes helplessly.

"Castus, Jesse is *our* son," Camila chimed.

Castus sat at a nearby stool at the bar and picked up a half-full glass of whisky and sniffed it.

"Oh, as I said, I never met him," he replied, downing the glass.

"In that case, the family reunion is over. Jesse, it's time to go." Lucifer grabbed Camila's hand and walked a few feet away from Castus.

"Wait, we can't just leave him here. Isn't he coming, too?" Jesse expressed growing concern for his mindless father.

"No, he's staying. Someone will be coming by soon to pick him up. Which is why it's crucial we leave now." Lucifer tried to hurry things along.

"Who's coming?" Jesse turned to Camila for answers.

"Maggie. She agreed to help us. She'll know what to do." Lucifer explained half right. It was indeed, she'd agreed to help. But it was regarding the little black book, not Castus. The Prince of Darkness talked Mendulous into the exchange with Castus which he was certain he and Maggie would eventually cross paths tonight. Lucifer wanted Mendulous to see the Destroyer of Worlds with his own eyes.

His plan of retrieving the little black book, taking Castus back to the Underworld, and having Maggie and Mendulous in the same room was working. It was a win, win, across the board for him. However, there was only one thing the King of manipulation wasn't anticipating. Someone was already three steps ahead of his master plan.

"Jesse, we must leave now," demanded Camilla.

Jesse took one look at his dad and lowered his eyes in dismay. It was clear their interaction was not what he ever expected.

"It was nice to finally meet you, Dad," he said over his shoulder before joining Camila and Lucifer in a half-circle.

An oblivious Castus grinned heavily and waved them farewell like an innocent child.

Before Lucifer could disappear, two angry intimidating beings manifested within the mist of magic before them, interrupting their exit.

The short woman angrily stared at Lucifer as if she were shooting flamed daggers at his head. If looks could kill, Lucifer would have expired on sight. Without hesitation, she quickly approached him and forcefully grabbed him by the arm, showing him that she was now in charge.

"Going somewhere, dear brother." Helen's teeth clenched tightly as if she were trying to shatter them to pieces.

"Blimey!" was Lucifer's last word as he realized things had just gotten interesting.

CHAPTER 19
THE DEMON DIVIDED

Mendulous' stern baritone voice resonated fear in even the bravest of men. When he spoke, all ears were open and all eyes, whether fiery or confused, were on him.

"I hope you weren't thinking about leaving with this boy and the little black book." Lucifer could have sworn the walls themselves had trembled in fear as Mendulous spoke. "Were you not going to honor our agreement, old friend?"

"Why, Mendulous, of course, I was. Have you forgotten? I am a man of honor." Lucifer grinned from ear to ear, trying his best to lighten the mood. He pointed at Castus who was sitting at the bar, oblivious to everyone around him as he threw peanuts in the air and caught them with his mouth.

"There is Castus patiently waiting. As agreed! Now, you have to hold up to your end of the bargain. This young chap belongs to us." Lucifer pulled his arm away from Helena and patted Mendulous on the shoulder in a friendly gesture. "Good to see you all, but I must scatter. In case anyone has forgotten, I have a Hell to run. Good day!"

"You're not going ANYWHERE!" Helena furiously stomped her foot causing the floorboards underneath Lucifer to shake and rise like a mini tidal wave. Lucifer lost his footing and tripped over the rising boards, causing him to land hard on his hands and knees like a dog on all fours.

"Fuck, I hate when she does that," he said to Camila as she desperately ran over to him to help him back up on his feet.

"Who are they?" Jesse asked Lucifer, trying to hide the quaver in his voice.

"That is your grannie and Mendulous, the Hand of my Father."

"Whoa…this is unbelievable. Angel told me all about her parents and the Hand of Father. I can't believe they are actually here!" Jesse went from concern to excitement within seconds. "This is turning into a family reunion."

"Don't get so excited, she isn't the most pleasant of angels." Lucifer couldn't escape the Debbie Downer tone in his voice.

With a swift glide, Helena moved next to Castus who was now licking the salt out of the small empty peanut dish without a care in the world.

"Oh, hello!" Castus ignorantly smiled at his mother and reached over for another dish of peanuts. "Peanuts?," he offered.

Helena irately slapped the peanut dish out of his hand and drew closer to his face, examining his features. She gazed deeply into his pale-blue eyes and slowly ran her fingers through his short blond hair. The faint scent of decay and sulfur reeked from his pores. Castus continued to eye her in return, still smiling like an unaware child. She noticed one fine detail about him while caressing his head, something no one else would have noticed—the two tiny lumps that were peeking out from his skull and hiding under his ruffled hair.

Still holding the look of death on her face, Helena glided back over toward Lucifer. She grounded her feet and eyed him as if he were the only one standing in the room. Before he could utter a word, she quickly sucker-punched him in the gut. The punch hit him like a lightning bolt to the intestines. His eyes teared from the impact as he hunched over to block any more blows to the midsection.

Helena then swiftly locked her arm around his neck and tightened him in a headlock.

Mendulous chuckled at the comedic scene. It was as if he were watching them wrestle as they did in their childhood, except this time Helena was not holding back.

"WHERE IS MY SON?" She yanked Lucifer's head lower and lower, nearly bringing him down to the ground. She tightened her grip around his neck and squeezed with all her might. Lucifer could feel his breath diminishing as he gasped.

"STOP IT!" Camila's screams were only temporary as her fight instinct kicked in. She instantly intervened by jumping on Helena's back, sending blows of fury to her face and arm in a vicious attempt to get her to release her grip. But Helena's magic was stronger than she had anticipated. With one quick jolt, Helena sent ripples of electric shock waves through her body, causing Camila to convulse as though stung with a high-voltage stun gun.

Jesse watched in disbelief as he witnessed his mother fall to the floor and collapse like a ragdoll. He kneeled to her side out of instinct and checked for a pulse and heartbeat as the chaos continued around them.

"YOU ASSHOLE! Do you think I don't know my own son? That thing there has horns and reeks of rotting death," Helena shouted, not loosening her grip. It was going to take an army of angels to break up their sibling fight.

Mendulous turned his attention to the imposter Castus, who shot up from his stool and hastily threw the barstool at Mendulous, causing more of a distraction.

Jesse frantically dragged an unconscious Camila and hid beneath a nearby table. His wits were smart enough to tell him to stay away from a celestial vs. demon bar fight.

Imposter Castus shed his human figure and turned into a red-faced, blood-hungry, raging demon in the blink of an eye. He stood a few feet taller than Mendulous, and his strength was slightly stronger. The two fought mercilessly like two gladiators in the Colosseum.

Seeing Camila still unconscious brought out Lucifer's inner devil. With all his might, he lifted Helena off her feet and went for an unexpected body slam. The floorboards cracked beneath them, and the room rattled as these two celestial beings geared up to go blow for blow. Helena lay in pain for less than a second. She wasn't easily intimidated; battling her little brother was a walk in the park for her. She speedily rose to her feet and magically manifested a bow staff in the palm of her hands.

"I've been waiting for this moment for a very long time, little brother. Come on!" Helena extended her hand and waved her opponent forward, daring him to come closer.

Lucifer's hollow, devil eyes pierced through her as he cracked his neck and adjusted his suit. He readied himself into his famous warrior stance and balled his fist, conjuring all his power to his fingertips. "With pleasure, dear sister," his voice was filled with an undying hatred.

BOOM!!! The entire fiasco came to a screeching halt when the front doors to O'Riley's Pub were blown off their hinges. Maggie, Angel, Master Anu, and Keiko all charged into the bar. Tables, chairs, and stools flew across the room, as did the rest of the demons and celestials.

"JESSE!" Angel called out, her tone panic-stricken.

A coughing Jesse crawled out from underneath the scattered tables and chairs and gave his proof of life.

"MOM, I'm over here. I'm okay. I think," he struggled to say between his coughs. Through the dust and debris, Keiko rushed to his aid and walked him over to Angel. She handed him his glasses that she found broken and with a cracked lens on the floor.

"Where is Lucifer?" demanded Master Anu.

"I don't know. Probably buried under all this mess," replied Jesse, still hacking up dust from his throat.

Maggie and Keiko surveyed the perimeter and found Camila unconscious, lying on top of a banged-up Helena.

"Get this demon OFF OF ME," Helena commanded, extremely annoyed, trying her hardest to push Camila's dead weight from her chest along with the tabletop that pinned them together like a ham and cheese sandwich.

Maggie mentally flicked the tabletop and Camila as if they were annoying bugs and helped her to her feet. Helena nearly wobbled over but righted herself in a cool and collective manner.

"Who are you?" Maggie addressed Helena, ready to attack her if necessary.

"That's your grandmother," Angel replied, glancing at her mother from head to toe. "Hello, Mother."

"Daughter, Eden must be shining its light upon me. I'm so happy to see you." She embraced Angel awkwardly as if she wasn't sure what to do at that very moment.

Angel returned the hug, knowing it was exactly what she needed, her mother. She quickly broke away as soon as she saw her old friend Camila finally regaining consciousness.

"Uggh, my ears," Camila moaned, wiping streams of warm liquid that were gushing from her ears, then shuddered at the sight of blood on her hands.

"Camila, are you alright?" Angel bent beside her to examine her wounds.

"Angel? You're here." Camila's eyes widened. "I...I...I had no choice..."

"Stop!" Angel interrupted. "Maggie already told us everything. You don't have to explain." She half-smiled and held out her hand to assist Camila and to also indicate that she had no ill feelings.

Camila hesitated before she finally planted her bloody palm into the helping hand.

Keiko sized up Camila then whispered into Master Anu's ear.

"I'll keep my eye on her. I'm positive the devil's lover cannot be trusted."

He nodded in agreement.

From within the rubble of more broken chairs and tables, emerged Lucifer and Mendulous. The two stared at each other for less than a second, then charged toward one another like two angry bulls.

Maggie, feeling like she'd already had enough, rapidly morphed into her demon side and jumped in between the two powerful beings.

"ENOUGH!!!" The thickness in her voice shook the fixtures on the walls and caused cement particles to fall from the ceiling.

"This shit needs to STOP! I'm fucking tired. This is your chance to talk this out. We're all here, even my grandmother. Just explain what the fuck you want already, Uncle Lucifer, so we can all move on with our lives," Maggie pleaded.

"Do you think it's that easy, child? He's caused so many problems it will take his entire existence to come back from it. We owe him nothing." Mendulous straightened his stance and pressed down on his black leather warrior tunic. The muscles in his arms seemed to pulse from the rage he held inside in wanting to pulverize Lucifer.

"You must be Mendulous, the mighty Hand of Father," Maggie walked a little closer to him to get a better look at what she was up against. She stared into his chocolate eyes and examined the needle-sized warrior scar on his left cheek.

"Uncle Lucifer has told me so. Much. About you." She walked around him as she spoke and nearly touched the deep, long warrior scar on his right arm that stretched from the top of his shoulder down to the tip of his elbow. The scar was a vivid reminder of the many wars he'd fought and survived in the name of Eden.

"And don't you think *you* need to redeem yourself, as well? Erasing an innocent girl's memories and leaving her in the hands of a demon. I'm the product of that situation," Maggie schooled. "I'm *your* mistake."

Mendulous looked past Maggie, maintaining a hardened expression.

"LOOK AT ME!" Her eyes turned a bloody red as the purple veins on her temple expanded down to her cheeks. She wanted him to see her for what she was, a ferocious demon who would never have the opportunity to step foot into Eden and rejoice with her family, thanks to *his* careless mistake.

Mendulous stared into Maggie's eyes, his stern gaze never disappearing.

"I saved Angel."

"Sure, you did," Maggie stated sarcastically.

"I don't blame you, Mend. What's done is done. I just want Castus back," Angel spoke up, reassuring him of her willingness to move on from the past.

"He never forgave himself for what he did. And for a long time, I didn't forgive him either. Your words mean everything to him, Angel." Helena gently touched Mendulous' strong arm in confidence.

"Now, Brother, where is my son?" Helena furrowed her eyebrows, getting back to business.

It was at that moment the huge, red-faced demon erupted from behind the bar. He busted through the wood as though it were a piece of thin paper. Maggie, Master Anu, and Keiko all charged at it like soldiers running into battle. However, Lucifer instantly poofed it away with a wave of his fingers and brought it kneeling by his side like a well-trained lion.

Everyone turned to face Lucifer who had the demon gripped by one hand. The demon seemed to be hanging its head in shame.

"This is Castus." Lucifer reminded everyone again for the millionth time.

"That thing is not my son," retorted Helena.

"You're lying. He made me give that demon Castus' soul," said Jesse.

Camila rushed over to Lucifer's side, hoping to calm the situation.

"Tranquilo, everyone, please. That is Castus. Just give Sire a chance to fix the situation." Camila darted a worried glance over to Lucifer. It was obvious it was time to reveal the truth.

The floorboards rattled beneath everyone's feet for a few seconds as tainted, thick, black smoke emerged from the cracks of Hell and consumed the huge red demon. As the tar-colored smoke slowly made its way back through the crevices, the clearance unveiled a pale-faced Castus.

Helena was the first to rush beside him. She clasped his head in between her hands as Lucifer set him free from his grip.

"Castus? Castus, my darling son, is this really you?"

The rotten scent of death and sulfur no longer lingered in the air.

"Mom?" he whispered in response. "Mom, what are you doing in Hell?"

"You're not in Hell. Not anymore, my son."

Salty tears of joy streamed down Angel's cheeks as she joined her mother and wrapped her delicate arms around Castus, nearly squeezing the breath out of him.

"It's really you. I can't believe it's really you."

"Angel? HA! HAHA! This is... Oh my... HA...HA." Castus was so overwhelmed with emotion, he didn't know how to respond.

Angel and Helena slowly helped him up. He took a moment to fully observe his surroundings and take in his environment. O'Riley's Pub was the place that started his nightmare and hopefully where it would end. Castus nodded at Mendulous and shot Lucifer a dirty look.

"I will never forgive you; you are no uncle of mine." He said with much disdain. "You took everything from me. Even the woman I loved."

"Castus, you betrayed my rules and my world. What did you think would happen? And, for the record, Camila was never your woman. She was your mere fling who got bored with a boy and found comfort in the arms of a real man." Lucifer put his arm around Camila as if he had won first place in a grand contest.

Hurt and jealousy washed over Castus' face. He couldn't hide his expression even if he tried. It was obvious even to the blind that Lucifer got under his skin.

"Your punishment was the harshest. You took my soul!" Castus balled his fist tightly in indignation.

"That I did. But I gave it back, and your son over there did the honors," Lucifer pointed to Jesse who was silently watching the drama unfold next to Master Anu and Keiko.

"YOU gave me my soul then possessed me with a demon. WHY? Why the FUCK are you so vindictive?" Castus was going on an angry rant, letting his emotions flare out at anyone that wronged him.

Castus swiftly turned to Camila and insulted her as if she were the gum stuck to the bottom of his loafers. "Thank you for making my first encounter with our son a huge disappointment, you despicable waste of space."

With quick feet, Lucifer glided up to Castus while everyone drew closer to protect him.

"Watch your mouth when you talk to her before I send you back to bloody Hell without your FUCKING balls," Lucifer threatened.

"Try it, dear brother. And I will rain a war against the Underworld like no other," Helena shot back as she positioned herself in a fighting stance.

"I already love your mother," Keiko whispered to Angel, clearly entertained.

Lucifer glanced at all the hardened faces around him. Seeing that he was outnumbered, he stood back beside Camila and firmly held her hand.

"Time to go, love. This party has become rather dull. Jesse, come along," he called out.

The whispers grew louder among the group as Jesse slowly stepped forward. Castus rushed over to him and quickly embraced him, not letting him go. Tears rolled down Jesse's cheeks as he finally received the embrace he had longed for.

"My son, what is going on?" whispered Castus.

"I made a trade. Your life for mine. I'm going with Camila."

"No. No, you can't. I fought for you to never go there. I will go back. I will suffer a thousand more years if it means I get to save you." Castus wiped the tears streaming down Jesse's face. The moment of sacrifice was hurting the hearts of everyone there.

"I don't care what deal Jesse made with you. He's not going anywhere." Master Anu declared with authority, but it seemed to fall on deaf ears.

"Ohhh," Lucifer turned to Master Anu, acknowledging him for the first time. "I almost forgot you were here. I didn't think Angel let you speak."

"I speak on my own terms very well, thank you." Anu retorted, appearing to fall victim to Lucifer's witty insults.

"Then listen here, Vampire. A deal with the devil cannot be broken. There is nothing you or Eden can do about it since they have also agreed to the same deal." replied Lucifer, flashing his eyes towards Mendulous.

"It's alright, Master Anu," chimed Helena. It's the double-cross we've been expecting. My brother agreed to release Castus and give Eden the little black book in exchange for Jesse. However, he never intended on giving us the book. I always knew that. And he needed to find a way to get to Jesse. The only way he was going to accomplish that was by some way, somehow, bypassing Angel." The room went silent and the air grew thick as Helena looked at each hardened and confused expression before her.

"He used me," Maggie finally answered as she put the puzzle together. "Lucifer used me to get to Jesse. He brought me to the Underworld, and fed me stories about the power of the book. He's been following me, he knew where Jesse would be because of me. I unknowingly led him here. But our agreement was for him to leave Jesse behind as long as I got him the book."

If a coin accidently dropped from the distance it would be heard as Maggie momentarily paused to jog her memory. She stared towards Lucifer's direction, "But you never actually agreed to leave

Jesse behind. Your exact last words were, *"we will let Jesse decide where he wants to be."* You conned him. Just like you tricked the rest of us." Maggie couldn't help but to feel played. "You brought us all here together so we could wallow in our sins and guilt. We would have the joy of having Castus back but then suffer the heartache of losing Jesse. By possessing Castus you knew he would never be able to enter Eden. He would be just like me, an abomination."

Hearing her say those words out loud for the first time nearly caused a tear to shed from the corner of her eyes. However, her anger wouldn't allow her to shatter to a million pieces in front of the man she wanted to kill on site, Lucifer.

"You would have caused a vicious cycle of family hatred, just to fulfill yours and Camila's selfish desires." Angel added to Maggie's unrealing of the final truth.

Lucifer smirked, as if seeming pleased to have conned everyone around him. He inhaled deeply and clapped his hands together proud and loud as if congratulating Maggie for finally getting something right in her life.

"Here, here, Magdalena. Who would have known, that you, out of all people would have figured it out. You're not a twit after all," he slyly smiled.

Maggie's orbs glowed a fiery red as she tried to control the rage that was burning her heart. Keiko gently placed a hand on Maggie's slender shoulder hoping it would ease the heat coursing through her body.

Helena stepped forward, "All this, and yet, you want us to believe that you won't use the little black book for your own games."

"You'll just have to trust me then, dear sister," winked Lucifer.

"I was never good at trusting you, my dearest brother." Helena walked toward Camila admiring her beauty. "You're like Helen of Troy, causing all sorts of wars."

A surprise expression washed over Camila's face. "You know Helen?"

"Don't we all?" smirked Helena. Without warning, she quickly shoved Camila toward Mendulous as hard and fast as she could. A startled Camila went flying into Mendulous' strong arms as he tightly held her in a bear hug and vanished into thin air, leaving nothing behind but white, floating, angel feathers.

Everything happened within seconds. Lucifer didn't have a chance to react. It was as if time was against him, and things moved with lightning speed.

"WHAT DID YOU DO?" Lucifer rushed Helena, knocking her to the floor. His devil face and his hands glowed a bright red.

Helena flipped herself into a fighting position.

"She's in Eden. Since we will never see the little black book, you will never see the love of your life. Isn't revenge a bitch!"

"Bring. HER. BACK!" Lucifer roared. He pointed his fiery hand toward Castus and cocked it back. "The BLOODY HELL WITH YOU!" He shot a large thunderbolt at him as if he were the root of all problems. Angel quickly jumped in the way to protect him.

Master Anu, using his Vampire speed, intercepted her and took the bolt to the chest instead. His chest glowed from the inside as he exploded into heavy ashes.

The sounds of Keiko's screams echoed throughout the room. Angel's face was covered in black ash as she landed hard on her bottom. She frantically wiped her face, and her hands shook uncontrollably at the sight of what used to be Anu.

"NOOO!!!" Maggie, feeling nothing but rage flowing through her veins, bellowed a battle cry and hurtled into Lucifer. They bashed through two cement walls with Keiko, in demon form, racing behind them. Before she could catch up, they disappeared into a smoke-filled void.

CHAPTER 20
MY MISTAKE!

The suffocating smell that saturated the air was the result of ash and despair that circulated throughout the room. Angel sat silently on her cream-colored couch in a catatonic state, her gaze remaining fixated on her tar-colored knuckles and fingertips that encased her trembling hands. It was as if she was reliving Master Anu's final moments in her mind like a horror movie stuck on repeat. Neither the loud conversations nor Keiko's aggressive behavior was enough to elicit a reaction from her. Her entire being—every cell and molecule of her mind and body—appeared glued on the grey and black ashes she held tightly in her palms of what used to be her husband. Her face drew a blank as her eyelids lowered and her breathing went silent. She was completely dead inside.

Helena sat next to Angel, her gentle arms wrapped around her stiff shoulders as she desperately tried to console her as only a mother could. She whispered comforting words of sympathy and tried to ease her pain with her angelic aura, but nothing seemed to help soothe Angel's broken heart.

The living room around them was wrecked like the painful aftermath of a chaotic hurricane as Keiko raged around in her demon form, ripping the satin curtains from their rods and screaming in the twisted tongues of a long-dead language. She smashed everything she could get her claw-like hands on. End tables were turned upside down, books were tossed out of windows, and anything glass was shattered into tiny pieces. Her loud wails could rupture the ears of mortal beings.

Many of the servants and V guards began peeking into the room, trying to figure out what was happening. Even the panthers ran toward the commotion.

Jesse ordered everyone away and shut the French doors in their faces, leaving the servants to their own assumptions and disbelief.

"We're going to have to find a way to snap mom out of this and calm Keiko down. We have to address the house and break the news about Master Anu and Maggie."

Before Jesse could say another word, a grey, marble lamp swooshed past his head, smashing into large fragments and chipping the cement wall behind him. His neck cracked, and he nearly suffered whiplash as he turned to look at what could have been his just barely missed head.

"THAT'S MY FATHER. THAT'S MY FATHER. DEAD! DEAD!" Keiko repeated in her furious, slithering demon voice. Her grief had finally circled back to a language that everyone could understand. Her words were never in full sentences; it was like trying to make sense out of a three-year-old's dialogue.

When there was nothing else to throw, smash, or destroy, Keiko resorted to punching the concrete walls until her knuckles bled and tiny fragments of paint began to peel away. She cursed under her breath as she continued to jab the wall away as if it was her personal punching bag and she was training for a championship fight.

Castus stood three feet away from Keiko and examined her like she was a complicated puzzle. She hissed at him and blew tar-like smoke from her nostrils causing him to flinch backward and bump into Jesse, nearly knocking him over.

"I wouldn't stand too close if I were you," warned Jesse.

"Sorry. I kinda got that!" Castus straightened his blazer. "She's not like any of the demons in the Underworld. Are you sure she's a demon?"

"Master Anu made that assessment. Maybe she isn't from the Underworld. Maybe she's from another dimension. Who knows!" Jesse shrugged his shoulders, brushing off the comment.

"Perhaps," replied Castus, keeping a close eye on Keiko, "but I know for a fact she doesn't belong to the Underworld. From the color of her purplish skin to the skunk-like scent of her smoke, she's not one of them."

Jesse glanced at Keiko, making mental notes about her different demon characteristics. He was interrupted by Helena who brought everyone back to the matter at hand.

"We can deal with the demon later. What are we going to do about Angel? I know that no matter what I say, nothing will ever bring back Master Anu. Mendulous and I had to take Camila. It was the only way we could secure his word in getting Castus and Jesse back and never using the little black book. We didn't expect anyone to get hurt."

Jesse folded his arms tightly across his chest with an expression of deep thought.

"This isn't anyone's fault. Lucifer planned this. He got us all there —in one place. He always knew what he was doing," said Jesse. "But what he wasn't expecting was to be outwitted. Which is the reason why we all should be concerned. I don't know what will happen moving forward. But right now, we should mourn Master Anu and Maggie, as well."

Jesse casually walked through a white adjacent door in the far corner of the room. He reappeared within seconds with a bottle of aged vodka, three glasses, and a few loose pages of white paper. He poured himself a shot and offered a glass to Castus and Helena, but they politely declined.

The sound of the crisp alcohol being poured into a crystal glass captured Keiko's attention, and her ears twitched at the sound. Her nose sniffed about until it led her to the clear bottle of vodka. She picked up the empty glasses and resumed smashing them against the wall.

"Goodness, does that thing never tire?" Helena stated in annoyance.

Keiko snatched the bottle from Jesse and cocked her hand back, ready to swing it at Helena.

"Whoa, whoa, I think it's time you chill out." Jesse grabbed the bottle before further damage was done. "Throwing things at me is one thing, but let's not make it a habit to throw at others. This is exactly the fire that Lucifer wants to ignite between us. Let's put it out before it begins."

Keiko paused, making sense of Jesse's words. She morphed back to her original self and yanked the bottle of vodka from him. She cut her eyes toward Helena then poured the warm alcohol on her bleeding knuckles before gulping from the nozzle as if the liquor belonged to her.

"And this *thing* never gets tired," Keiko spat between her hard swallows.

Helena remained quiet, keeping her arms around Angel.

"What are those pages you're holding, Jesse?" Castus inquired curiously.

"Notes that Master Anu and I took about the little black book. I wanted to share them with everyone. The book may be gone, but what we have here is golden." Jesse shook the pages in his hands as if he were holding the map to the lost city of Atlantis.

Helena quickly stood and reached for the white pages. Her eyes swiftly scanned over every sentence as if she were storing data in her memory bank.

After a few seconds, she gasped and held her hand over her mouth, fear seemed to wash over her body.

"Dear Eden! You two have cracked the code to the Unknown Worlds. How did you do this?"

"Master Anu is how. He was pure genius. But that's not all we cracked. There is a way to close the Unknownworlds for good! Anu confirmed that Maggie was the key. I brought the little black book to O'Rileys to show Maggie the symbols. Stupid me, I should have brought the damn pages instead. Now with Master Anu and Maggie gone, I'll never be able to figure the rest out on my own." Jesse plopped next to Angel and rested his head in his hands, seeming defeated.

"Don't beat yourself up, son. We'll figure this out." Castus gently patted and rubbed Jesse's back, signaling that the situation would eventually get better.

Angel blinked a few times as if she was coming back to her senses. She closed her eyes tightly then opened them wide, seeming to push herself out of her catatonic state.

"The Underworld," she said, almost in a hushed whisper.

Everyone grew silent.

"Lucifer. He branded Maggie. She has a passage in and out of the Underworld. I'm sure in her rage that's where they vanished. She isn't gone forever, not like Anu." Angel held back tears.

"Then I will send Mendulous down there to help her," replied Helena, as if she just conjured a master plan. "They will fight side by side, and together they can retrieve the little black book. Lucifer can sit in the Underworld hating himself again for all eternity. If I know anything, it is that my brother is a piece of..."

"NO!" Angel fumed. She quickly stood as everyone watched her speak with ash-smudged lips. Her face was covered in dirt and her hair fell, tangled and unkempt, past her shoulders. She was in far worse condition than the rest of them.

"This needs to STOP!" Angel pleaded. "We've already lost too much. I lost my daughter, again, and now Anu. Keiko lost a father; this house lost a leader. Innocent people have died because of our shit. This is my torture. This has been nothing but mayhem since the day I got here. Uncle has gone too far. This family has gone too far. Greed, power, and revenge have been the only things fueling us, and I've had ENOUGH!"

Everyone remained silent as they hid inside their own thoughts. Angel assessed the damage in the room, shaking her head at the destruction Keiko left behind. She couldn't blame her; she would have gladly joined her if she hadn't spent the first hour in a state of shock. If only she could reverse the hands of time, if only she could go back and save everyone, then she could avoid this tragic ending. Then the idea hit her from the far left.

Angel turned to Helena and spoke with conviction and in a commanding tone that was unfamiliar to her. "As the Queen Guardian, I DEMAND to speak with Grandfather!"

"So, you're really doing this, huh?" Keiko approached Angel as she rinsed the dirt and ash from her bronze skin. It was obvious to anyone observing that it was killing her inside to wash away the last bit of Master Anu. It was even harder to watch. The porcelain, white bathroom sink stained quickly, streaked with the ultimate testament of misery and defeat.

Angel paused at the sound of Keiko's voice and quickly turned to face her. Her disheveled appearance drowned out the beauty that once radiated from her.

"Yes, I'm willing to do anything. Even if that means begging my grandfather until my knees bleed. I only need one day back in time to fix things. I can prevent Maggie from vanishing to the Underworld and reverse Anu's death," replied Angel.

"And you truly believe the Ol' Mighty man himself will grant you that wish?" Keiko shook her head from side to side, doubting Angel's plan.

"He's sent me to the past more times than I can count. I know he can."

"He can, but I'm sure he won't." Keiko tightly folded her arms across her chest.

"He will!" Angel snapped.

"How can you be so sure? Have you stopped to think about what you're asking? You're asking to be sent back in time to save your 'husband' and half-demon daughter. I'm sure in your world marrying a vampire is not even a thing, especially breeding a half-demon. Maggie will probably be looked at as an abomination."

Angel slid past Keiko, storming toward the next room. Keiko followed in her wake while continuing her rant of righteous disbelief.

"It's a waste of time. We need to face the facts. We've been defeated. We need to inform the house that my father is gone and the Vs are one leader short..."

"NEVER! As long as I'm still breathing, this isn't over." Angel pointed her finger in Keiko's face in frustration then swiftly shot it down. Keiko never flinched; she held her stern demeanor, determined to intimidate her opponent.

Angel took a deep breath, gathering every ounce of patience she had left.

"Do not tell anyone in this house that Anu and Maggie are gone. I will get them back. If word gets out about Anu's death, the Vs will be looking for someone to blame, and it might be me. You have to trust me. I'll bring them back." Angel pleaded, "Please Keiko, have faith in me."

"No, I can't do things your way anymore. Count me out!"

"KEIKO? Keiko, wait!" Angel hastened to keep up with Keiko as she double-timed toward the front entrance of the house.

A warm breeze pressed against their hardened faces as the front wooden door swung wide open with one glare of Keiko's angered eyes. She nearly stuck one foot through the threshold when Angel soared past her like a peregrine falcon and slammed the door shut with one hard push of her hand, preventing Keiko from making a mistake she may regret. The two women glared at each other. The air around them grew thin as they both seemed to anxiously wait for the other to take the first cheap shot.

"Angel, you need to move before I make you." Keiko demanded as her nostrils flared with irritation.

"I can't believe how you're just giving up on me. But not just on me—Anu and Maggie, too. How can you walk away from your family?"

"My family is dead. The final piece of my family died back at that shithole bar along with my heart," Keiko retorted.

"That's not true. I'm your family. Jesse, the Vs, Maggie. We don't want you to leave. We all need you...I need you." Unexpected tears streamed down Angel's cheeks as she poured her heart out to the only demon she respected. Originally, she and Keiko hadn't gotten off on the right foot. It took a while before Keiko finally accepted her. And when she did, it was mutual. But after losing Anu, it was clear she was throwing in the towel.

The cascade of falling tears and the scent of heartache and despair weren't enough to change Keiko's icy heart. She hardened her face and dismissed the misery that was attacking what was left of her soul. Internally, she was holding back the river of tears that threatened to escape from the corners of her narrow eyes. She swallowed her heart as it tried to break free and rain on her with sorrow. She refused to crumble and wallow as humans do when they watch their loved ones get buried.

Keiko slowly placed her smooth hand over Angel's and moved it away from the door almost in slow motion. Like a human experiencing a bad break-up, Angel shook her head no and tried to reach for the door again. She hesitated and reached for Keiko instead, who had already slipped away.

"Then I'll see you in the past," sniffled Angel.

"If you make it that far." Keiko snapped. She walked out into the darkness without looking back at her distraught friend.

Two shiny black panthers trotted out of the nearby shrubs, blocking Keiko's path. Their dark eyes seemed to question her actions as they maintained their imposing stance on the concrete.

Coco, the sleeker panther, let out a low growl under her breath. Her sister Pearl, the more muscular of the two, displayed a fierce look of anger as she huffed heavily, trying not to out-growl her sibling. Nothing was getting by them without an explanation. Keiko raised her right eyebrow in her best Master Anu manner. She placed her hands on her hips, not taking their antics seriously. What she was about to do; she couldn't do it alone.

"So, you two wanna come hunt some demons?"

The two panthers conceded and followed her into the darkness.

"FUCK!" Angel punched a hole through the entrance door in her rage and fury. In one day, she lost the three most important people in her life. Her world was rapidly caving in on her. Castus, Jesse, and Helena stood a few feet away from her, watching, seeming at odds. They had witnessed her disagreement with Keiko and secretly judged Keiko's rash decision to abandon them during this crucial time.

"Angel," Castus' voice was almost unrecognizable now that he had matured into manhood. His voice was no longer the cracking, squeaky tone it once held in his teenage years. It was deep and soothing, like their father, Luke. "I will go back in the past with you. We'll change things. Just like old times," he mused.

Angel gazed at her brother and took his hand in hers. His palms were clammy just as they were when they were kids. Her heart rate settled as she realized that the person she missed the most was standing by her side ready to conquer the world. Despite her insufferable loss, having her little brother back gave her hope. Her face softened as her lips split into a half-smile.

"Then we better get going," she replied.

THE END!

EPILOGUE

Camila

The sounds of exotic birds happily chirping, mixed with the scent of fresh flowers and honey-filled air, is what gives Eden its touch of unique paradise. Angels and souls rejoiced under the sun singing soothing classical songs. Many danced gracefully with the children under the cherry blossom trees as they laughed and giggled under the falling blanket of pink petals. Everyone was pleasantly cheerful, from their huge bright smiles to their constant kind pleasantries, as they greeted each other while passing on the busy roads.

Eden was a place of pure tranquility—an escape from violence, there was a deep devotion of love, trust, and commitment among the community of souls—yet Camila hated every moment of it. For decades she pondered why her soul had been doomed to the Underworld, but after spending so much time there, she had assimilated well and it had become her home. She missed the smell of sulfur, the constant darkness, the screams of the damned as she and her demon friends tortured the crap out of them, and the raging parties. But most importantly, she missed her lover. It pained her so much to be without him. It felt as if a thousand needles were pricking her bleeding, aching heart.

Camila sat silently on glittering rocks by a steady, crystal-clear stream that quietly flowed through Eden's enchanted forest. The cool water washed over her delicate feet as she let the bottom of her chiffon, ice-blue dress drown alongside it.

Feeling annoyed, she examined the bottom of her dress one last time and hastily ripped it open into a deep slit that reached the beginning of her lady parts. She smiled triumphantly knowing that the tear of her gown was bringing her one step closer to dressing like her old self.

"I don't think that dress will be up to code," said a smooth male voice startling Camila from behind.

She quickly spun around and gasped in disbelief. She couldn't believe the angelic sight standing before her. Fragments of words swam around her head as she tried her hardest to figure out the right thing to say. She was beside herself. Never in a million years would she have anticipated having to face Dom.

"Hello, Camila." His silky dark hair blew naturally in the light breeze. He grinned brightly without a care in the world. After all, he was already dead. Thanks to her and Lucifer.

Camila swiftly shot up and nearly toppled backward into the flowing stream, but Dom caught her fall. She stared into his deep, dark eyes feeling a hint of guilt washing over her body. She instantly pulled away.

"Dom," was all she could mutter.

"Yep, in the flesh!" Dom spread his arms out as if inviting someone for a hug.

"How did you know I was here?"

"Everyone knows you're here. You're the talk of the town. One thing you're gonna learn about this place is that we have a lot of time on our hands. And with that time, all we do is gossip." Dom chuckled.

"Great!" It was more sarcasm than excitement. "So, I guess you already know I had something to do with your death and now you're here to...kill me?" Camila urged as if killing her, again, would land her in Hell.

"Don't be silly." Dom walked past her and knelt by the stream. "I'm here to finish my fishing. You just happened to be in my way. Besides, I can't kill you. Even if I wanted to, Eden wouldn't allow it. This place surely knows how to embed inner peace into us. Trust and believe I have no desire for revenge." Dom felt the cool water rushing through his fingertips. The reflection of the bright sun beamed on several freshwater fish swimming down the stream.

Dom removed his leather backpack and reached for a net and a sack that peeked from his bag.

"Hold this for me, will ya!" he asked as he shoved the sack into Camila's hands. He continued speaking as he caught several fresh fish from the water and threw them in the bag. "Mendulous told me about my death. About Maggie, her parents, and everything in between. Lucky me to fall in love with trouble. I was pretty angry in the beginning. Being dead before the age of twenty-five really messed me up. I didn't even get to live my full life. And I didn't get to say goodbye to my mom and sister." Dom placed his net in the water and stared off into the magical forest. Looking around at its beauty was beyond words and anything one would see on a Hallmark card.

"I know what you mean," chimed Camila, relating to his grief. "I died at the age of eighteen. Trust me, you'll get used to being dead."

Dom slightly shrugged, "I'll have to admit that being here isn't so bad. I'm with my dad. Seeing deceased loved ones is the best thing about this place. Which reminds me. Your husband is looking for you." Dom grabbed the sack of fish from Camila and tied it tightly as she wiped her wet hands on her dress.

Even the mention of the word husband sent shivers down her spine. Being in Eden had reunited Camila with her first love, the man she originally killed herself over many centuries earlier. It was her suicide that landed her in the Underworld to begin with. She'd been avoiding him like a disease ever since she came to Eden.

"Please don't tell him you've found me," she pleaded.

"I've never seen you," Dom reassured.

The sounds of loud bells gonging repeatedly interrupted their friendly chat. Camila looked around in confusion, trying to find the source of the noise.

"That noise only goes off when angels from Earth return to Eden," Dom schooled. "If you paid attention to the gossip, the Guardian of Eden is coming back home."

"Angel?" Camila was stunned.

"Yep, she requested a meeting with the man himself. And thanks to Mendulous, I got a front-row seat to the action. It was their drama that got me here in the first place. I better get going. It was nice chatting with you."

Camila blocked Dom's path and snatched the sack of fresh fish out of his hands. Her eyebrows furrowed as she quickly shifted her attitude.

"Take me with you. Or I'll make sure this fish becomes my next dinner," she threatened.

Angelina

Father and his council sat on their white thrones, positioned as if Angel was approaching a judge and jury. They all stared with stern expressions as Angel, Helena, and Castus stood before them ready to plead their case.

The marble room gleamed brightly as the sun shone heavily inside the open space. It was as if they were standing on the sacred ground of Mount Olympus except they were not on the top of a glorious mountain. Instead, they were atop the highest hill in Eden.

Angel held her head up high, maintaining a straight warrior face, preparing for the unexpected. She scanned the room and took mental pictures of the faces she recognized and the few she did not.

Mendulous approached the trio in silence. His long, brown cloak dragged on the ground as his bare feet heavily hit each marble tile with every step he took. He turned and bowed before Father and introduced everyone as if it were their first time there. Angel could never get used to the structure and formalities of Eden. Even as a child, she despised how she couldn't just walk into her grandfather's house unannounced and sometimes unaccompanied.

"My dearest granddaughter, Angelina. To what do I owe the honor of your visit?" Father's voice was deep and welcoming as he sat tall behind his marble bench. The top of his bright white tunic was tied in a pristine bow against his chest. He smoothed his long, silver beard and locked eyes with Angel, appearing as if he was prepared to cast judgment.

"I will have to respectfully disagree. It's *my* honor to stand before you, Grandfather. Thank you for agreeing to see me," Angel schmoozed, hoping it would help her case.

"Of course! Anything for the Guardian. I see you have managed to successfully return Castus home." He then casually addressed Castus as though he had never been stuck in the Underworld but, rather, on a long vacation. "You look well, Castus," he grinned brightly. "You seemed to have turned into a fine young man."

Castus nodded his head in acknowledgment before he responded, "Thank you, Grandfather."

Angel shifted the leather satchel that hung around the middle of her corset like a high-waisted belt and pressed her hands together. She had almost forgotten how uncomfortable her warrior clothing in Eden was. Her entire attire felt heavy as she took a few steps forward to approach the shiny, marble bench.

"Grandfather, I come before you today to beg for a new mission," Angel's heart began to beat outside of her chest.

"And what mission is that?"

"To go back in time to save my daughter, Magdalena, and a man named Master Anu Du'shun."

The room roared in loud whispers and confused chattering. It was as if they all knew something she didn't.

Castus glanced around the room and noticed a slender Camila peeking behind a pillar in the far corner of the room. When she noticed that she had been spotted, she quickly tried to hide again. But it was too late, he had already seen her.

Castus slightly leaned over to Helena and softly whispered, "Camila is here. Hiding. Behind the pillar."

Helena quickly glanced over but did not see anyone. "If she's still here, we will deal with her afterward," she whispered in return.

"SILENCE!!" roared Father, interrupting them. "There is no need for weak chatter. I have already made my decision. Angel, your request for a new mission is denied."

"I second that motion," erupted a councilman who rose from his seat and pointed a finger at the three of them. The room, again, began to sound like an overcrowded cafeteria as everyone began speaking at once.

"Grandfather, WHY?" cried Angel, needing answers. "That is my daughter I need to save."

"QUIET!!" commanded Father as he rose from his seat demanding order.

"Angel, this daughter of yours is an abomination to both our world and Earth. The fact that she is stuck in the Underworld with Lucifer is a blessing to our worlds. And this *Master Anu* of which you speak is a Vampire that has no place in Eden or the Underworld. To speak frankly, you have made a mockery of us all."

Angel gasped at the irony. Keiko had told her this might happen, yet she pushed through anyway. "How? I did everything in my power to keep the Earthen world safe."

"Marrying the enemy and having a demon child is not protecting Earth. It is making things worse," Father retorted.

"Anu is not an enemy or a monster. He is a good man. It is because of his orders and rules that the Vs are not exterminating the humans. Maggie is not an abomination. She is my daughter, my flesh, and part of this family." Angel spoke out of turn with much conviction, similar to her Uncle Lucifer when he had challenged her grandfather several centuries ago. "If you do not honor my request, the Vs will blame our species for his death. They will hunt us down for sport until their revenge is satisfied. Be that as it may, as the Queen Guardian, I will not be able to save us all."

Father stared directly into Angel's eyes. She could see the specks of fiery fury beginning to form an angry dance in his pupils. "Then let them come. As of today, you are no longer the Queen Guardian and are stripped of your reign."

The council members exploded into pandemonium. Many agreed with Father as they clapped and rejoiced with his decision. Castus and Helena appeared shocked like two deer staring into bright, oncoming headlights.

"I will send a new Guardian, one appointed by *me* to wipe out these despicable Vs FOREVER!" Father roared, his voice thundering as if he were Zeus himself.

Burning rage filled Angel to the core. Her body shook with indignation as she allowed her mind to go into complete madness.

Without thinking, she pulled out a red, flaming dagger from her satchel and charged at Mendulous from behind. She quickly and furiously kicked his feet out from under him, sending him falling to the ground like a limp doll. She put her right knee on his neck with all her might and held the flaming dagger to his eye.

Mendulous surrendered, understanding that it was best for him to comply.

"One pierce or prick of this flame will send Mendulous to the Underworld for eternity. And there will be nothing in your angelic magic that will be able to set him free." The threatening tone in Angel's voice was unlike anything they had ever heard.

Helena drew closer to Angel. "Stop this madness, daughter. Think of what you're doing," she urged worriedly as the words escaped her quivering lips.

Angel ignored her pleas. She positioned Mendulous on his knees, as extending to his full six-foot three-inch height was not an option. She tightly, yet carefully, pressed the fiery dagger to his neck as droplets of sweat trickled down from his temples onto the burning dagger.

"The world does not need another Guardian. What they need is me. I begged and pleaded with you, Grandfather, for years to help and guide me out of my despair. But my pleas fell on deaf ears. Now I come to you in the flesh, begging again, and yet I'm seen as nothing but a disgrace and a bearer of an abomination. I hope one day everyone here will find it in their hearts to forgive me, but now, I am demanding that you send me back in time. Or I will dispose of Mendulous."

Everyone remained silent as they fixated on Angel's threat. The air around her felt suffocating as she inched the dagger closer to Mendulous' neck.

Father glared at Angel and exhaled heavily. He whisked his hand toward her and released a glowing tiny white speck from his fingertips. The tiny orb grew larger as it floated and paused two steps before her. It slowly grew to the size of a door and transformed into an oval, green-and-silver shimmering portal.

"I don't know how far back in time this portal will send you, nor do I care. But for your sake, I hope you make the most of it. You have twenty seconds to leave my sight before I change my mind and outcast you to a place worse than the Underworld," Father stated, his tone desperately working hard to sound calm.

Angel nodded at Castus, giving him the green light to quickly enter the portal.

"Apologies," she whispered in Mendulous' ear as she removed the burning dagger and released him.

For the first time, Mendulous half smiled, seeming as if he were secretly proud of her rebellion.

Castus took one last look at Angel, "Just like old times," he stated, nervously smiling.

"Just like old times," she repeated.

As Angel and Castus began to walk through the portal together, Camila came crashing through head-on like a runaway bull. She broke between Angel and Castus, shoving him with all of her might so that he fell to his side and slid yards away from the portal. Before they could stop her, she dove through headfirst as if she were an Olympic swimmer. Angel grabbed on tightly to the last inch of material waving from the bottom of Camila's chiffon dress.

"Castusss..." was Angel's last word as the portal sucked her in then disappeared from sight.

Magdalena

"Hell makes me feel so alive!" Maggie blurted as she danced around Lucifer's lair feeling powerful. "This place is heightening my energy. Everything feels so magnified, intense. I can feel the adrenaline coursing through my veins."

Lucifer continued reading the little black at his desk, ignoring her every word.

"Uncle Lucifer, you're not listening to me," she interrupted, needing attention like a neglected feline.

"Yes, yes, gal, high adrenaline," he said dismissively, not looking away from the book.

Maggie turned to face the golden floating torture mirrors. The horrific scene never once frightened her; instead, she chuckled internally at the fate of their doom.

"When are you going to let me join the fun inside the torture chambers?" she pouted.

Lucifer finally lifted his head from the book and rose. He approached the mirrors and pointed in annoyance, "Those chambers are no place for you. I have other plans, bigger things we need to focus on other than this disaster."

Maggie folded her arms tightly across her chest. "Like what?" Her demon, bloodshot eyes stared directly into Lucifer's black soul. "If you're expecting me to help you with anything that will benefit *you*, the answer is HELL NO! Just because I'm stuck down here, which I'm not complaining about because I actually like this place, doesn't make us friends." She stared at her reflection in one of the golden floating mirrors, admiring her long, dark horns, bloodstained eyes, and large, black silk wings. "This place makes me feel sooo good at being sooo bad," she stated out loud while puffing her curls over her shoulders.

Lucifer leaned against his desk, seeming to ponder her last statement. He removed his suit jacket and gazed around his lair before setting his eyes back on Maggie.

"Maybe Hell could use a little co-parenting," he proposed.

Maggie's eyes widened and her ears peaked with delighted interest, "Go on."

"My plans will not only benefit me but you, as well, while I figure out a way to return Camila. How would you like to help rule the Underworld?" Lucifer grinned slyly from ear to ear.

CHARACTER GUIDE

1) *__Angel (Birth name Angelina)__:* Daughter to Helena and Luke, trusted warriors of Eden. Chosen by the Divine Right as the protector of the angels and the humans on Earth. She is also known as the Queen Guardian and is the wife of Master Anu Du'Shun. *__Supernatural Strengths:__* Can see into the past and the future, with limitations. She is a healer and can feel people's emotions. Has the ability to worsen one's physical pain.

2) *__Camila Del Rio:__* Jesse's biological mother. Human that lives in the Underworld and is branded as a demon. Lucifer's lover and most trusted demon. *__Supernatural Strengths:__* None

3) ***Charlotte Devery:*** Maggie's best friend who was robbed of her site at a young age. She is a scholar of religious studies and mythology. Although she is blind she is extremely intuitive and insightful.
Supernatural Strengths: None

4) ***Dom (Dominique Kim):*** Korean name Kim Dae-Seong. A human DJ and boyfriend to Maggie.
Supernatural Strengths: None

5) ***Gia:*** An angel Warrior of Eden. A soldier to Angel on Earth. The ex lover to Lucifer.
Supernatural Strengths: Ability to read minds, angelic warrior strength.

6) ***Helena:*** Mother to Angel and Castus. Sister to Lucifer and eldest daughter to Father.
Supernatural Strengths: Warrior of Eden, can instantly heal herself and others.

7) ***Jack:*** Rouge demon from the Underworld. Father to Maggie and step father to Jesse. Lover to Ruby Jane the Ultra witch.
Supernatural Strengths: Master charmer, ability to track anyone around the world.

8) ***Jesse:*** Son to Camila and Castus. Half human and half angel.
Supernatural Strengths: Absorbs information faster than the human mind, possesses supernatural strength, and is a master in chemistry.

9) *Keiko Meiji:* She is a half human and half demon born in the early 1800's. The biological daughter to the Japanese Ruler, Emperor Meiji. Adopted by Master Anu Du'Shun at the age of ten. Top adviser and loyal solider to the Du'Shun vampire line.
Supernatural Strengths: Telekinesis abilities, can pause people for a short period of time, transforms into a ferocious demon when angered.

10) *Lucifer:* Ruler of the Underworld. Uncle to Angel and Castus. Brother to Helena. Father's second youngest son.
Supernatural Strengths: The power of charm and manipulation. Master to the demons in the Underworld, the ability to diminish people and things on site.

11) *Maggie (Magdalena):* Daughter to Angel and Jack. Half demon and half angel. Is the key to destroying the Unknown worlds.
Supernatural Strengths: Power of manipulation, possesses angelic and demon strength, can counteract certain angelic powers, telekinesis, and temporary force shield abilities. Extremely powerful in demon form.

12) *Master Anu Du'Shun:* Ancient Vampire from the Carib Indian tribe. Leader of the Vampire species. He is a scientist, researcher, and collector of supernatural beings. Married to an angel and father to his adopted half breed daughter Keiko.
Supernatural Strengths: Vampire strength and speed, able to walk under the sun. Ability to

manipulate the human mind by erasing memories and using hypnosis.

13) **_Mendulous:_** The Hand of Father and his most trusted advisor. A warrior of Eden.
Supernatural Strengths: Possesses the power of tranquility and peace. Combatant fighter with angelic strength.

14) **_No Nose Tommy:_** Trusted demon to Lucifer and a soldier of Lucifer's Eyes.
Supernatural Strengths: Demon strength, ability to possess a human body.

15) **_Pearl and Coco (Sisters):_** Protectors and loyal soldiers under the Du'Shun vampire line.
Supernatural Strengths: Shifters.

16) **_Pierre_**: An angel Warrior of Eden. A soldier to Angel on Earth.
Supernatural Strengths: Ability to slow down time.

17) **_Ruby Jane:_** Ultra/Supreme queen witch of her coven. Lover to Jack.
Supernatural Strengths: Master of black magic, spells, and conjuring demons from the Underworld.

Acknowledgments

Thank you Stephanie Larkin and the Red Penguin Team for assisting me on another project. It's been an exciting journey filled with several teachable moments.

Jodie Etra and Dana Doan Stein, you two have been the best beta readers one could ever ask for. Thank you for all of your healthy feedback and suggestions; it never goes unnoticed.

Shamaine Henry, thank you for always giving me your undivided attention and helping me along my writing journey. Although we didn't see eye to eye on certain parts of this book, it was nice to come to an understanding. You are amazing.

My husband Christopher, thank you for always being supportive, loving and understanding.

Gini Lee, thank you for proofreading this book, giving me helpful insight, and being a great author friend. I'm so lucky to have met you.

To all my readers, thank you for supporting me and writing honest reviews. Without you, Angel's journey could not go on.

About the Author

Bernice Burgos currently resides in the State of New Jersey with her loving husband, two teenage kids, and her fur baby Fancy. She began her writing journey as a poet, then ventured into writing fantasy.

Angels, Demons, Vampires, Witches, and Shifters are just a few of the magical characters a reader would find in her books. If you're looking for an escape into a fictional version of New York City, the Underworld , or Eden, then pick up a copy of her books. They will not disappoint!

**You can visit her website at berniceburgosauthor.com
**Instagram berniceburgos_fiction_author
**TikTok @bethewriter

www.ingramcontent.com/pod-product-compliance
Lightning Source LLC
LaVergne TN
LVHW041700060526
838201LV00043B/499